My Dearest Sons,

If this letter ever finds you, I hope you are together.
I hope you are well. And may you have it in your
hearts to forgive your mother her greatest sin—
loving you too much to keep you both.

Please know the choice I made was not easy. It has
haunted me since the day I kissed you goodbye, dear
Nicholas. My arms still ache to hold you one more
time. I pray that your new parents were good and
kind and that they loved you enough for me, as
well. And Gabe, I'm sorry, too. I realize you had to
know some part of me was missing after your brother
went away. I'm sorry if I wasn't there for you as a
mother should be. I'm sorry if you ever felt you
weren't loved enough.

I pray that time and fate has brought you together
once again. But perhaps the distance between you
will be greater than even a mother's love can bridge.
Find it in your hearts to embrace one another as
brothers. Forge a family. Forge on.

And forgive me. Forgive me.

Love always,

Mother

Dear Reader,

Have you ever been to a family reunion where you're amazed at how many relatives you have? That's the way it is with the Randalls, a family I created a few years ago. When Harlequin asked for more hunky cowboys, I at first said no. But then I couldn't resist and my fertile mind came up with some more, and off we've gone on another adventure. So here they are. More Randalls. But these two Randalls didn't grow up under the eyes of Jake and his brothers, though they've made them part of the family now. And the two women who fall for these Randalls were adversely affected by their own family bonds.

Family relations have always been important to me, so this family is right on target. If you have family, you know what I mean. There are days that family members are not always a benefit. And when you're not used to dealing with all those bonds, you have a lot to learn. So join me while Nick and Gabe learn about Randalls and family all at the same time. I'm pretty sure the good will outweigh the bad. And there might be a few laughs along the way.

Best,

Judy Christenberry

Judy Christenberry

UNBREAKABLE BONDS

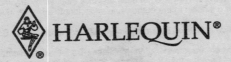

HARLEQUIN®

TORONTO • NEW YORK • LONDON
AMSTERDAM • PARIS • SYDNEY • HAMBURG
STOCKHOLM • ATHENS • TOKYO • MILAN • MADRID
PRAGUE • WARSAW • BUDAPEST • AUCKLAND

ISBN 0-373-83509-4

UNBREAKABLE BONDS

This edition published by arrangement with Harlequin Books S.A.

® and TM are trademarks of the publisher. Trademarks indicated with ® are registered in the United States Patent and Trademark Office, the Canadian Trade Marks Office and in other countries.

Visit us at www.eHarlequin.com

Printed in U.S.A.

National bestselling author **Judy Christenberry** has penned over fifty novels for both the contemporary and Regency markets. A B.A. in English literature and an M.A. in French literature, combined with a love of reading all her life, made writing seem a likely career for this mother of two. Though now a resident of Arizona, this native Texan enjoys writing about cowboys, which just seems to come naturally. Judy, who has survived a twenty-year teaching career, currently contributes to both Harlequin American Romance and Silhouette Romance.

Unbreakable Bonds is dedicated to my hard-working, supportive editor, without whom this book might not have appeared. Melissa Jeglinski planted the seed and nourished its growth, helping me grow as a writer. Her faith in me is greatly appreciated.

THE RANDALLS

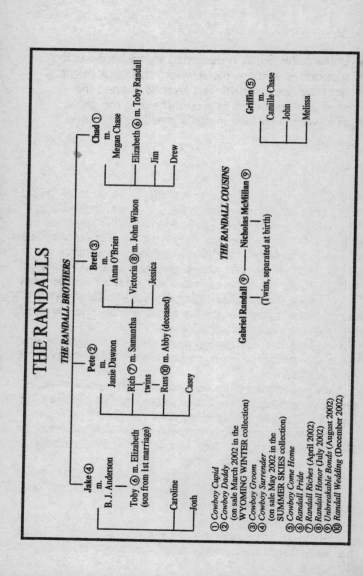

THE RANDALL BROTHERS

Chad ① m. Megan Chase
- Elizabeth ⑥ m. Toby Randall
- Jim
- Drew

Brett ③ m. Anna O'Brien
- Victoria ⑧ m. John Wilson
- Jessica

Pete ② m. Janie Dawson
- Rich ⑦ m. Samantha
  - twins
- Russ ⑩ m. Abby (deceased)
  - Casey

Jake ④ m. B. J. Anderson
- Toby ⑥ m. Elizabeth (son from 1st marriage)
- Caroline
- Josh

THE RANDALL COUSINS

Gabriel Randall ⑨ ———— Nicholas McMillan ⑨
(Twins, separated at birth)

Griffin ⑤ m. Camille Chase
- John
- Melissa

① *Cowboy Cupid*
② *Cowboy Daddy*
(on sale March 2002 in the WYOMING WINTER collection)
③ *Cowboy Groom*
④ *Cowboy Surrender*
(on sale May 2002 in the SUMMER SKIES collection)
⑤ *Cowboy Come Home*
⑥ *Randall Pride*
⑦ *Randall Riches* (April 2002)
⑧ *Randall Honor* (July 2002)
⑨ *Unbreakable Bonds* (August 2002)
⑩ *Randall Wedding* (December 2002)

CHAPTER ONE

Nick

STROLLING INTO RAWHIDE, Wyoming's general store, Nicholas McMillan couldn't keep a smile from his lips. This place was nothing like what he was used to. He shopped the expensive specialty stores in Denver when he did any shopping, which was as seldom as possible.

Oh, well, he wasn't shopping today, except for information. Over the rows of goods for sale, he caught sight of a young brunette industriously straightening a pile of garments. His boots made no sound on the floor covered by well-worn indoor-outdoor carpet.

He noted her trim figure, which didn't seem surprising since she seemed to be in perpetual motion. He tapped her on the shoulder.

She spun around so quickly, she almost toppled over. He reached out to keep her from falling, but slowly drew his hand back as she straightened herself.

It wasn't her quick recovery that stopped his movement. Her gray eyes, fringed with lush brown lashes, widened in surprise and then anger.

He hurriedly began his request, hoping it would soothe whatever had upset her. "Pardon me for interrupting, ma'am, but I wanted—"

"How dare you!"

Before he could respond, her right hand connected with his bare cheek with a smacking sound that startled even

him. His skin stung, and he saw her draw her hand bac
again for a second turn.

He grabbed her hand to stop her attack. What could h
have possibly done to have offended her? "Whoa, ma'an
there's no need to get violent."

"Get out! Get out and don't ever come back!" sh
screamed, tears coming to her eyes.

Nick couldn't remember the last time he'd made
woman cry. Well, there was the time he turned dow
Mindy's marriage proposal, but that hadn't really been hi
fault. "If you'll just tell me…" he began, but when h
didn't respond to her verbal command, she wrenched he
wrist from his hold and began pushing him with both hands

He had to move his feet or she would've shoved him t
the floor. She didn't stop until they reached the shop's fron
door. Before he knew it, he found himself standing on th
sidewalk, staring at the door closing in front of him.

The sign on the door read Welcome.

"It should read Welcome to Everyone But Nick Mc
Millan," he muttered, which drew him a few curious look
from shoppers on the street. *She* hadn't had any shopper
at all in *her* store. And he could understand why, if sh
treated them all like she'd treated him.

A man on the sidewalk squeezed by him with an "excus
me" and entered the store. Nick leaned forward to pee
through the door's window and watched the brunette giv
the patron a beautiful smile.

With a frown and a shrug of his shoulders, Nick decide
to put this strange experience behind him. He caught sigh
of a café on the next block. The town wasn't large and h
figured he'd have more people to ask about the informatio
he was searching for if he tried there.

He entered the busy café and looked around the roon
full of diners. He'd talked himself into a meal as he'
walked down the street, but the place was so crowded ther

was not an empty booth in sight. Then two guys in the
back started waving him over.

Strange town. First a woman slaps him and now strangers were inviting him to join them. Bizarre. But he wasn't
going to turn down a chance to eat. Halfway through the
crowded tables, he got a good look at the men and realized
just how lucky he really was. These men were Randalls
and exactly whom he had hoped to find during his visit.

"Hello, Pete, Toby," Nick said, using their first names,
which he had memorized. "May I join you?"

Pete grinned. "Of course. We just ordered. And if you're
ordering you're usual enchiladas, you'll get your food with
ours. If they weren't so darned good, the café wouldn't be
so crowded on Enchilada Day!"

Before Nick could ask what Pete meant by getting his
"usual" or even agree, a waitress arrived at the table.
"You want the special, hon?"

"Yes, please." Before he could order a drink, she
walked away.

"Wait!" he yelled, but she never looked back. Maybe
he'd lost his charm. He'd been successful with the ladies
in Denver, but that was certainly proving not to be the case
here.

"What's the matter?" The man named Toby asked.

"I wanted a cup of coffee."

Almost as he spoke, the waitress returned with a cup and
saucer and Toby lifted the pot of coffee that was already
on the table and began pouring. Pete was staring at him.
"What's wrong with you, Gabe? You know coffee's in-
cluded with the special."

Gabe? What was going on?

"How's your barn coming?" Toby asked. "We're planning on coming over Saturday."

"What?" He knew he'd asked the wrong question. They
looked at him as if he was crazy.

"What's wrong with you, Gabe?"

Time to come clean before he got the same response as the one the lady delivered. Only these two guys could deliver a knockout punch. "My name's not Gabe."

"The hell it's not!" Pete responded.

Nick sighed. He didn't know what was happening, but it had to be connected to why he was here. He pressed on in spite of the angry looks he was receiving. "I'm Nick McMillan from Denver, attorney-at-law."

"But you knew us?" Toby asked, a deep frown on his face. "Is some bozo suing us?"

"If so, you can take your cup of coffee and drink it on the street," Pete added. Now their expressions looked quite similar to that of the woman who had slapped him.

"Wait a minute. No one is suing anybody. My visit to Rawhide has nothing to do with my profession."

"Then why are you here and how do you know us?" Toby demanded.

"I'm here to—to find my family. And I recognized you from this." Nick reached into his back pocket, pulled out a rolled-up magazine and put it on the table.

Toby and Pete stared at their pictures on the cover. The magazine was named *Rodeo,* and it had done an article on the Randall family and their lifelong involvement in rodeoing.

The waitress arrived with three plates piled high with steaming enchiladas. She set them down in front of each of the men and hurried away, returning immediately with a bowl of chips. "Enjoy!" she muttered, as if it was required to say that, and disappeared.

"She's always rushed on Wednesday," Pete said, as if he was afraid Nick would take offense.

"Okay, so that's why you knew our names," Toby said, "but that doesn't explain the family thing."

"Yeah," Pete added. "You wouldn't be the first one who tried to lay claim to our ranch or try to get some of our money or something."

The two Randall men just looked at each other. Then Toby said, "Chloe!" and they both laughed as if sharing an inside joke.

"Who's Chloe?" Nick couldn't help asking.

"My dad's first wife," Toby said. "Because of her, the family almost died out."

"Aw, Toby, it wasn't that bad. Besides, I'd already gotten Janie pregnant. I just didn't know it."

Nick was taken aback by their conversation. "You know, if I represented you two, I'd tell you not to reveal any more family secrets."

Toby and Pete laughed even harder. Finally, Pete said, "You've never been to a small town, have you?"

"Of course I have."

"Well then, you've never been to Rawhide. Hey, Connie," he called as the waitress came close to their table. When she turned to look at him, impatient, Pete asked, "Connie. How many kids do I have?"

"You lost your mind? Three, of course. Casey and the twins."

"Thanks," he said, and she hurried away.

"Hey, Dick," he said, leaning toward the next table. "Did you come to my wedding?"

"You know I did, Pete. We was all discussin' what you was gonna name the baby and whether Janie's daddy was gonna shoot you with that old shotgun of his for gettin' his little girl pregnant." The man sat back and roared with laughter.

Pete waved his hand at the man and turned back to Nick. "See? There aren't any secrets in a small town."

"Okay," Nick said. "If there are no secrets, then can you tell me why you called me Gabe when you first saw me?"

Pete and Toby exchanged a look. Then Pete asked, "You don't know who Gabe is?"

"No."

"But you came here to find him?"

"I'm not sure who I really came to find." Nick suppose
he'd have to open up a little, but it didn't come easily. Afte
all, he'd been raised by a lawyer father who had examine
every word he spoke and a socialite mother who kept ev
erything to herself so she wouldn't be an object of gossip

"Okay, I'm going to tell you why I'm here."

"That'd be a good idea," Pete drawled.

Nick drew a deep breath. "I was adopted. My parent
told me about it when I was young but they didn't wan
me to look for my 'real' family. Then my father died
couple of months ago and among his things was a lette
addressed to me. It had my real mother's name. Her las
name was Randall."

He paused, watching the two men take in his words
"And…my father wrote that I'd had a twin brother. My
adoptive parents didn't know his name. And they tried t
adopt him, too. But his mother wouldn't let him go."

"Were you born in Rawhide?" Pete asked, his voic
rising in shock.

"No. Kansas City."

"Then what are you doing here?" Toby asked.

Before Nick could answer, Pete spoke. "Because h
found out his mother is dead. And his brother doesn't liv
there anymore."

"Yeah," Nick agreed, staring hard at Pete.

"Something wrong with the enchiladas?" the waitres
asked, pausing by their table.

"Naw, they're great!" Toby said gustily, and shovele
a big bite in his mouth. He nodded toward Nick, and i
didn't take a lot of brainpower for Nick to realize he shoul
take a bite, too.

They quietly continued to eat for several moments. The
Toby whispered to Pete, "Gabe? You think it's Gabe?
mean it has to be. Look at the resemblance."

Nick's heart began thumping in his chest. He'd wanted to ask the question, but he hadn't dared.

Pete didn't answer Toby's question. Instead he ordered, "Eat up and let's get out of here."

Nick could only stare at the two men eating their lunch, as if their conversation hadn't been important. He guessed it wasn't to them, but it was to him. But maybe he was making a mistake. Besides, his possible brother must be a real son of a gun if that woman in the store's violent reaction was any indication. She'd obviously mistaken him for this Gabe, as well. What had this Gabe done?

He figured he had a right to at least ask one question. "Okay, so you won't help me. But at least tell me why I got slapped just for walking into the general store."

That remark got them to stop eating, Nick was glad to see. "Well?" he prompted when they continued to stare at him.

"Was it a blonde who slapped you?" Toby asked.

"No, a good-looking brunette."

"Of course it was," Pete said, adding a long-suffering sigh.

"Of course?" Nick asked.

Toby asked the same question, which surprised Nick.

Pete stared at both of them. "She's protecting her baby sister."

That seemed to satisfy Toby, but Nick wasn't happy at all. "What did this Gabe do to her?" *Her baby sister?* "Damn, how old is this sister? Don't tell me he's the kind of man who likes 'em real young?"

Pete grabbed his napkin, wiped his face and stood up. "That's it. Come on."

Pete strode to the counter, taking out his billfold.

Nick stared after him, stunned by his stormy exit. Toby grabbed his hat and rose, grimacing at Nick as if offering an apology and a goodbye.

Nick sighed. Well, at least he had a name. That was more

than he had when he came in here. But maybe he'd better think about whether or not he wanted—

"Nick, get your carcass over here!"

Nick turned his head to see Pete standing by the door, hands on his hips, staring at him. Was the older man going to take him outside and punch him for asking questions? So be it. He could give as good as he got.

He jumped to his feet and strode to the door, measuring Pete's muscles as he did so. For a man his age, probably forty-five or fifty, he was in good shape. Maybe he could take him. But if Toby joined in, he was in real trouble. He stopped when he got to Pete, his fingers curling into fists to be ready.

Pete gave him a look of disgust and shoved him through the open door. Toby was right behind him.

"What's wrong with both of you? Toby, I expected better of you. But you're an attorney, Nick. At least you say you are. You should know better."

Nick stared at the man. He was chewing him out the same as Toby. Like he was family. Pete was walking away and Toby hurried to catch up. Nick decided to do the same.

Pete had reached a beat-up truck. He slid behind the wheel, but before he started the engine, he said, "Get in."

Toby and Nick looked at each other and hurried to obey.

Nick kept expecting Pete to yell "Not you!" but he didn't.

When he'd closed the door, Pete backed the truck out and headed up the main street.

"Um, my car—"

"We'll bring you back."

"Uncle Pete," Toby finally said after several minutes, "What did we do wrong?"

Nick was glad Toby had asked. It didn't make him feel so dumb for being completely bewildered.

"We don't discuss family secrets in public. You know how much everyone gossips in town. And this isn't even our secret! And I couldn't get you two Chatty Cathys to shut up!''

Nick opened his mouth to protest, but Toby was faster. ''You're calling us girls!'' he said, clearly outraged.

''Well, you were gossiping like girls. And Nick here asking if Gabe messed around with young girls right there in public.''

''I thought that was what you meant. It sounded like it.''

''You didn't mean that, did you, Uncle Pete?'' Toby asked.

''Toby Randall, you know Jennifer is twenty-six. I don't think that makes her an innocent child. And what two consenting adults do in private is none of our business.'' He paused, his steam fading a little. Then much to Nick's surprise, he grinned. ''If it were, I'd be in jail myself.''

''You're talking about you and Janie, right?'' Toby asked, and Pete threw on the brakes.

''Of course I am and don't you ever suggest any different. I wouldn't betray Janie for any reason and don't you forget it!''

Nick was beginning to wonder if insanity ran in this family. Suddenly it occurred to him to ask, ''Uh, where are we going?''

''You two are going to drive me crazy! I thought you wanted to see Gabe. Did you think I'd let you just walk in on him? Of course not. I'm taking you to his place.''

Nick turned and stared out the window. Gabe, his brother, maybe, was a lucky man. Pete was a good friend. Hmm, maybe he should say ''relative.'' ''Are you kin to Gabe?''

''Yeah. And you, too, I'm thinking.''

''Hey, that'd make you my cousin,'' Toby said with a grin. ''Except not blood cousin. I was adopted, too.''

Nick was surprised. ''You were?''

''Yeah, Jake married my mom and took me on, too.''

''You know he wouldn't have it any other way, boy,''

Pete said matter-of-factly. "He's proud as he can be of you. Except back there in the café, when you, along with this one, were intent on spilling your guts about the family."

"Sorry, Uncle Pete."

"I didn't mean to upset you, either, Pete...I mean Mr. Randall."

"No need to get formal now, boy. What did you say your last name is?"

"McMillan."

"You were raised in Denver?"

"Yeah."

Pete chuckled and Nick asked, "What's funny about that?"

"Jake went to Denver to find wives for us. And you come from Denver. Guess there are more Randalls about than we knew."

"But I'm a McMillan."

Pete leaned forward and stared at him. "Nope, boy, you're a Randall through and through."

Nick glared at Pete, a little resentful of his dismissal of his life in Denver and his adopted parents.

"You'll see what I mean," Pete told him as he turned the pickup off the highway onto a dusty track.

CHAPTER TWO

Gabe

HIS SHOULDERS SLUMPED and his head hanging low, Gabe Randall drove his battered pickup home.

Life had turned sour ever since he'd quit rodeoing and tried to settle down. And today he'd just received another blow. Damn it! The bank had turned him down on his request for a loan. The place next to his was on the market and he wanted to buy it and expand. But he hadn't had his own place long. Only a couple of months. And he understood their reasoning.

But that didn't mean he had to be happy about it.

He threw the bank's letter on the car seat and almost stripped the gears in his anger. He'd better be careful because there wasn't any extra money for a transmission job. He was trying to get his barn finished before winter came in earnest. The summer heat was already dwindling and it was only August. Everything else could wait until next spring, but the big barn needed to be finished soon.

He'd been too ambitious, probably. He remembered the day he'd found out he'd managed to get his loan approved to buy the place. He'd immediately gotten into his truck and driven to town to try again with Jen. She'd told him she wouldn't marry him while he played hero at the rodeo.

It hadn't occurred to him that she'd refuse to marry him because of his occupation. She'd loved following him around, everyone wanting his autograph. He'd thought she'd be proud to be Mrs. Gabe Randall. Instead she'd said some ugly things. And he'd gone away mad.

He'd been sure he'd get over her in no time. He hadn't. Jen was like no other woman he'd ever known. So, he'd waited until he found a place on the market near Rawhide and actually bought it. Two months had passed since they'd broken up, but with the deed in hand, he'd gone to claim his bride.

And she had said no. Again. He hadn't even had a chance to tell her about the ranch. She'd told him there was someone else.

He'd called her a liar, having believed that she wouldn't be able to get over him any easier than he would've gotten over her. But she'd insisted.

A month later, when he'd heard she was pregnant, he'd finally given up. And he hadn't been into town since. He'd sent Blackie to town for supplies for the ranch, but insisted his ranch hand not say who owned the place.

The Double Moon. Gabe's place. The small lake on the ranch reflected the moon at night. He'd been stupid and named the place for the double moons that seemed to appear, thinking there was a moon for him and one for Jennifer.

Now he was stuck with the stupid name and the stupid thought. It made him think of Jennifer every time the moon shone on the lake.

And things had gotten worse ever since.

As he reached the ranch house, Gabe figured he'd better get out to the barn and get to work. Forget about his silly dreams. He'd make it without the place next door. Just like he'd make it without Jennifer.

Damn straight he would. He wasn't going to let some woman ruin his life.

A FEW HOURS LATER, Gabe was discussing his barn roof with Blackie when Pete Randall appeared in the doorway.

"How's it going, Gabe?" his older cousin asked.

He wanted to tell him about the loan rejection, but a man didn't cry about his failures. He'd told Blackie, of course, though only casually. As if it didn't matter. "Fine," Gabe said, smiling. "Just messing with the roof."

The Randalls were his neighbors to the south and also his distant cousins. But besides the fact that they were family, they were also nice people.

"What brings you by?" Gabe asked.

"I've got someone I want you to meet."

Gabe frowned but waited for more. He expected Pete to extend an invitation over to the Randall place. He hoped it wasn't regarding a woman Pete and his notorious matchmaking brother were trying to fix him up with.

Pete paused. "Now."

"You mean here? Is it a man needing a job? I can't take on any more men right now, Pete. Sorry, I wish I could."

"I think you'll need a couple of more if you're going to take on the Baker place," Pete said cheerfully. "But that's not what I mean. Come on up to the house."

Gabe shot Pete a strange look. Then he nodded in agreement before looking at his manager. "You come, too, Blackie. It's about time for your break."

Blackie, who was somewhere in his sixties, hated the fact that the doctor had told him to take breaks twice a day. Gabe tried to keep him to a lighter workload whenever possible.

As they strode toward the house, talking weather, a popular subject for ranchers, Gabe dropped a piece of information into the conversation. "By the way, Pete, I got turned down for the loan so I guess I won't be buying the Baker place, after all."

Pete shot him a scrutinizing look, and Gabe made sure he kept his face clean of all emotions.

"Sorry to hear that," Pete said just as casually.

They reached the house and Gabe held open the door.

"I'll have Letty put the coffee on. Let me tell her we've got company."

His housekeeper was a wonder. She worked hard all day but she made it look easy. Until she'd come to the Double Moon, nothing had been easy for him and Blackie. But now the food was good and ready when they were, and their clothes were sweet-smelling and clean. He was lucky, in spite of getting turned down for the loan, he reminded himself.

Pete motioned for Gabe to precede him into the kitchen as if there was a surprise for him.

Gabe saw Letty beaming at someone sitting at the table and he swung his gaze in that direction.

And came to a complete halt.

Gabe didn't know who was playing a trick on him, but he didn't much like it. Seated at his kitchen table was a stranger who looked like an exact copy of himself.

"Who are you?" Gabe's voice was gruff and unwelcoming, and he didn't care.

"Nick McMillan," the man said. Gabe noticed he didn't extend his hand, and he was glad.

Pete frowned and spoke. "I guess we should explain, Gabe. I knew it'd be a shock but—"

"How do you know him?" Gabe couldn't take his eyes off the man. They said everyone had a double, but *exactly* the same? Maybe the man's hair was shorter, more expertly cut. Blackie usually took the scissors to Gabe's. But other than that, he couldn't see any difference. It was unnerving.

"What do you want?" Gabe demanded. He always faced trouble head-on. It was the only way. He'd never had protective parents to shield him, or a big family to back him up. It was him against the world.

"I was looking for you," the stranger responded.

"So you've found me. Now what? If you want money, I don't have any."

The man looked puzzled.

"Gabe...I wouldn't have brought him here if I thought he meant to hurt you," Pete explained.

"Why else would he be here? I don't know him."

"I think you may be my brother," said the stranger with his face. "My twin."

"I don't have a brother," Gabe replied bitterly. "I don't have—"

"Well, I'll be!" Blackie, once his mentor and now his only family, interrupted.

Gabe turned to his old friend. "What is it, Blackie?"

"Look at him!" Blackie ordered. Everyone at the table did so, including Letty.

She said, "All I see is the mirror image of Gabe, Blackie. Is that what you're talking about?"

"Naw. That's obvious. But what does he do when he's worrying on something?"

While they looked, the stranger jerked his hand down to the table.

"You're right, Blackie," Pete said suddenly. He turned to Gabe. "You rub your eyebrow when you're worrying."

"So?"

"That's what Nick was doing."

"A lot of people do that," Nick said.

"Why do you?"

"It's a habit," Nick said hurriedly, and clamped his mouth shut.

"That doesn't prove anything. Why do you think we're kin to each other if you've never seen me before?"

Nick looked around the table, then spoke. "My parents told me I was adopted, but nothing else. But my dad died a couple of months ago, the last of my family. He left me a letter. It gave my real mother's last name...the fact that I had a brother out there somewhere. A twin brother."

"And what did he do, leave you directions to my home? That doesn't make sense. I just settled here about two months ago. He wouldn't know that."

Nick said, "He didn't know where you were. Or your first name. Just that your last name was Randall."

"Then how did you find me?"

Pete laid his arm on Gabe's shoulder. "Take it easy. He'll tell you."

"I'm an attorney. I had someone check in Kansas City for birth certificates for twin boys born on my birthday, to a couple named Randall. The father was listed as deceased at the time of the twins' birth. Then, with my mother's first name, we found her death certificate dated twenty years ago."

"What's your birthday?" Gabe asked.

"November 2, 1970."

Everyone's gazes focused on Gabe. Blackie spoke, "Well? Is that your birthday? You never mentioned it."

"It's not a day I celebrate," he said bitterly. Seeing sympathy in the eyes of those around him, he tried to move the conversation away from that subject. "Okay, you found me. What now?"

"I'd like to get to know you."

"Why? Because you've run out of family? That's nothing to cry about."

Letty protested. "Gabe!"

"Sorry, Letty," he said, his voice gentling. He wouldn't hurt Letty's feelings for anything. "If you're looking for a place to spend a few days free of charge, we've got an empty spot in the bunkhouse." Then he headed for the door. He had a lot to think about.

"Just a minute, brother."

Gabe stopped, resenting the ease with which the man called him that.

"Seems some lady mistook me for you this afternoon. I'd like to know what you did for me to get slapped at the general store today. And whether or not that's likely to happen in town again."

Gabe lunged at Nick, his hands formed into fists, but Pete and Toby caught his arms, holding him back.

"You stay away from there, do you hear me? Don't go near her." Then he wrenched his arms free and stomped out of the house.

"Reckon I'd better go make sure he don't knock down all the work we done today," Blackie said. He looked at Nick, as if debating whether or not to offer his hand. Finally, he said, "You can have the extra bedroom here. Letty will show you. But I'd avoid Gabe for now. He'll settle down after a while."

Blackie followed Gabe out the door.

Nick shoved his chair away from the table. "I think I'd better get a room at a hotel."

Letty protested again. "That's too far. You and Gabe would never get to know each other."

"I thought town was just about thirty miles from here when Pete drove out today."

Pete took over the discussion. "It was, but Letty's talking about Buffalo."

"The town of Buffalo? Why would I stay there?"

"It's the only place nearby that has a hotel," Pete explained.

"How long a drive?" Nick asked in clipped tones.

"Well over an hour."

Nick sat there drumming his fingers on the table.

"Of course," Pete continued, as if Nick had asked a question, "you could pay for your room by pitching in with the work. If you can do any?"

Nick was hurt by that question, as if he were defective by the Randall standards. Which were his, of course, he hurriedly told himself. "What kind of work?"

"Gabe's trying to get his barn together before winter. Only he doesn't know much about carpentry. The neighbors are coming over to help him Saturday."

"I know a bit about carpentry," Nick said briefly.

"Good, it's settled. Letty, show Nick the room, and if he needs anything else, he can get it in Rawhide when he picks up his vehicle."

Letty nodded and started out of the kitchen. Nick quickly followed her.

"This room's not fixed up. I'll get it clean, but finding matching linens may be hard. There wasn't much here when Gabe bought the place, and he hadn't had a home before."

"I'll get some linens. Anything else?" he asked politely.

"A bath towel, or two. Things you need for your shower."

"No problem."

"How am I going to tell you two apart? Even your voice sounds the same," she explained.

"I'll smile. That ought to make it easy."

He expected a chuckle. Instead, Letty came to an abrupt halt, her hands on her ample waist. "Don't you make fun of Gabe. He's had a hard life!"

Nick's eyes softened. "I apologize, Miss Letty. I won't do that again."

Her gentle smile returned and she reached out to pat his arm. "Good. I'm working on softening him up, but it takes a while."

"Tell me about his life," he suggested.

"No," she said. "I'm not one to tell tales. If you want to know about Gabe's life, you can ask him. But I wouldn't if I was you. Not now. He has to get used to you."

Then how in hell was he supposed to find out anything? he wondered in frustration.

Letty opened a door and he stepped into a small, dusty room with a twin bed frame and mattress made about fifty years ago, he figured. Damn, a bad motel would outrank this place.

"I know it looks bad," Letty said apologetically.

"Blackie suggested you stay here 'cause people will talk if Gabe puts his own brother in the bunkhouse."

"You and Blackie take care of him?"

"The best we can. He doesn't have anyone else."

"But I thought he's kin to Pete and Toby?"

"They're distant cousins, but Gabe doesn't like charity."

She opened the door to a narrow closet and then showed him a small chest of drawers. "Don't you forget that, either."

"Yes, ma'am." He didn't ask how she knew he had money. He figured the tweed jacket he wore with his jeans could pay for Gabe's entire wardrobe from what he'd seen.

"When should I expect you back?" she asked. "We go to bed early out here 'cause we work hard all day, and we get up early. Don't expect breakfast at ten o'clock around here."

"Yes, ma'am. What time is breakfast?"

"Six-thirty sharp. Dinner the same time twelve hours later."

"Got it," he assured her, and followed her back to the kitchen.

"I'm ready to go if you are," he told Pete and Toby. "Sorry to cause you an extra trip."

"No problem."

Nick got the impression there wouldn't be much conversation on the way to town. Nick's reception from Gabe obviously had the other Randall men worried.

CHAPTER THREE

Sarah

LEANING AGAINST THE STACK of jeans she'd just straightened, Sarah Waggoner let out a heavy sigh. It had been a difficult day. But then most days seemed that way lately. When had that feeling started?

She knew. When her life began falling apart. For the second time. She'd been a happy child. But her mother had died when she was ten, and suddenly she'd become the woman of the house. Her father had expected her to do the house chores and care for her sister Jennifer, three years her junior.

And she was still trying to take care of Jennifer.

A sound on the stairs shook her from her thoughts. "How was your nap?" she asked her sister.

"I couldn't sleep. Sorry I didn't come help you, but I was just too tired."

Sarah straightened her shoulders and said crisply, "Jon said a little exercise might make it easier to get some sleep."

Their local doctor was the husband of one of her best friends, Victoria Randall. Of course her name was Victoria Wilson now, but once a Randall, always a Randall, in Rawhide.

"What does he know? He's never been pregnant," Jennifer muttered as she came to the counter and morosely propped her elbows on it.

"No, he hasn't been pregnant. That would be a modern miracle since he's a man. But he is a good doctor, and you know Victoria successfully went through her pregnancy under his care."

"It's different for me," Jennifer said. After a moment, when Sarah didn't reply, she asked, "What are you fixing for dinner?"

Sarah stiffened. She knew she was responsible for Jennifer's dependence on her. When their father had died when Sarah was twenty, his last words had been "Take care of Jennifer." Well, she had. So much so, that Jennifer expected Sarah to do everything for her.

She'd decided lately to make a change. "I'm too tired to cook dinner tonight, Jen. What don't you see what you can pull together. I've been working since seven this morning, you know."

"But I'm pregnant!"

"Pregnancy doesn't make you incapable of cooking. Please? I'm really tired."

"Oh, okay. But it won't be good. I can't cook like you." She turned and started back up the stairs.

"Oh, Jen, Gabe came in today. I—I sent him away and told him not to come back." She hurried through the words and neglected to mention that she had slapped the man, hoping Jen wouldn't get upset, but she knew it hadn't worked when she saw tears already forming in her sister's eyes.

"Gabe came here? Did he ask to see me? Maybe he wanted to apologize."

"I didn't ask him why he was here."

"Sarah! I'm sure he wanted to see me. You shouldn't have sent him away!"

"Jen, you said you told him about the baby and he laughed at you and walked away. He said he didn't want anything to do with you or the baby. Didn't you?"

"Ye-es, but he might have changed his mind."

Sarah felt a headache coming on. She had liked Gabe Randall. But he was a traveling man, always going from one city to another, anywhere there was a rodeo. She'd warned Jennifer about pinning her hopes on Gabe. Of course, at the time she hadn't known Jen was sleeping with him. It hadn't even occurred to innocent, stupid her. When had she ever dated? She'd always played the role of Jennifer's "mother." What did she know about life?

"Jen," Sarah said with a sigh, "if Gabe walked out on you and the baby, I don't understand why you'd welcome him back."

"Because I'm pregnant and unmarried. I'm too embarrassed to go out in public."

They'd had several arguments about that. "So if he puts a ring on your finger, all is forgiven?" Sarah ground her teeth. "Maybe any man will do, then. Shall I offer you to any single man who comes in?"

"Why are you being so mean to me? Besides, you know nothing about real life. All you do is work here in the store. You're good at that, Sarah, but you don't understand men."

Sarah wanted to scream. Didn't Jennifer realize that she knew nothing about men because she'd been trying to raise Jennifer? No, she knew she didn't. Jennifer thought Sarah hid behind her father's last words because she was shy. She sighed again. Maybe Jennifer was right. Whatever the case, life had passed her by. She was almost twenty-eight. And there was no romance in sight for her.

The bell over the door jingled and both sisters looked up, each with a different reaction.

"Gabe!" Jennifer sang out with more life in her words than Sarah had heard in months.

"I thought I told you not to come back," Sarah said sternly. She was embarrassed about her earlier behavior, but she'd meant what she said.

The handsome man ignored Jennifer's reaction, which

seemed strange, and came to Sarah, his arm extended,
something in his hand.

"What is this?" she asked as he drew closer.

"My driver's license. My name is not Gabe."

"Really, Gabe," Jennifer said in a chastising tone as she
came back to the counter, "you don't have to go that far
if you want to see me."

The man nodded to Jennifer, acknowledging her for the
first time. "You're a pretty sight, lady, but I'm telling the
truth. I'm not Gabe Randall."

Sarah took the driver's license he held out. It had been
issued in Colorado and listed the man's name as Nicholas
McMillan. She stared at the photo and then at him. He was
well dressed, much more than Gabe had ever been, but—
his features were the same.

"You could be twins," she muttered.

"We are."

"Don't be ridiculous, Gabe Randall," Jennifer protested.
"You don't have any close relatives and I know it. You
told me so yourself." She came from around the counter
to face him, which surprised Sarah. Usually she hid behind
it so no one could see her stomach.

He nodded to Jennifer again until she reached him. Then
he frowned, staring at her stomach. "You're pregnant?" he
asked in surprise. "Are you having Gabe's baby?"

Jennifer began to back away. "Oh, my word. You aren't
Gabe!"

"Look, I don't want to get in the middle of Gabe's business. I'm just here to make some purchases—without taking a beating," he added, with a slanted look at Sarah.

She turned bright red.

Jennifer said politely, "Then I'll leave you to Sarah's
care." At that, she hurried up the stairs.

"Well, I at least made friends with one lady," he said
with a sigh.

Sarah had to clear up something. "I apologize for my

earlier behavior—'' she paused to look at the driver's license "—Mr. McMillan. Regardless of who I thought you were, my actions were uncalled for." She handed back his license and moved behind the counter. "Now, how may I help you?"

"Aha, the mighty dollar weighs in."

She didn't appreciate the scorn she heard in his voice. She bowed her head and took a deep breath. Much to her relief, the front door opened.

"Excuse me," Sarah muttered, and moved toward the new customer. "Good afternoon, Mrs. Winslow. How may I help you?"

The lady was looking for a zipper to put in a dress she was making, and Sarah led her to exactly what she needed. Then the two of them returned to the counter, Sarah going to the cash register.

"Oh, you're another of those Randalls, aren't you?" the lady asked Nick brightly. "Such a lovely family. Didn't you just buy the Harper place? I believe I heard that."

"Yes, ma'am," the man who had just claimed he was Nick said with a polite nod.

"Good. Another family settling down. You are married aren't you?" Mrs. Winslow watched him as if she were a bird about to pounce on a worm.

"No, I'm not."

"You must meet my niece. A lovely girl. She has a wonderful personality."

He grinned. "I'm sure."

Mrs. Winslow turned to go, after trying to pin him down on a time and place. But she didn't succeed. When they were alone again, Sarah began, "So you *are* Gabe?"

"No. I told you I'm Nick."

"You didn't tell Mrs. Winslow that."

"No, because the explanation would've taken too long. She won't know the difference."

"When she ropes Gabe into a blind date with Susan Winslow, *he'll* know the difference."

"True. I'd better be back in Denver by then."

"Are you really Nick McMillan and not Gabe Randall?"

"Really."

Sarah shook her head to clear it and avoided looking at him. "Well, then, how can I help you?"

"Ah, back to business? Not even going to ask me to explain?"

"It's none of my business, Mr. McMillan." She wanted to ask, sure that it would be a fascinating story. And she also wanted to know when Gabe had bought the Harper place. She hadn't known he had settled in the area. She wondered if Jen knew.

"Do you have any sheets?"

She stared at him in surprise. "Sheets?"

"Yes. I'm staying with Gabe and he's a little short on linens, according to Letty." Nick McMillan smile was even more devastating than Gabe's, because he was more...polished, she decided finally. She dropped her gaze, sure it would be best to avoid that smile.

"Twin-size."

That answer turned her gaze again to his big, muscular body. "Twin-size? Won't that be—" She blushed again and brought her mind back to business, ignoring the flush in her cheeks and hoping Nick would do the same.

"Ridiculous, isn't it," he answered. "But beggars can't be choosers."

"How true," she murmured, keeping her gaze lowered. "Of course we have sheets. This way, please."

She found him his sheets, white only, of course. She didn't have room to stock much of a selection. And a pillow when he added it. A blanket came next. She started for the counter when his bed was completed.

"Where are you going?" he asked. "I need more things."

"I'll be happy to help you, Mr. McMillan, but I can't carry any more. Let me place these on the counter and we'll continue. Um, will you be paying with cash or credit? I'm afraid I don't take out-of-state checks."

"Nicely done, Miss Waggoner."

Her cheeks flushed again. He must've noticed their name on the outside of the store. "I don't know what you mean, Mr. McMillan."

"I mean how subtly you questioned me on my ability to pay."

"I don't believe I asked that, Mr. McMillan. I simply wanted you to know I couldn't accept your check."

"Not even if I'm kin to the almighty Randalls?" he asked.

"So you say." She put the bedding down on the counter and turned to face him. "What else can I help you with?"

"Some work clothes."

"What kind of work?"

"Are you by any chance interested in me?" he asked, grinning.

"I need to know the type of work to know the kind of clothes you're talking about," she replied primly. Of course she was interested in him. She might have avoided men in the past, but it wasn't because she had no interest. Especially in one as handsome as him.

"I'm planning to do some work on Gabe's ranch," Nick stated. "I'll need some work shirts and a couple of pairs of jeans. Work gloves, work boots, a hat."

They spent half an hour picking out what he needed. Finally, she said, "Gabe has really bought a ranch?"

"Yeah. He's building a barn and I'm going to help in exchange for my room and board."

"You could probably find a permanent job around here if you've got any skills."

They moved to the counter and she began ringing up his purchases before he said anything.

"Thanks, honey, but I don't think I'm cut out for this kind of work permanently."

Sarah couldn't help but wonder why Gabe had bought a ranch. She would've sworn he was crazy about Jennifer. Why would he decide to settle down here in Rawhide without her?

"Something wrong?" he asked

Sarah realized she'd been staring into space, not moving. "Oh, no, sorry, I—I got distracted."

"No problem. When do you close?"

Sarah checked her watch. "Oh! We usually close at six. I didn't realize it was so late." They were ten minutes past closing time. She excused herself and went over to change the Welcome sign to Closed. Then she returned to finish Nick's—Mr. McMillan's—order.

"Sorry to make you run late. Will it take you long to get home?"

She looked up and blinked her eyes. "Oh, no, my sister and I live upstairs."

"Oh, good." He stood silent, watching her industriously tally his bill. When she looked up and gave him his total, he handed over his platinum card.

She carefully examined his card and then ran it through the card reader, something she'd added to the store five years ago. It quickly gave her approval of the large amount. She handed him back the card with a brief smile and began sacking everything while the sounds of the register processed the bill.

When everything was done, she finally looked at him again. "Thank you, Mr. McMillan. Come back to see us."

"I certainly will, Miss Waggoner. Now, can I ask you something?"

"Of course." She waited eagerly, glad for something to extend their conversation for a few minutes.

"Will you go to the café for dinner with me? It's the only place I know in town and I hate to eat alone."

"Why aren't you eating at Gabe's?" she asked, though she had no business being so inquisitive. It gave her time to stall giving him an answer. She hadn't been asked out in several years. Her fault, of course, since she'd rejected every invitation any man had ever extended.

"Will you hold it against me if I tell you the truth?" he asked.

"No, of course not."

"Everyone thought it would be best if I avoided Gabe for a while. He's not too happy to discover he has a brother."

"Oh." How sad. Even though Jennifer had caused her a lot of work, she wouldn't want to be without her. If Gabe had married her and taken her away... Oh, dear. Had she ruined Jennifer's romance in order to keep her sister here? Could she be that selfish?

"What's wrong?" he asked.

She looked at him in surprise. "What?"

"You looked like you'd just lost someone or something. I don't know, but you looked upset." He leaned toward her and she took a step back. It wasn't that he didn't smell good, because he did. Or that she wasn't attracted, because she was. Oh! Her thoughts were spinning around and she couldn't—

"Look, Miss—damn it, what is your name? I can't keep calling you Miss Waggoner."

"Sarah."

"Pretty name to match a pretty girl," he said softly.

Almost automatically she said, "Oh, no, Jennifer's the pretty one." He gave her a strange stare and she realized what she'd said. "I mean—I'm sorry."

"Sarah, Jennifer is pretty, but so are you."

"Uh, thank you." She looked away.

"Will you have dinner with me? Take pity on me?"

"I would but—it would be awkward. You see, Jennifer dated Gabe for a long time and everyone would think—"

"Is there somewhere else we could go besides the café?"

"There's the steak place. It's part bar, part restaurant, but during the week it's pretty quiet."

"Perfect. Come with me?"

CHAPTER FOUR

Jennifer

SHE STARED AT THE CONTENTS of the refrigerator with dismay. Sarah always did the shopping, so Jen wasn't sure what she could make for supper.

"Jen?" Sarah's voice floated up from downstairs.

She closed the fridge door and walked over to the top of the stairs outside the kitchen. "Yes, Sarah?" She looked down to see her sister standing beside the man who claimed he wasn't Gabe. Boy, didn't he look just like him, though, she thought.

"I—I'm going to dinner with Nick. I'll be back later. You'll be all right?" Sarah looked at her, her face flushed. What had Sarah said? She was going to dinner with a man? And leaving her behind? "You're going to dinner with Gabe?" She was so stunned she hadn't realized she'd called the man by the wrong name.

"I'm not Gabe," the man said. "But I'll see him later tonight if you want me to deliver him a message."

She didn't know if he was telling the truth, but she had no intention of letting Gabe think she wanted him or needed him. "No! I'll be fine." She turned and walked back to the kitchen, her head held high. She wasn't going to cry. She ignored the fact that she'd cried several times today and Sarah had known about all of them.

What was wrong with her? She never used to cry. Jon said it was her hormones. He was a good doctor, but some-

imes she didn't want to hear what he said. She rubbed her
stomach. She hadn't planned on getting pregnant. Oh, she'd
figured she'd have a baby sometime, but not unmarried and
alone.

She didn't want anyone to see her while she was pregnant—all red-eyed from crying over her ever-growing
stomach. She'd been known as the prettiest girl in Rawhide.
She'd enjoyed that title for a long time. She wasn't smart
like Sarah. At least, she wasn't as educated as Sarah. Sarah
had actually even gone to college for a few years. But when
their dad had died, she'd come home and taken over the
store.

Jennifer had continued being the prettiest girl in town. It
was her role. But she couldn't play that role while she was
pregnant. What was she going to do?

If Gabe had married her and built a big house for her,
she could've given up her role gracefully. Could have become the prettiest wife in Rawhide.

But now she was the unmarried pregnant girl in town.

She decided she wasn't hungry, after all. She'd just go
to bed, because thinking about her situation made her cry.
As she pushed away from the kitchen counter, she felt
something in her stomach.

Panic ran through her. There it was again! A flutter or
something. Was something wrong? She ran for the phone,
sure something was wrong.

Quickly she dialed the number she'd insisted Sarah keep
by the phone. "Jon? Jon, something's wrong!"

"Calm down. Who is this?"

"It's Jennifer Waggoner. I—I felt something."

"Describe it to me."

His calm voice reassured her in spite of her panic.

"It was like a flutter. And it happened *three* times."

"Did it hurt?"

"No," she said slowly, suddenly realizing it hadn't.

"I think you just felt the baby's first movement. It's a good sign."

"You—you mean that was my baby?" Being pregnant had never been a reality for her. It meant nothing more than growing fat. But the baby moving made her condition real all of a sudden.

"Yep. You're doing a good job, Jen," the doctor said. "You are getting a lot of sleep, aren't you?"

"Yes, of course."

"And exercise? Normal activity? You need to stay healthy if the baby is going to be healthy, you know."

"I know, I know."

"Okay, then, when's your next appointment?"

"Uh, in two weeks."

"Okay, I'll see you then," he said in a disgustingly cheerful voice.

Of course he was cheerful, she thought to herself. He wasn't pregnant. But that complaint was one she'd used almost from the beginning when she'd thrown up almost every morning and...and felt sorry for herself, Jennifer realized. Oh, dear, she must have been a pain for Sarah to put up with. Such selfless thoughts didn't occur to Jennifer too often, but as she rubbed her stomach, for the first time truly aware of what was inside her, she felt ashamed.

She hadn't thought of anyone but herself lately. Feeling ashamed, she tried to think of times when she'd thought of Sarah, done something for someone besides herself. She'd arranged for a surprise blind date for Sarah once. It had been a disaster, but she'd meant well. She used to help out in the store occasionally. But not often enough. Sarah had run it her way, and Jennifer had had other things to do. Sarah never complained or said anything, she hastily assured herself.

She felt the flutter again.

"Okay, little one, I feel you. You're safe."

Was the baby a boy or a girl? She hadn't even thought

that far ahead before now. They had tests for that. Should she be taking one? She reached for the phone to call Jon, then she lay back on the pillow. She'd already called him once. She'd call him at the office tomorrow.

"Supper!" Maybe her baby was hungry! She rolled off the bed and hurried to the kitchen. How selfish of her not to think of her baby. She quickly made a salad. Then she found some meat loaf wrapped in foil that Sarah had made last night.

She put it in the microwave and pressed the buttons, not sure how long to cook it. When she heard the microwave start, she was proud of herself. Until there was a big pop and a flash of light. She whirled around and saw the meat loaf on fire! She found the off button and hit it, then opened the door. She used a couple of big spoons to scoop her dinner into the sink and turned on the water.

The fire went out, but she had a sodden black mess in the sink. She should call—who could she call? She didn't have any girlfriends. The girls in town had always seemed jealous of the attention she got from men. Sarah was really her only friend.

Her perfect sister. Sarah knew how to make meat loaf. And lots of other things.

Jennifer couldn't help thinking that her baby would like Sarah more than her, its own mother. The only thing she could cook were cookies. Kids loved cookies, but babies needed more nutritious meals. She'd have to learn to make other things. She wanted her baby to be healthy.

She went back to the refrigerator. She found some sliced turkey to eat with her salad. And she poured herself some skim milk. She'd told Jon she didn't like milk, but he'd encouraged her to drink it.

"See, I'm being good for you, baby."

After finishing her meal, Jen decided to read up on babies. Jon had given her some pamphlets to read, but of course she hadn't read them. She'd put them away, forgotten all about them, sure this couldn't be happening to her.

Walking into bedroom, Jen dug through a drawer until she found the brochures. Then she settled down to read but couldn't keep her mind from wondering to Gabe.

Their baby would be so beautiful. She sobbed and then quickly pulled herself together. If Gabe didn't want their baby, it was okay with her! Her conscience lit up like a firecracker.

Okay, so when he'd come to see her several weeks ago she'd told him there was someone else. But that was only because he'd gone away in such a huff when she'd told him she wanted him to settle down and buy them a place to live. She hadn't known she was pregnant at the time, but Sarah warned her that she might not like traveling with Gabe from rodeo to rodeo.

She actually thought it might be fun for a while. No house to clean, no dishes to do. Not that she really knew how to keep house. But she'd learn. She just didn't have to right now, because Sarah took care of everything. She wanted to…didn't she?

She didn't like all this soul-searching. She'd talk to Sarah in the morning. She could get up when Sarah did, at seven. She'd been sleeping in until nine or ten. Maybe that was why she wasn't ready to go to sleep now.

Or maybe it was her conscience still bothering her.

When Gabe had come back to town, she'd decided to make him pay for leaving her alone when he went chasing after yet another rodeo championship. She'd stamped her foot at him, told him she wanted him to settle down, and he'd gone away.

She'd thought he'd surely be back in a day or two. But weeks passed and then she'd found out she was pregnant. By the time Gabe got around to coming to see her, she was so angry she couldn't see straight. She decided she'd show him! She told him there was someone else. He couldn't neglect her like that and get away with it.

"Stupid!" And she wasn't talking about Gabe. She'd only hurt herself with her lies. Gabe had gone on his merry way, as usual, probably finding a new girl at every rodeo, and she'd sat home getting fatter by the minute.

But she'd never believed the baby was real. Until tonight. It was like waking up from a dream. Or a nightmare.

She'd have to tell Gabe she was pregnant. It was his baby. He had a right to know. And maybe he'd come running to her. Hold her in his arms, as she'd loved him to do. Rub her tummy and talk to their baby. Having a baby might not be so bad if Gabe was there.

"Your daddy will love you, baby. I know he will."

She grabbed the phone. Where could he be? Maybe she'd call—one of the Randalls would know. She dialed the number for the Randall ranch.

"Um, may I speak to Elizabeth?" she asked sweetly. She was Toby's wife and a very pleasant woman.

"Hello?"

"Elizabeth, this is Jennifer Waggoner. I wondered if you and Toby know what rodeo Gabe is at this week. I need to talk to him." Why hadn't she thought of this earlier? Just tell him the truth and he'd come back. Dear Gabe.

"Um, just a minute, Jennifer. I'll ask Toby."

It took a while to ask Toby, and Jennifer got nervous. When Elizabeth came back on the line, she asked quickly, "Well?"

"Um, Jennifer, Gabe happens to be in town. Here's his number." Elizabeth rattled off a number that Jennifer hurriedly copied down in surprise.

"Thanks, Elizabeth, that's wonderful." She said goodbye and disconnected.

He was in town. He could be with her tonight. Her loneliness and anxiety would be over. The two of them—no, the three of them, would be together.

She dialed the number and was startled when a woman answered the phone.

"Randall ranch."

She guessed Gabe was staying with one of the Randalls. She didn't know which, but it didn't matter. "Is Gabe there?"

"Yes. Just a minute."

Jennifer couldn't stand waiting. When she heard someone pick up the phone, she said, "Gabe, is that you?"

"Yeah. Who's this?"

That took some of her happiness away. "It's Jennifer! Who did you think it was?"

His response was complete silence.

"Gabe? Are you there?"

"I'm here, Jennifer."

"You—you don't sound surprised to hear from me."

"Sorry, what do you want?"

This wasn't going the way Jennifer had pictured, but she hurried on. "I wanted to tell you—that is, I know it was wrong of me, but I lied to you when you came to see me all those weeks ago. I haven't been seeing anyone else. There's only been you. And now...we're having a baby."

She waited for an outburst of pleasure.

Instead, she got a gritty voice filled with anger. "You must think I'm really stupid, Jennifer. What's the matter? Did the new boyfriend decide not to marry you? Think you could foist your baby off on me? Think again, sweetheart." Then he slammed the phone down.

"No! No, Gabe, you've got it wrong. That's not what—" Finally realizing he'd hung up, she sank back in a heap of tears on the bed. That wasn't what was supposed to happen. She didn't want—what she wanted didn't matter. Sarah had once warned her about telling a lie. She'd just discovered the truth of that old wives' tale about it coming back to haunt you.

She sobbed for several minutes.

Then she felt the baby move again. "I'm so sorry," she said, touching her stomach. "I'll make it up to you. I'll be a good mother. I'll become more responsible. I'll read books about how to take care of you. I'll do everything to make you happy. Maybe someday I'll find you a new daddy. But your real daddy doesn't…love me…at all," she said, hiccuping her sobs.

"But we'll be all right. I'm going to do right by you to make up for…what I did. Just be patient with me. I'll make it up to you."

She fell silent, cradling her stomach, her legs curled up underneath her. Gradually, her heart woeful, her lashes drifted down. Sleep relieved her of her pain and regret, and she gave her strength to meet the day as a new Jennifer, one focused on her baby and her promise.

CHAPTER FIVE

NICK BRACED HIMSELF for breakfast the next morning. He'd gotten up early to be sure not to miss the meal and hoped he'd have some time to speak to his brother.

When he sat down at the table, Letty and Blackie gave him a cheerful hello. Gabe barely grunted.

"Hey, bro," Nick said to Gabe, "I got worried about our working together—"

Gabe interrupted. "So go away."

Nick paused. Maybe Gabe thought he was acting too friendly for a long-lost brother. He tried again. "Gabe, I just thought that since we're carbon copies of each other, folks around here might need a way to tell us apart."

"We are not carbon copies!" Gabe shouted. "I'm me and no one else."

Letty gave Nick a pleading look, and he swallowed his automatic response and tried one more time. "Okay, I was trying to show you these." He held out a red bandanna and a blue one.

"So you've got bandannas. Do you think that makes you a cowboy?"

"No. I thought if you wore one color all the time and I wore the other, there wouldn't be any confusion," Nick snapped, his patience obviously thin.

"That's a smart idea," Blackie said, approval in his voice.

Letty added praise for Nick.

Gabe gritted his teeth. He seemed upset that Blackie was taking Nick's side. "Fine! Which one do I wear?"

"You get first choice. You're the boss." Nick stared at him, daring him to choose.

Gabe snatched the red one and tied it around his neck. "We'll need more than one. It gets hot and sweaty out there."

"I bought a dozen for both of us. Would you put the stack of red ones in Gabe's room?" Nick asked Letty.

"Pay him out of the household money" were Gabe's only words the rest of the meal.

Nick ate his breakfast. He wasn't a fool. It was going to be a long day under Gabe's rule. No question about that. He'd need all the fuel he could get.

Why was he going along with this plan? he asked himself. He had so many questions about his birth mother, the woman who had obviously raised Gabe. Who had decided to keep one son and give the other away. Why was Gabe so reluctant to even discuss their obvious relation? He couldn't help wondering if his brother was even worth getting to know. But he knew Sarah Waggoner was. Dinner last night had been a delight. She'd been brisk and businesslike at times. Other times, he'd think she'd never had a date, which was ridiculous. Yes, he decided, if nothing else, he'd stick around long enough to get to know Sarah better.

"You going to sit there all day?" Gabe's voice, sounding like an angry bull's jolted Nick from his thoughts.

Nick didn't answer. He wiped his face with a napkin, grabbed his hat from the back of his chair and followed his brother out of the room. Blackie followed, giving Nick a slight smile of apology.

WHEN LUNCHTIME ROLLED AROUND, Letty called everyone to the house. There were three other men working with them. Nick had got on with them fine. The only one he had trouble with was Gabe. Nick's experience with building didn't improve anything.

"I thought you said you were a lawyer," Gabe growled as he followed Nick into the house.

Nick knew it wasn't approval or gratitude for his good work that had Gabe speaking to him. "I worked for a builder in Denver summers during law school."

Gabe grunted but said nothing.

"You're a good worker, Nick. Really know this building stuff," Blackie said.

Gabe's face darkened. "We'll take a half-hour lunch and then I want everyone on the job!" Gabe snapped, and walked past the table filled with food to the hallway beyond.

Nick started after him, but Letty grabbed his arm. "Leave him be, Nick. He'll get over it."

Nick patted her hand, then removed it from his arm and continued on. He found Gabe's door closed. He knocked, then opened it, knowing Gabe wasn't going to invite him in.

He found the man staring out the window. "You want to drive off three good men or kill Blackie?" Nick asked casually.

"Get out of here!"

"I will. I'll go all the way to Denver if that's what it takes for you to treat your workers decently."

Gabe glared at him, but Nick didn't back down. "What irks you the most? The fact that I'm a good worker, or that I know more about building than you do?"

Gabe bowed his head and closed his eyes. Then he looked up and sighed. "I apologize. Go out and tell the men to take an hour." Then he turned back to the window.

Nick didn't leave. "Thanks, Gabe. You're a good man."

"I don't need your approval and I'm not trying to impress you."

"I know. That's why you did impress me. You did it

because I was right." He said the words softly and watched for Gabe's reaction.

"Yeah."

"What's wrong, Gabe?"

His brother shook his head but didn't respond.

"Is it me?" Nick asked. "I can leave if that's what you want."

"No. It's a personal problem. Has nothing to do with you."

"You found out about the baby?" Nick asked in surprise, then regretted his words.

Gabe's eyes seemed to turn into burning coals as he glared at him. "What do you mean?"

"Uh, I met Jennifer last night."

"I thought I told you to stay away from her!"

"I had to buy some things. They do run the only store in town."

"What things?"

"Bandannas, sheets, you know, things."

"Yeah, I guess I do." He stood there, his hands on his hips, and Nick still marveled that looking at him was like staring into a mirror. "How did she seem?"

"Jennifer? She looked good, though I have nothing to compare her to now, of course. Pregnancy seems to agree with her."

Gabe glowered. "Was the father of her baby there?"

Nick did a double take. "But she said you—" He broke off and cleared his throat. "I thought—"

"Well, you thought wrong. I'd never abandon my child. That's what our father did, even if he couldn't help it. And look what happened!"

He headed for the door and Nick followed, wanting to ask him to explain his words. But Gabe caught his eye, seemed to know what Nick was about to ask and quickly said, "I don't want to talk anymore about this!"

Nick followed him back to the table, where Blackie,

Letty and the three ranch hands awaited them. Gabe said, "Sorry, guys, I was mad and I took it out on you. Take an hour for lunch. And if it keeps getting hotter, we'll knock off early tonight."

The men gave a cheer, and in no time, everything was smoothed over.

Nick joined them at the table and was quickly asked by one of the men why the brothers had been split up. Nick told them how he'd been born with a clubfoot and had needed expensive surgery to walk properly. He told them that he had figured his birth mother had given him to a wealthy couple—his adoptive parents—so he'd be taken care of. He looked at Gabe for some type of confirmation, but his twin seemed to be staring off into space.

"Why are you working out here?" one of the hands asked, as if to break the tension. "Lose all your money?"

"Nope." Nick took a bite of the apple pie Letty had just served. "I'm here to find out about my past and—" he looked directly at Gabe "—get to know my brother."

No one brought Nick's past up again.

SARAH COULDN'T HELP BUT BE worried when she got up the next morning and found Jennifer in the kitchen, reading the directions on a box of oatmeal. "Jen, are you all right?"

"I'm fine," she said carelessly.

"Uh, I found the meat loaf in the sink last night. Did something happen?"

"It caught on fire, Sarah. Just because I put it in the microwave. We probably need someone to come fix it."

"No. It's because you put it in there with the foil around it. Foil is metal. You can't put that in the microwave."

Jennifer's face flushed. "I won't do it again. I'm sorry."

"I'm just glad you're all right," Sarah said. "I probably didn't tell you that."

"You're being nice, Sarah. We both know I've never learned anything about cooking. But I'm going to learn now. I'm going to be a good mother. And I'm going to work in the store, too, and earn a salary." Jennifer lifted her chin to let Sarah know she wasn't going to be argued out of her new plan.

"That's wonderful, Jen, but you get half the profits, you know."

"But I should earn them."

Sarah hugged her. "I like this new Jennifer."

"Oh. I need to learn about business, too, I guess. This may take a while."

"It's okay if you go slowly, but I'd really like you to learn. Sometimes I feel a little lonely trying to make the right decisions on my own," Sarah confessed.

"But you're so smart," Jennifer said, shocked.

Sarah laughed and hugged her again. "You really do have a lot to learn," she said teasingly. "Did I ever tell you about the order of microwaves I bought? It took us six years to sell all of them."

Jennifer giggled with her sister. "I know I've been a pain, Sarah, but I'm going to be better."

"I know you will. But tell me, why are you reading the oatmeal box?"

"I'm going to make breakfast."

She didn't make it by herself. Sarah had to show her how, but Jennifer caught on quickly. During breakfast, Sarah discovered the movement of the baby had brought on these changes in her sister. Sarah knew Jennifer might not always remember to help with things, but she believed pregnancy had forced her sister to do some major growing up.

Just as Sarah was about to get to work downstairs, Jennifer stopped her. "I have to tell you something before I lose my nerve," she said.

"What?" Sarah asked, a bad feeling in her stomach.

Quickly Jennifer confessed the lies she had told Gabe about being involved with another man.

"Honey, you're going to have to tell Gabe the truth. I'm not surprised by his reaction, but—but he has to know."

"I know I've been thoughtless in the past, Sarah, but will you forgive me? Will you let me and the baby stay with you?"

Sarah swallowed her sudden tears. "Always, Jennifer. But you still have to talk to Gabe. I know you love Gabe. And it is his baby. He has a right to know."

"He does know! I told him. If he doesn't want to believe me, then I'll manage without him. I can do this, Sarah, I know I can...if you'll help me." She added, "I'm sorry for being so clingy."

Sarah hugged her again. "Never apologize for needing me. I'm your sister. We both should do the best we can, but we don't have to apologize for asking for each other's help."

"Right—" Jennifer's shoulders straightened "—we're sisters. And I'm going to be a better one. I'll put the dishes in the dishwasher. Then I'll be down to help you in the store."

"Are you sure? Today is Wednesday. That's usually a busy day."

"I'm sure."

"There'll be a lot of people in the store," she added, watching Jennifer closely. Her sister had been hiding from most of the townsfolk since her pregnancy had begun to show.

"I'm sure. I think I'll wear those maternity pants and top you ordered for me. It won't shock too many people, will it?"

Sarah assured Jennifer she'd look great. Then she took Jennifer up on her offer to rinse the dishes and hurried downstairs more lighthearted than she'd felt in days.

The morning flew by. She got a lot done with Jennifer waiting on the customers. She saw some of them whispering behind their hands, but Jennifer didn't seem to notice.

A shipment came in and Sarah told Jen she'd be out back helping Boyd unload the truck. Boyd was a quiet man in his forties who lived nearby and worked during the day moving the heavy loads, doing simple tasks, making Sarah's life easier.

She checked in the order and directed Boyd where to store the items. "Bring this stack inside when you've finished, Boyd, please," she added before she went inside. She was excited about the order. She'd never carried dishes before. She'd ordered some for new brides, but she'd decided to order a basic set to keep in stock. They were completely white, but their unique shape made them rather fancy. She loved them.

She hurried back into the main part of the store, a smile on her face until she heard her sister's angry words.

"It's my baby and nobody else's. And if you don't like it, you can shop someplace else!"

Uh-oh. The bluebird of happiness from this morning had disappeared. She saw Jennifer run upstairs. Sarah rushed to the counter to discover a busybody she barely tolerated staring up the stairs where Jennifer had disappeared.

"Good morning, Mrs. Parker. May I help you?" Sarah asked.

"That sister of yours is very difficult. All I did was ask who the father is!" she said indignantly.

"And I believe she answered you quite sufficiently. Can I get you anything else or are you ready to check out?"

"She was quite rude to me!" the lady added, not satisfied with Sarah's words.

"Don't you remember how crazy your hormones got when you were pregnant?"

As if she were leading a surprise attack, Mrs. Parker said, "So you admit she's pregnant!"

"Why wouldn't I? Now, is there anything else?" she asked, and began ringing up the woman's minuscule purchases. Sarah suspected the woman bought only a few things each day so she'd have a reason to get out often. She lived alone and feasted on gossip.

By this time, a line had collected behind Mrs. Parker. Sarah helped them quickly, keeping a smile pasted on her face. Then Tori, the doctor's wife, grinned at her. "A long day?"

"Oh, yes," Sarah said with a sigh. "Can you stay a minute? The rush has passed. I'll go get us a cup of coffee." She had bought a small table with two chairs to put in one corner of the store. She called it her consultation area when people looked at some of the catalogs she had and placed private orders. But she and Tori had coffee there a lot.

"I was hoping you'd ask."

Sarah ran upstairs, figuring Jennifer would've gone to bed with her tears. Instead, as she got to the top of the stairs, she smelled fresh-baked cookies. She found Jennifer in the kitchen. The pot of coffee Sarah fixed each morning was ready and she reached for some mugs.

"You baked cookies, Jennifer? How nice. Will you let me steal a few for me and Tori?"

"Of course. Oh. Are you two having coffee?"

"Yes, we are. Uh, do you want to join us?"

"I'd love to," Jennifer said, smiling brightly. "I'll come down as soon as this batch of cookies is done. And I'll bring milk for me."

"Okay. I'll carry down a folding chair, so we'll have three."

Sarah carried down a chair, ran back up and got a tray with two cups of coffee and a plate of cookies. "Jennifer's joining us."

"Oh. How nice," Tori said carefully.

Sarah was grateful for Tori's tolerance. "She's doing much better. She's wearing maternity clothes and she just announced to Mrs. Parker that she was pregnant."

"I know. I was here," Tori reminded her.

"Oh, yes. I forgot. Anyway, she went upstairs and started baking cookies. So I brought us some."

"What a nice treat. And I brought back your accounts." Tori and her cousin, Russ Randall, were partners in an accounting firm down the street.

"How's Russ doing?" Sarah asked.

Tori looked sad and replied, "He's managing, but he's not happy."

"It takes time," Sarah said, remembering his wife's sudden death a year ago.

"I know," Tori replied with a sigh.

Just then, Jennifer came down the stairs, carrying her glass of milk.

"Um, I should apologize, Sarah. I was rude to Mrs. Parker."

"Don't worry about it. We'll work on our people skills later. A cookie will keep you sweet. These are very good."

"Yes, they are," Tori added. "I didn't know you could cook."

Jennifer looked at Sarah and they both broke into laughter. It had been a long time since Jennifer laughed like that and the sound made Sarah very happy.

"You've just seen my entire repertoire, Tori," Jennifer confessed with a grin. "Oh, no, I forgot, Sarah taught me how to make oatmeal this morning."

Tori laughed, too. "That's always handy. Oatmeal is multipurpose. It even makes great cookies."

"Are they difficult?" Jennifer asked.

"No more than these. Just read the recipe on the box," Tori explained, and Jennifer excused herself to head upstairs.

Sarah expected there would be more cookies to sample later. "Thanks to you," she said to Tori, "I think I'm going to be on a continuous diet of cookies."

"Maybe she'll move on to gourmet dinners," Tori teased.

Then a crash came from upstairs and Sarah rolled her eyes and replied with a laugh, "Maybe not."

CHAPTER SIX

AFTER HE AND HIS MEN had knocked off work for the evening, Gabe headed home. But after a quick shower he realized he had so much to do and to worry about, he didn't know where to begin. He couldn't get his mind off Jennifer's phone call.

There had been such hope in her voice. He knew she could be selfish at times, but he'd believed her when she'd said she loved him. What a fool he'd been. But he couldn't stop loving her, wanting to protect her. And now she was alone and pregnant and he wasn't taking care of her.

But it wasn't his job, he reminded himself. It was the job of the rat who'd gotten her pregnant! He jammed his hands in the pockets of his clean jeans and walked out of the house. He strode toward the lake, which was just a stone's throw from the house. He loved that lake. It represented a good resource, of course. But it was like the icing on a cake. He could get along without it, but it added a beauty and a richness he enjoyed.

When he'd first seen the lake, he'd imagined him and Jen having picnics by it. He could picture their children learning to swim there. Or maybe ice skating there. He'd never tried ice skating before, but he'd learn so he could teach his kids. In his dreams, they'd joked and played. He could've sworn he heard their laughter. It wasn't a sound he'd heard often in his youth.

After his mother died, he'd stayed with his stepfather a

couple of years. The man was a mean drunk. He hadn't hit his mother, but he'd hit Gabe a lot.

Finally, Gabe asked himself why he was staying. He couldn't find an answer and he'd slipped out at dawn with a few things to sell and thirty dollars he'd found in the kitchen. The last of the food money for the month. The rodeo had been in town and he'd looked for odd jobs, slept in the stables each night and managed to keep his stomach filled.

When the rodeo left town, he went with it. It was a hard life, but he soon met up with Blackie. Blackie had been a pretty good rodeo man in his time. He had some savings tucked away, but he had no family. He took Gabe under his wing. He told him rodeo stories, made sure he had a place to sleep, bought him food when Gabe didn't have any. Slowly he began teaching him the skills that he had learned over the years.

He'd paid Gabe's first entry fee when he was old enough to ride. Gabe had won. It was a small rodeo, not much competition, but Gabe took it as a good sign. He'd done well over the years, had enjoyed traveling from town to town. And then he had met Jennifer. Their romance had been sweet and he'd figured he was the luckiest guy in the world. But it had been a shock when Jennifer had told him he had to settle down if he wanted to be with her.

In the end, it had been easy. Gabe had been saving his winnings so he could afford to buy a place. Blackie agreed to settle down with him. In fact, the older man had confessed he was tired. Gabe had found Letty and hired her on to help Jennifer with the housework. Jennifer was like a butterfly. It was enough that she brought beauty to his world. It was more than he'd ever had.

And now he didn't have any of it.

"But I have my lake."

The other Randalls had a lake. But theirs was a lot farther from their home. He was lucky his was so close.

Yes, he'd have the lake and Jennifer would have the children. And he realized that no matter what else, it was Jennifer he wanted. So why had he turned her down?

"Want company?"

Gabe turned around to find Nick behind him. They were standing at the edge of the lake, but Gabe had been barely conscious of walking that far. "You followed me?"

Nick hesitated, then he said, "Yeah. I figured if I ran into a mad bull, you'd save me."

"I don't have any cows in this pasture right now. My herd is small, but when spring comes, I'll buy some good stock and start building my herd."

"Sounds like you know what you're doing."

Gabe smiled, surprising himself. "About as well as you know how to build a barn."

"Then you're in good shape, bro."

"Thanks." He relaxed a little, leaning against a tree.

"What were you thinking about?"

Gabe rubbed his eyebrow, as he was wont to do when he was thinking. "Look, Nick, I know you're looking for something from me, but I don't know what it is. I'm not used to sharing. I'm a loner. So maybe I can't give you whatever you're looking for."

Nick studied the lake in front of him. "Pretty place."

"Yeah."

"I might believe what you say if it weren't for Blackie. I see you watching him, worrying about him."

Gabe kept his eyes fixed on the shimmering water. "I owe Blackie a lot."

"So when you've paid the debt, you'll send him back to the rodeo?" Nick said casually.

Gabe exploded away from the tree. "I'll never be able to pay that—" He stopped because Nick was grinning at him. "What's funny?"

"I know there's more between you and Blackie than money. Tell me about him. When did you meet him?"

To Gabe's surprise, he found himself opening up, reminiscing about his growing up under Blackie's wing. "I guess he was like a grandfather, or maybe even a father. I'm not sure since I hadn't been around any of those kind of people until I met the Randalls. But we're pretty much stuck with each other."

Nick nodded. "You had a hard life, didn't you?"

"Not once I ran away."

"But you didn't get much education."

"No, I didn't get your kind of education. But I know animals. I know how to make my ranch run. I've learned from the Randall brothers since I met Toby a few years ago. I feel kind of complete, like I've found my kind when I go over there to dinner or something. It's a good feeling. I've always felt kind of odd man out, until then."

"I've always felt that way, too. Until I met you," Nick said quietly, and Gabe's jaw dropped.

"But you're a lawyer, like your father. Didn't he… wasn't he proud of you?"

Nick shrugged his shoulders. "I guess. I know at times he was, but it was expected of me. I had no choice but to go to law school."

"You probably feel pretty damn superior when you're around me," Gabe said dryly.

Nick squatted down and ran his fingers through the grass. "You think so? I don't know anything about ranching. Nothing."

"You could learn. But you'll make more money as a lawyer in a year than you will as a rancher in twenty."

"Then maybe you should think about going to law school."

Gabe grinned. "You got me there." After a moment, he said, "I had dreams of settling down, having—" He stopped abruptly. "Damn if you're not coaxing words out of me!"

"What's wrong with that?"

"How do I know I can trust you?" Gabe asked.

"We're brothers. You're my family. I don't have many close friends because I've always felt alone. Until I found you. Why would I ever betray you? Now, even if I leave here, I know you exist."

"Yeah. I guess it would be a shame not to get to know each other."

"I guess," Nick agreed casually.

"It doesn't mean you have to work on the barn. You can stay here without working for your keep."

"Or I could pay you rent."

"Naw, I'm fine."

"Just as I thought. You don't mind me leaning on you, but you would never lean on me."

Gabe looked at him. "I don't need to lean."

"The day you do, remember me, okay?" Then he added, "And I'll be working on that barn tomorrow. If I don't, you might wind up with a doghouse instead of a barn."

Gabe laughed at his teasing and Nick joined in. For the first time since he'd seen Nick sitting at his table, he relaxed a little...until he thought of Jennifer.

"WHAT DO YOU THINK?" Sarah asked as she stood back and looked at her arrangement of the dishes she'd received the day before.

Jennifer came over and stared at the neat stack of dishes. "Well, it's—very neat."

"And has a good personality?" Sarah added on.

"What do you mean?" Jennifer asked.

Sarah laughed. "That's how people describe girls who aren't blessed in the looks department, like you are."

"Well, it's a nice thing to say."

"No, that's the point. Everyone knows that if you're described as having a good personality, you're ugly."

"Oh," Jen said, her cheeks flushing. "I didn't mean that your arrangement was ugly, Sarah. Really, I didn't."

"You may not have meant it, but it is. Why don't you see what you can do? I imagined something striking that would catch everyone's eye, but this isn't it."

Jennifer watched as Sarah approached a customer and offered to help her, exchanging polite pleasantries. That was one of Sarah's special talents, Jen thought. She could make anyone feel welcome and at home. Jen wasn't so good at it, though she was making an effort to be better. But making transitions in every part of her life was hard. And discouraging.

The baby had something to say about that as she kicked Jennifer. The kicks were becoming a bit more forceful as if her baby was growing stronger. And Jen realized she was growing stronger, too. She wasn't staying up late at night, crying nonstop. She fell asleep when she got into bed, exhausted from work. Lately, she'd been thinking wistfully about those naps she used to complain about. Maybe she *was* trying to change too much too fast.

Baby kicked again and she rubbed her stomach. Jen decided she'd best try her hand at arranging the dishes before she fell asleep standing up. She removed some of the dishes, stacking them carefully on another shelf. She thought Sarah, in her enthusiasm, had tried to show every piece of china at once.

When she finished the arrangement, she was pleased with her efforts, but she'd have to see what Sarah had to say about it. She took the pieces she didn't use to the front window. Sarah filled the window to overflowing, too.

"I've finished the dishes, Sarah," Jennifer said after Sarah left a customer's side.

"Oh, thanks, Jen, I'll—oh, Jen, that's terrific. Exactly what I had in mind!" Sarah enthused. She'd been very careful to be positive about all Jennifer's efforts, but Jen heard real enthusiasm in Sarah's voice.

Jen hugged her sister. "I'm glad you like it."

"I love it, and I think it will draw a lot of eyes."

"Then would you mind if I worked on the front window? I'd like to make some space to put some of the dishes there."

"That would be terrific, Jennifer. I think I didn't spend enough time on the display, but I have so much to do."

"I know you do, Sarah, that's why I want to help you around the store. Thanks for the chance."

"Honey, you've been doing a lot. It's been a great week, but I'm worried about you doing too much."

"We'll talk later. And don't worry about me, I'm excited about this job."

They exchanged smiles and Jennifer returned to her task. At least she'd found something she could do without causing a disaster.

Their meals this week had been spotty, at best. She was learning, but not without a few burnt offerings. She'd never learned to do anything in the kitchen except make cookies before her mother died. Now she was an adult and supposed to know a few things, but she was still a novice. "Good thing I didn't marry Gabe. He would've divorced me after the first week."

She blinked quickly to keep the tears from falling. She'd vowed to be happy for her baby, but that had been one promise she really struggled with. She was reading books about childbirth in the evening. But there was always a picture of the happy mother supported by the happy father.

It was a good thing she had four more months to get the hang of all this, and store up her courage to go through the birth alone.

But she wouldn't be alone. She had Sarah. They were much closer after only one week of her trying to be more mature. And she loved it.

Yet she still couldn't keep Gabe from her thoughts. How she missed him. How she loved him. Only he didn't love her. That much was clear.

With all her promises to herself and her baby, she had

to admit now that she'd made some of those promises in hopes that Gabe would change his mind and call her. But he hadn't, of course. He never would.

She began removing all the new items Sarah had put in, or maybe she should say thrown in, the window. Jennifer got so wrapped up in her work, she didn't even notice the people passing by. She was in her own happy world.

A knock on the glass shocked her, and she jerked her head up to find Gabe staring at her, a smile on his face. Gabe! Was she dreaming? She reached for her hair, sure it was a mess, worried that he would think her ugly in her maternity clothes. "I have to get out of the window," she muttered, shoving things out of her way to go meet Gabe. He'd come. He'd finally come!

She got out of the window and ran toward the front door as it opened. "Gabe!" she called, beaming at him.

She'd almost thrown herself in his arms, but he said, "No, I'm not Gabe."

She stood there, her mouth open, until Sarah came over and said, "It's Nick, Jennifer."

Jennifer stared at her, her words not making sense.

What did she mean? Couldn't Sarah see it was Gabe? Couldn't she remember the way Gabe looked, his strong muscles, those brown eyes that twinkled when he teased her? Then her memory caught up with her excitement. Gabe had a twin. Sarah had gone to dinner with him.

Jennifer had never even asked her sister about her evening out. Too much had been going on in her head. That had been selfish of her. She turned to the man who looked so much like Gabe. "Is Gabe with you?" she asked, her voice shaking.

"Uh, no, I'm afraid not."

Even his voice sounded like Gabe's. "Is—is he well?"

"Yeah, he's fine. Working on his place."

"His place?" Jennifer asked, surprised.

The man looked at Sarah, as if wondering what to say.

Sarah again spoke softly, as if she were afraid to upset Jen. "Gabe has bought the Hunter place. I told you, remember, honey?"

Jennifer felt her head spinning. Gabe had a place? He hadn't come for her? He had a place without her and the baby? She felt herself falling, but she couldn't seem to stop.

SARAH GASPED AND REACHED for Jennifer, but Nick got there first, scooping her into his arms before she could hit the floor.

"Oh, dear, thank you, Nick. I think seeing you was a shock to her system. She's been so tired lately. Could you carry her upstairs for me?"

He grinned. "Of course."

Sarah led the way, wondering if Jen had made the beds this morning. She took turns with Sarah now, making the beds while the other did the breakfast dishes. She found everything neatly in place. "Put her down here, please, Nick, and thank you so much for bringing her up."

"No problem. Is there anything I can do? Should we call the doctor?"

"No, I think she just got overwhelmed. She's been working hard this week. I'll be down in a minute. If there are customers, would you tell them?"

"Sure. I'll wait for you downstairs."

Sarah was relieved when he disappeared. He affected her breathing, which was ridiculous. "Jen?" she whispered, stroking Jennifer's forehead. "Jen, can you hear me? Wake up, honey. I want to see if you're all right."

Jennifer stirred, much to Sarah's relief. "Are you all right?" she asked.

"What happened?" Jen replied, staring around at her bedroom.

"I think you've worked too hard. Then when Nick came in you thought—it was Nick, honey, not Gabe."

Jennifer's eyes widened as she hurriedly responded. "Oh. Yes, of course. Nick. I remember."

"You don't need to sit up so soon, Jen. How do you feel? Is the baby okay?"

Jen looked slightly panicked, but then she cradled her stomach. "She's moving, so I guess she's okay. Should we call Jon?"

"Do you want me to?" At Jen's negative shake of her head, Sarah said, "Well, since Nick kept you from hitting the floor I think you're okay. You're just tired and doing too much. Why don't you stay in bed. I'll go close up and then I'll fix us some supper."

"It's my turn to cook."

Sarah smiled. "And you've done a great job this week, but I told you earlier I think you're overdoing it. I think we need to rethink our schedule. We'll discuss this tomorrow."

"Okay," Jennifer hazily agreed, letting her eyes close.

Sarah covered her with a light blanket, waiting until she was sure her sister was asleep before she went down to close up the store.

Not to see Nick, she told herself staunchly, but those sparkling brown eyes were the first thing she looked for when she got downstairs.

CHAPTER SEVEN

SARAH RECOGNIZED THE WAY her stomach constricted when she looked at Nick. The same thing had happened when she'd accompanied him to the café last Wednesday night. But her hope that he'd held any romantic interest in her had soon been dashed. He'd spent the night asking a lot of questions about the Randalls and the town of Rawhide. Nothing about her.

She might be low on dating experience, but even she knew that asking questions about a person indicated interest. And conversely, no questions meant zero interest. She'd thought about him since then, she admitted, but a week and a half of silence only reinforced what she'd realized. He'd wanted information and some company during a meal, but it hadn't mattered who he got these from.

So she shushed the excitement in her stomach and made her tone matter-of-fact as she thanked him again for helping out with Jennifer.

Nick smiled as he watched Sarah come down the stairs. She was so sweet. At least his second reception at her store had made him feel better. Today hadn't been so good.

"Is everything okay now?" he asked, referring to Jennifer's condition.

"I think so. She's going to stay in bed tonight. Were there any customers?"

"One lady and she said she'd come back tomorrow. How are you?" He hadn't talked to her since they'd gone out the night he'd come to town. He'd wanted to call her, but it was awkward being out at Gabe's place.

"I'm fine. Thank you for taking care of the customer. I think it's time to close. Did you want something?" She leveled her gray eyes at him, and he wanted to tell her the truth and nothing but the truth, but he figured it would shock her. Somehow, he didn't think she'd appreciate him voicing just how much he wanted *her*.

"I came to extend an invitation," he said instead, smiling.

"Really?"

"Yeah, we're having a barn raising at Gabe's place tomorrow evening. Letty says there'll be a lot of eating and dancing. Sounds like fun, doesn't it?" he asked, but he noticed Sarah wasn't smiling. "What's wrong?"

"Are you suggesting I come to the barn raising?" she asked stiffly, crossing her arms over her chest.

"Well, yes, I—what's wrong with that idea?"

"You don't know? My sister is upstairs hurting because she's still in love with Gabe. She's carrying his child that he rejected, and you want to know what's wrong with it? Don't you think my attending a function at Gabe's place would be a betrayal of my sister?"

"I think you're making too big a deal of it. You're a member of the community. I think you should go."

"No, thank you," she said tersely, and moved toward the front door. "I'm locking up, so you'd better get on the other side of the door."

"Just like that, you're refusing? If you're worried about leaving Jennifer alone, I can hire someone to stay with her. Just give me a name."

"No, thank you."

"The Randalls make up a large part of the community. You can't ignore them."

She swung the door open and stood waiting, not responding.

He debated what to do. "I want to make a purchase. I need another blanket. I got cold last night."

She closed the front door and walked to the section of the store where she kept the blankets. "Does color matter, sir?" she asked, pulling a blanket from the shelf.

"Sir? You're going to be formal? Or maybe you don't want my business. I have a lot of money, Sarah. You'd be a fool to turn down my patronage...or my friendship." He stared at her.

She stared back at him for several seconds. Then she placed the blanket back on the stack and walked to the front door. "I'm sorry, Mr. McMillan. We're closed for the evening. Perhaps you can come by on Monday."

He lost his temper. "No. I damn well won't. If necessary, I'll drive into Buffalo to make my purchases. From someone who knows the customer is always right."

"The customer is always right at our store—when the customer is buying an object, and not a person. Good night, Mr. McMillan."

"Goodbye, Miss Waggoner!" he snapped as he strode past her.

There was no response, except the click of the lock turning.

Damn, damn, damn! He'd lost his temper and acted like a spoiled child. Just because he was wealthy wasn't a reason for her to kowtow to his wishes. He knew that, but obviously he'd gotten spoiled in Denver. Women didn't usually turn him down.

He'd already been warned by Letty that Gabe had a lot of pride. Apparently, Sarah did, too.

He turned back toward the store and banged on the door. Better to apologize now than let her go to bed thinking he was a total jerk. But though he rapped on the door several times, there was no answer. No movement in the store.

Okay, so he'd have to send flowers. He didn't see a florist shop anywhere on Main Street. Life wasn't as handy in Rawhide as it was in Denver. For him. Denver was a town where a lot of money bought almost anything you wanted.

He'd been thinking he could ensure Gabe's approval of him by helping his brother get the ranch he wanted to purchase. Blackie had told him about Gabe's recent disappointment at not getting the bank loan. He could take care of that without much damage to his pocket.

Now he realized he was wrong there, too. Gabe would throw it back in his face. He wasn't a person who could be bought. Neither was Sarah.

"She's probably holding out for marriage," a little voice said.

"She'd have a long wait." Again he was talking to himself on the sidewalk in front of her store. He wasn't cut out for marriage. His father had wanted him to marry and have children. He'd refused. He was too unsettled, looking for something that he couldn't identify. Then, when he'd found out about a twin brother, he'd wondered if that had been the cause of his unrest.

And he'd tried to buy Gabe, or planned to, like he'd just tried to buy Sarah.

He was embarrassed that he'd been so crass.

Wandering into the café, Nick ordered some dinner. He'd told Letty he'd eat in town. Might as well.

He ate slowly after his food was delivered thinking about what he should do about Gabe's situation. He had money, more than enough to share with Gabe. They were family. Brothers. Twins. He could ensure Gabe's success.

When he couldn't figure out what to do, he decided to visit the Randalls tonight and ask Pete. He didn't mind letting them in on his plan to help Gabe. He figured they knew his brother better than anyone else in town. The Randalls would surely have some advice for him.

He paid his bill and got back in his car, a new Lexus.

He'd thought about trading in his car for a pickup, to fit in more with what the locals drove, but he liked his comfort.

Half an hour later, he turned off on the gravel road that led to the Randall stronghold. He figured he should've called first, but after all, he was family. Sort of.

When he knocked on the front door, several minutes passed before it opened. A distinguished man, similar to Pete in features and build, stood there.

"Is Pete here?" Nick asked.

"Yes, he is. You must be Nick. I'm Jake, Pete's brother and your cousin. Come in."

"Thank you."

"By the way, next time come to the back door. We wouldn't have heard your knock except I was passing by on my way to the kitchen."

"All right, thank you." His mother would've laughed at the Randalls' countrified ways.

Nick followed Jake through a swinging door, into a huge kitchen where all the Randalls seemed to have gathered to eat. There were a lot of people in the room. About half of them were cooking, and three men were sitting at one end of a big table.

"Pete, Nick's here to see you," Jake announced. Then he added, "These are my two other brothers, Chad and Brett. Join us."

Nick was a little unsure of what he should do. He had intended to speak in private to Pete. But obviously that idea didn't occur to Pete as he remained in his chair. Nick pulled out a chair and sat down.

"You getting used to life on the ranch over at Gabe's?" Pete asked.

"It's a little spartan," Nick said, smiling, "but I'm getting used to it."

Jake's eyes narrowed, but Pete said nothing. The other two brothers listened politely.

"I, uh, Blackie told me about the ranch next door to

Gabe that he wanted to buy. I wanted to offer to help him out, but he's a little touchy." He cleared his throat, finding his question hard to ask. "I wondered if you could tell me who to talk to at the bank to take care of this."

Pete opened his mouth to speak, but Jake raised a hand and Pete sat back, saying nothing. Jake asked, "How would your talking to someone at the bank make a difference? Are your powers of persuasion that strong?"

Nick felt as if he'd just been insulted. "No, but my bank account is." He stared back at Jake, not about to be intimidated.

"Really?" Jake asked, not appearing impressed.

"I inherited my father's estate, and I also have my own investments. I could help Gabe, maybe become a partner."

"You know anything about ranching?" Brett asked.

"No. But I could learn."

Pete and Jake exchanged a look. Then Pete leaned forward. "I'm sure Gabe would appreciate your offer, Nick, but we took care of it."

"What do you mean you took care of it?" Nick asked, surprised. "You offered him money?"

"No. Gabe wouldn't take money from us."

"Then what did you do?"

Jake leaned forward. "We had a talk with the bank."

"And that did the trick?" Nick asked, a little doubt in his voice.

"You could say that," Jake drawled.

Chad took pity on Nick. "Jake's the president of the board of directors."

"I see," Nick said stiffly. He stood. "I'm sorry I wasted your time," he said as he headed for the door.

"Nick," Pete said quietly, and waited until Nick turned around to face him.

"Gabe's a bit touchy about money. He made a lot in the rodeo, but most of his life he had nothing. I'm pretty sure he went to bed hungry more than once. He knows the power money has. And he doesn't like not having that power himself."

"Does Gabe know you have money?" Brett asked Nick.

"No, he doesn't."

"So you're going to make him look like a fool when word gets around," Chad suggested.

"No!" Nick protested. That hadn't been his intent, but he guessed he could see how Gabe might think that. So his money, instead of winning him his family, was going to cost him?

Pete nodded his head. "Gabe offered you a place to stay because he thought you were down on your luck. You didn't tell him differently."

"Hell! If I had, he'd have thrown me out. I wanted to get to know him!" Nick thought that was a good-enough reason.

"Why?" Jake asked. "Because you're going to settle down here, be a part of his life?"

"No! I don't know. I haven't decided. I mean, I'll always be his brother. If I go back to Denver, we'll still keep in touch."

"Keep in touch? Why did you come here if you don't want to be closer than that?" Chad asked.

"Not all families are as close as you Randalls! I don't have to live in the same town for us to be family."

"It sure helps. Gabe's been alone a long time. Blackie's stuck by him, but until Gabe moved here, he's been about his only family," Pete said. "We were all happy for him when you showed up." Pete gave him a quelling look. "But I guess we assumed too much. You're a city man. Our town isn't big enough for you, and our people aren't rich enough for you."

Nick knew he was being judged and fell short of what they thought he should be.

"I'm sorry I don't meet your standards. That doesn't happen to me often. Since I can buy most anything I want."

He hadn't meant to brag, but he didn't like their criticism.

All four men exchanged smiles. Then Jake stood and offered his hand. "Good for you. Come see us before you leave."

Nick could tell he was being dismissed. Still, he found himself asking, "Does Gabe know about his reprieve, thanks to you?"

"No," Pete said. "We'd appreciate it if you didn't say anything. The banker will be out Monday to inform him."

"I see. Thank you for helping him." Then Nick walked out the back door. Clearly he hadn't impressed the famous Randall brothers.

He drove home slowly, not liking the results of trying to throw his weight around. He'd thought it would be a simple thing, to make life better for Gabe. But, though they were brothers, Gabe was more like the four men he'd faced tonight. He was a self-made man. One who had confidence because he'd faced many challenges and obviously overcome them.

Nick parked his car beside the unfinished barn, then leaned back against the headrest. Was he going to stay? He didn't have an answer. He thought he might. He might be a better man for it if he did.

The summer his father had told him to go to work for the builder, he'd wondered why he would do such a thing. By the end of the summer, he was much more confident of himself than he'd been before. He'd told his father he'd enjoyed it and thanked him. He'd been proud of his maturity. His father had said good, since he'd be working there again the next summer. He hadn't understood why.

Now he did. Maybe he owed his father another word of thanks. He could add a thanks for the information about his brother, too, if it wasn't already too late to form any kind of bond with Gabe.

SARAH HAD JUST OPENED the door the next morning when a huge vase of red roses was thrust at her face.

"These are for you, Sarah. Biggest order for an individual I've ever had. Hope you like 'em," the delivery man said before handing her the vase and walking away.

She figured she knew who they were from. After all, he'd said he had money. But she wasn't going to think about him anymore.

Jennifer came down the stairs. Sarah had suggested she stay in bed this morning, but she'd refused.

"My, those flowers are gorgeous. Who are they for?"

That question certainly demonstrated more change in Jennifer than Sarah had thought. In the past, Jennifer would've had no doubt the flowers were for her.

"Me," Sarah said quietly. "I'll take them upstairs if you can take care of things down here for a minute."

"Of course. Who are they from?"

"I haven't looked, but I'd guess Nick." She hadn't said anything to Jen last night about the conversation she'd had with Nick.

"Wow! How romantic! He must be crazy about you, Sarah. Roses are for love."

"No. I think they're for an apology."

In a stern voice, Jennifer demanded, "Did he try to get fresh with you?"

"No, Jen, he didn't. He bragged about his wealth and expected it to change my answer to yes." She sent her sister a rueful look.

"What was the question?"

Sarah had considered not telling Jen about the barn raising, but she knew she'd hear about it. "He wanted me to go to the barn raising at Gabe's this afternoon."

Jennifer looked a little sick to her stomach and Sarah moved toward her. "No," she said, waving Sarah away. "There's no reason you shouldn't go, Sarah. I'll manage the store for you. I can do it. I learned a lot this week."

"I know you did, Jen, and I'm sure you could," she said. "But I'm not going."

"But you could see Tori and the rest of your friends."

"Did you notice Tori didn't mention meeting me there?"

"She didn't? Why not?"

"Because she knew I wouldn't go. And she knows why. Nick didn't understand, even when I told him. Which tells me he's not the kind of man I would be interested in." She'd kept telling herself that all night long when she couldn't get to sleep.

"I'm sorry, Sarah. I didn't mean to upset your big romance."

"You didn't do any such thing! Let me put these upstairs and then we'll get to work. I can't wait to see how good the front window looks when you're finished."

Once upstairs, she put the roses in her room. She didn't want them where Jen could see them and get upset all over again. Then she unpinned the note and slowly opened it.

"I apologize for my hardheadedness. Please forgive me. Nick."

She folded the note and put it in her desk drawer. She didn't have a collection of love letters. Only Nick's note. But she'd keep it, if for no other reason then to remind herself of how foolish she'd been, thinking the man cared for her.

CHAPTER EIGHT

GABE WAS GETTING A BIT ANTSY about the barn raising. He'd told Letty about the onslaught of people sure to arrive, and she'd been cooking since yesterday to be sure there was plenty of food for everyone. When he came into the kitchen, Gabe couldn't help but grab himself a warm brownie with chocolate icing.

"Gabe Randall! Keep your fingers off my cooking. It's for our guests!" Letty shouted.

"How do you know it's Gabe? I'm Nick, and I'm a guest!"

"I heard that!" Nick shouted from the doorway. Then he took a brownie, too, and sank his teeth into it. "Man, Letty, these brownies are great!"

"Scat, you two, before you destroy all my work," she told them with a smile.

Gabe bent and kissed her rosy cheek, and Nick did the same. Then he followed Gabe out the door.

"Gabe? Have you got a minute? I'd like to talk to you."

Gabe looked over his shoulder to see a serious look on Nick's face. "Sure. Is something wrong?"

"Kind of."

"Want to walk down to the lake? No one will bother us down there."

Nick nodded and they walked down the hill, their strides matching perfectly.

"You worried about meeting everyone today?" Gabe asked, hoping that was all Nick wanted to say. But the serious look on Nick's face worried him. In just a week, he'd gotten used to having him around.

Once they reached the lake, Gabe turned to face his mirror image. "Well?"

"Do you remember when you offered to let me stay here? You said if I was down on my luck, I could stay?" Nick asked.

"Yeah. Are you worried about that? No need. You've more than earned your keep. The barn is almost finished since you know what you're doing. It's looking good."

"No, it's not that. I'm not down on my luck."

"Good for you. I wondered why you would be, since you seem so sharp."

"I'm the opposite of down on my luck." Nick stared at him, as if waiting for some reaction.

Gabe returned that look. "Are you damn wealthy? If you are, just say so."

Nick's mouth fell open. "You already know, don't you?"

"Why are you so surprised? Do you think I'm stupid? I know what a Lexus costs. I've shopped for a nice jacket once or twice in my life. I've heard of a Rolex," he pointed out, looking at Nick's wristwatch.

"Why didn't you say something?" Nick demanded.

"It was your business. Has nothing to do with me."

"But it could. I could buy you that place next door."

"Why should you?"

Nick stared at him. "Don't you think I should do something for you?"

"Why?"

Nick gave him a wry smile. "Because I'm your brother."

Gabe thrust his hands into the pockets of his jeans and looked out at the lake. "I'm glad you came to find me since I didn't know you existed. And I hope, some day, we'll really get to know each other. But just because we came from the same gene pool doesn't make us real brothers.''

''I hope we will be,'' Nick said, his voice hoarse as he laid a hand on Gabe's shoulder.

''Me, too,'' Gabe whispered.

''Will you tell me about our mother?''

''I wish I could tell you she was happy. But she wasn't. I know now she mourned losing you, even though she made the choice. I think she regretted it every day for the rest of her life. I didn't understand. I kept trying to make her happy.''

Nick wanted to tell him he hadn't known his mother was suffering, but Gabe knew that.

''At night, she'd help me say my prayers. She always prayed for our family, even those we didn't know. I guess those prayers were meant for you.'' Gabe gave a shaky laugh. ''It's a relief to know that it wasn't that I failed her.''

''I think she'd be very proud of you, Gabe. You were strong and found your own way.''

''And she'd be thrilled about you. Every mother wants her son to grow up to be a success. I just wish she could've known it.''

''So it was just the two of you?''

''No. She remarried when I was ten. My stepfather was a miserable man. He was mean to me, but he treated Mom okay. I think he truly loved her, but he knew she didn't love him.''

''So you ran away and found Blackie?''

''Yeah. Blackie gave me a life.''

''I think you made your own life.''

Gabe shrugged but said nothing.

''I had a much easier life, Gabe. I can share my wealth with you. I have more than I can spend.''

Gabe shook off his sadness. ''Wait until you get married. I've heard a wife can spend more money than even you can imagine. Are you going back to Denver to get on with your life?''

Nick said nothing for a minute. Then he said, "I don't know. Are you throwing me out?''

''Never. But I know this life isn't what you're used to. I might even come see you sometime, if you wouldn't be ashamed of me.'' Gabe looked at him, knowing he'd see the answer in Nick's face.

''No, I'd never be ashamed of you, Gabe, and you're always welcome. But I'd like to stay a little longer, if you don't mind.''

''Why would I mind? You're a good worker!'' he assured him, grinning.

''But your barn is going to be finished today.''

''Yeah, but the house could use some work.''

''You've got a deal,'' Nick said, extending his hand.

''Let me know what supplies you need.''

''I can buy—''

''No, I pay my own way, Nick. I'm trading your spectacular accommodations for your labor.'' He grinned again. ''That's fair for how ever long you can stand it. But you're free to go when you're ready.''

Nick hugged his brother for the first time. "Deal.''

The noise of several vehicles arriving caught their attention. "I think our guests are arriving. We'd better get to the house or Letty will scold us,'' Gabe warned, and they turned and walked back up the hill.

A number of people were there by the time they reached the house. "Maybe you'll find the perfect lady for you here today and stay in Rawhide,'' Gabe teased.

Nick didn't laugh. Instead, he regretted how poorly he'd handled his last meeting with Sarah.

''Don't like that idea?'' Gabe asked, curiosity in his voice.

''I wasn't at my best when I saw Sarah last night.''

"You saw her? You were at the store? Did you see Jennifer?"

"Yeah, I carried her upstairs after she fainted."

"She fainted? Is she all right? Did they call the doctor?" Gabe asked, grabbing Nick by his arms.

"Sarah said she was okay."

"But did they call Jon, the doctor? I need to know she's all right." He looked around him and suddenly began running, Nick right on his heels.

"Jon! Jon! Wait!" Gabe had seen the doctor and his wife, Tori, one of his favorite cousins, going into the barn.

"Hey, Gabe, how's everything?" Jon asked, extending his hand. Gabe grabbed his hand and held on.

"How's Jennifer? Is she all right? She didn't hurt herself?"

Jon frowned. "What's this about Jennifer? What are you talking about?"

"Nick said she fainted last night. Didn't she call you?"

"No, I didn't hear from Sarah or Jennifer last night."

Nick stepped up and extended his hand. "I'm Nick, Gabe's brother. You must be the doctor."

"Dr. Jon Wilson, my wife, Victoria. Welcome to Rawhide," Jon said as he took Nick's hand.

"Thank you. I don't think Jennifer was hurt. I caught her before she could hit the floor."

"Do you know what brought on the faint?" Jon asked.

Nick looked at his brother's anxious face. "Well, she thought...it seems she thought I was Gabe. I told her as soon as I realized her mistake. And—and she just crumpled."

Gabe stared at him, then he walked away.

"Gabe," Jon called, walking over to where he'd stopped. "I'm sure she's all right, but I'm going in the house and borrow your phone to check on her. Is that all right?"

"Yes. I think that would be a good idea."

Jon told Tori he'd be out in a few minutes and the two men walked off. Nick stood there, wondering what to do.

Tori turned to Nick, slipping her arm through his. "You get the privilege of escorting me into the barn. I hear you're the real carpenter around here."

Nick found himself introduced to more people than he could possibly imagine.

"Oh, have you met the other twins in the Randall family?" Tori asked.

"I didn't know there were other twins. Where are they?"

"Only one is here tonight. Rich and his wife, Samantha, just arrived. Come on, I'll introduce you."

"Why isn't the other one here?" Gabe asked, curious.

"Russ doesn't…socialize much anymore. His wife died eighteen months ago, pregnant with their child. He's my partner in the CPA firm in town, but he doesn't go out much."

"I'm sorry to hear that. I'd like to meet him."

"Maybe you'll join us for lunch one day. Unless you can't get Gabe to give you time off."

"I think I can arrange that," Nick said with a laugh, and then followed Tori across the big barn to meet another twin.

SARAH AND JENNIFER WERE having a quiet dinner, seldom speaking. Jen couldn't keep her thoughts from Gabe and his new home. But she didn't want to admit as much to Sarah.

When the phone rang, Sarah answered. Jen couldn't think of anyone who would be calling them. All their friends would be at Gabe's.

"Hi, Jon. Yes, she's fine. Of course."

Jennifer looked at Sarah, wondering why Jon was calling. She took the phone when Sarah held it out.

"A little birdie told me you fainted last night."

"Jon! I'm fine. You didn't need to call."

"Are you sure?"

"Yes, of course. I was trying to do too much. I'm learning all sorts of things and I forgot to be careful."

"Are you busy Monday morning?"

"I'm working in the store," Jennifer told him, ignoring Sarah's attempt to tell her she shouldn't.

"Can you come in about eight-thirty? I'd feel better if I checked you. We could even do the sonogram, since I had an emergency during your last appointment."

"Are you sure that's all right? Then Sarah could come with me."

"It'll be perfect. I'll see both of you Monday morning. And take it easy until then, okay?"

"All right, I will. I plan to keep my feet propped up."

"Good for you. See you Monday."

Jennifer hung up the phone. "Jon's going to see me Monday morning at eight-thirty. And you should come with me because he's going to do the sonogram. We might find out the sex of the baby." She smiled and blinked to keep the tears from her eyes. Gabe should be going with her, but she was finally accepting that she would walk the parent path alone.

"Of course I'll go with you. You know, he may put you on a diet. I don't see you eat much, but the baby is getting big. Maybe that means she's really healthy."

"Are you hoping the baby's a girl?" Jennifer asked anxiously.

"No, honey, as long as it's healthy, that's all that matters. We may know more about girls, but if it's a boy, we'll manage."

"That's right. We'll manage."

"SHE'S FINE," JON SAID to Gabe as he hung up the phone. "I'm going to check her Monday morning."

"You'll tell me what you find?" Gabe asked.

"Well, I can't do that, Gabe. Doctor-patient confidentiality. But you can ask Jennifer. She might tell you." He cleared his throat. "Seems like she was anxious to see you when she mistook Nick for you."

"I can't do that. I can't take the place of the father of her baby. He should be there."

Jon shook his head. "He hasn't shown up yet. I hate to see a single parent. Taking care of a baby is a tough job. Jennifer doesn't seem strong enough."

"She's not, damn it!"

"If you love her, why are you letting her go through this alone?" Jon asked.

"I don't—I mean, it's the baby's father's job."

"I guess so." Jon paused and then said, "Come on. Let's go join the party."

NICK SETTLED INTO HIS narrow bed late that night. Gabe had told the household to sleep in the next morning. He'd certainly take advantage of that invitation, though he suspected Letty's coffee would be perked and waiting whatever time he got up.

Gabe was a lucky man. He had both Letty and Blackie to help him make his way. And they did so not because he paid them, but because they loved him. After today, he thought maybe Gabe was wealthier than he was. Not in money, but in terms of friends, loved ones and self-confidence.

Nick believed he was a good lawyer, but he'd never been sure. After all, he'd had a place waiting for him when he finished law school. He hadn't had to work his way up the ladder. He'd been handed a partnership in one of the most prestigious law firms in Denver.

His father had been pleased with him, but what he did was expected. His mother wanted him to marry, and he'd definitely failed her. And he'd brought sorrow to his real mother. He knew it had been beyond his control, because he hadn't even known she'd existed. Or Gabe. At least his parents, his adoptive parents, had given him that piece of knowledge. He was growing closer to his brother.

What should he do now?

Stay here and do carpentry work?

Return to Denver and practice law?

Neither of those combinations interested him.

Should he give up law practice? He was qualified to practice in Wyoming also, since a lot of their clients had places in Wyoming. Could he open a law firm on Main Street in Rawhide?

His heart beat a little faster. Did he want to stay here? Yeah, he did. He tried to ignore the picture of Sarah Waggoner he held in his mind. She'd never speak to him again and he deserved that.

And there might not be enough work to sustain a law office. But he didn't need to make money. He needed to find a life that suited him. He could offer free legal help to anyone he thought needed it, charge modest rates for those who could pay.

He'd have to ask around, see if there were other law firms in Rawhide. He didn't want to run anyone out of business. He felt sure Tori would know since she ran a business on Main Street with her cousin.

He'd met Rich and his wife last night. A nice couple. He was interested in meeting Russ. He'd like to know he and Rich got along, being twins. How they managed to help people tell them apart. Maybe he'd have lunch with them on Monday.

Since Tori was married to Jon, she might know something about Jennifer, too. Gabe seemed to still be hung up on Jennifer, but he was determined not to marry her since she'd gotten pregnant by another man.

But he was going to be miserable without her. Which was a good reason for Nick to forget about Sarah. He didn't want to be miserable. He could build a life here and be comfortable. He'd have Gabe as his brother and friend. And he'd have his work. That's what he'd do.

He closed his eyes, realizing he was happier in the narrow bed with its thin mattress than he'd ever been in Denver in a luxurious apartment.

For some reason, he was more at home here than he'd ever been in Denver.

CHAPTER NINE

GABE WOKE AT HIS USUAL TIME the next morning. He'd intended to go to church this Sunday, to become a part of the community. But he couldn't quite face everyone in church, feeling as he did about the man who'd gotten Jennifer pregnant and abandoned her. If he knew who he was, he'd seek him out, beat him within an inch of his life.

Maybe he should go away, put his place up for sale, return to the rodeo. That choice hurt. He'd settled in. He wanted to build a family, like his cousins had done. But he'd always pictured Jennifer at his side. Could he replace her with another woman? He couldn't imagine doing that. He didn't even know any other females except Randall women and the Waggoner sisters.

There had to be other women. One of the waitresses in the café? Maybe one of Jon's nurses? He'd have to ask him if there was anyone available. Or he could ask Jake. He'd heard Jake was behind most of the matchmaking that went on in their family, starting with Jake's own brothers. If that was true, Jake did a good job.

Gabe threw himself from the king-size bed he'd bought and began pacing the floor. He couldn't go hunting for another woman when he wanted Jennifer. Not yet. Maybe after she gave birth to her baby, or after she married the father. Then he could marry some other woman, have his sons and build a future.

But not now.

He headed for the shower, hoping to wash away those

thoughts. For now, he'd build his home. Nick was going to fix up the house, and he'd concentrate on preparing the ranch for winter. It wouldn't take much hay for his small herd, and he could keep them close this winter. Then in spring, he'd buy some stock from the Randalls. They had the best herd in the valley.

Yeah, thinking about cattle was better than thinking about Jennifer.

When he entered the kitchen, wearing jeans and a plaid shirt, he found Letty at the stove and Nick and Blackie sitting at the table, plates heaped with bacon and eggs, toast and jelly in front of them.

"Morning, Gabe," Letty sang out. "I thought you were going to church this morning."

"Changed my mind. I'm going to wait awhile."

Blackie was dressed in dress pants and a white shirt, with a tie around his neck. "But Gabe, it's a nice church."

"It must be. You sure took to it right away," Gabe grumbled.

When he heard laughter from Letty and saw Blackie's red face, he stopped reaching for food. "What's going on?"

Letty spoke up. "He's got his eye on Hazel Caldwell. She's a widow."

"Mind your own business, Letty, or I'll start telling tales about last night." Blackie kept his head down, taking a big bite of toast.

"I see," Gabe said. "And what was Letty up to last night?"

No one answered.

"Letty?"

"I enjoyed myself. There's no law against that." She put a full plate in front of him. "Eat up. I want to do the dishes before I go." She took her apron off and walked out of the kitchen.

"Well? Are you gonna tell me?" he asked Blackie.

The man kept chewing and shook his head no. "Said too much."

"I'll tell you what I know, but it's not much," Nick said. "I saw Letty dancing a lot with a gentleman who seemed interested. *Real* interested. I asked who he was and someone said he was the doctor's father."

"Bill Wilson! I hadn't thought he was interested in Letty. Not that I mind, but I'd hate to lose her."

"She deserves her happiness," Blackie grumbled.

"You're right," Gabe agreed.

They ate in silence until Letty came back into the room, a sweater over one arm, her hat on her head and sparkly earrings in her ears. "You look nice, Letty," Gabe said. "Don't worry about the dishes. Since I'm not going to church, I'll do them after I finish breakfast."

"I can't let you do that, Gabe. It's my job," she protested.

"Don't worry, Letty. I'll help him," Nick promised.

"Between the two of you, I'll have no dishes left. Nick, I doubt you've ever washed a dish in your life!"

"I'll admit I'm not as experienced as Gabe, but I've got to learn somehow."

"True, or no lady will want you. Modern ladies expect their men to be able to wash clothes, cook and clean, help with the children. Maybe I'd better leave the dish washing to you two just once, so you'll be able to find a wife."

She waved goodbye and left the kitchen.

Blackie stared at the two of them. "You two planning on marrying? You never said anything, 'cept for Jennif— uh, I mean, uh, lately."

"I'm suspecting you'll be married before us, Blackie. Maybe you'd better practice washing dishes with us," Nick joked, but his gaze was on Gabe's face, which had darkened, looking harsh and sad at the same time.

Blackie gave a nervous laugh, looking at Gabe, too.

"Not this morning. I've got a date." He stood, slamming his hat on his head, and hurried out the door.

Gabe stared at the wall across from him, saying nothing. He chewed methodically, putting in more food when he'd swallowed the first bite.

Nick followed suit. After a few minutes, he said softly, "He didn't mean to upset you."

"I know," Gabe said with a sigh, lowering his fork to the table.

After a few more minutes, the two men gathered the dirty plates and carried them to the sink. While Nick dried and Gabe washed, Nick remembered a request he wanted to make. "Uh, Gabe, since we're finished with the barn, what do you have planned for tomorrow morning?"

"We're going to check the fences on the nearby pastures."

"By truck?"

Gabe stared at him. "No, by horseback. Why?"

"I don't know how to ride, so I don't think I'll be of much use. I thought I might go to town, maybe have lunch with Tori so she can introduce me to Russ."

"Sure. You're free to do what you want, Nick. I told you."

"Thanks. Hey, do Russ and Rich look very much alike?"

Gabe shrugged. "They used to."

"What do you mean?"

"When Russ's wife died, he pretty much closed in on himself. There's a haunted look in his eyes now. And some of his hair has turned gray."

"That's tough."

"Yeah, Abby was a sweet lady. She was a school teacher, like Elizabeth, Toby's wife."

"That reminds me of another question I had. Is Elizabeth or Toby the Randall?"

Gabe grinned for the first time that morning. "They both

are. Toby is B.J.'s son from her first marriage. When she and Jake got married, he adopted Toby, who was about five at the time. Elizabeth is Chad and Megan's daughter. Toby fell in love with Elizabeth when they were young, but he left town, figuring they could never be together. When Elizabeth got engaged to another man, Toby came home. Soon after, Elizabeth broke off her engagement, and before we knew it, she and Toby were married. There's no blood relation between them.''

"They seem happy and suited to each other," Nick agreed.

"They're so happy they already have two kids, a boy and a baby girl."

Nick frowned.

"What?" Gabe asked as he rinsed out the sink.

"Do you ever get the impression this place is a matchmaking heaven? Everyone seems to be married."

"Not everyone," Gabe said, his voice hard.

"Right," Nick agreed quietly, and put the last of the dishes away.

"I'm going for a ride," Gabe told him, and hurried out the door.

"Good job, Nick," Nick said to himself in disgust. He'd actually gotten a few laughs out of Gabe. Then he'd brought up the subject of marriage again, throwing Gabe back into a foul mood.

AFTER A QUIET WEEKEND, Sarah and Jennifer got up early Monday morning and dressed for work. But before they opened the store, they were going to the doctor's office.

"Remember, you're only working half a day," Sarah told her sister. "After lunch, you go straight to bed."

"We'll ask Jon. Maybe an hour or two, but I don't need the entire afternoon in bed. I'll get too soft."

Sarah smiled. "Listen to you. You've certainly changed, Jen. For the better."

"Thank you very much. I still have a long way to go with my cooking, and you can't deny that."

"True," Sarah said with a chuckle. "But I didn't bother to teach you anything, so I have to share part of the blame."

"Maybe I'll do better this week. Oh, I went to the library yesterday afternoon." The town had a small collection of books in the saddle shop two doors down. Everyone called it the library. "I actually found a book on knitting. I'm going to teach myself to knit."

"Sorry I can't help you with that. I never learned."

"I know. You were too busy doing everything else."

"Not everything. I know nothing about babies. I borrowed one of your books last night."

Jennifer rubbed her stomach. "You already know about the throwing up. I complained enough for five pregnant women."

Sarah threw her arm around her little sister as they went down the stairs. "Don't worry about it. That's in the past, and the result is well worth the effort. After all, I get a niece or nephew."

"And maybe we'll soon know which." Jen stepped outside into the sunshine. "I guess I'll deliver at Christmas. Santa will bring a special gift down the chimney. Maybe we'd better widen that chimney before it gets cold."

With a laugh, Sarah linked her arm with Jennifer's and they started down the street the two blocks to Jon Wilson's clinic.

The clinic was quiet when they went in. Usually the waiting room had one or two patients. It had taken the citizens of Rawhide and the surrounding ranches a little time to get used to the change in doctors. Doc was enjoying his retirement, but he still had people calling him because they didn't trust that "young doctor." Doc still filled in for emergencies, but Jon was accepted now.

"No waiting, I guess," Sarah joked. They pressed the doorbell on the door that led to the examining rooms and waited for it to open. Jon's regular nurse swung open the door. "Come along. The doctor's ready," she said, leading the way to the first examining room.

Inside, she handed Jennifer a gown to change into. "I'll be back in a minute."

Jennifer hurriedly slipped out of her denim jumper and blouse. Sarah helped her into the gown and tied the strings in the back.

"This is so exciting, Jen. This sonogram test could let us know if the baby's a boy or a girl. We can start getting the nursery ready as soon as we find out."

Jennifer stared at her sister, tears gathering in her eyes. Then she reached out and hugged her. "Sarah, you're the best sister in the world."

Sarah grinned. "I don't think so."

"I was afraid you'd hate me for causing problems in your life," Jennifer muttered.

Sarah withdrew from the hug. "I'm getting a niece or nephew, Jen. More family. We're a little short on family these days. Of course I'm happy for you." She paused, then carefully added, "It would be better if the daddy were here, too, but I'm not throwing out the baby with the bathwater."

They hugged again as the door opened.

"Up on the table with you, Jennifer. The doctor's coming," the nurse announced calmly.

Jennifer sat on the end of the table, suddenly anxious, rubbing her tummy. "Sarah said I'm getting pretty big," she confessed. "I promise I'm not eating too much. Do you think I'll have to go on a diet?"

"The doctor will decide, my girl, and you'd best do as he says."

There was a sharp rap on the door and the nurse swung it open as if royalty were visiting. "She's ready, Doctor."

"Good. Hello, Jen, Sarah. Still feeling okay?" Jon waited for Jennifer's answer. She appreciated the time he gave to his patients. He'd never lectured her or made her feel bad about her baby. Just like Sarah.

"I'm fine, Jon."

"No more fainting?"

"No," Jennifer assured him. She'd had no reason to faint. Gabe…or his brother…hadn't come near her.

Jon had her lie down on the table. Then he measured her stomach and listened to Jennifer's assurance that she wasn't eating too much. Sarah hurriedly seconded her words.

"But she seems to be getting bigger," Sarah added. It wasn't that Jennifer looked like a bowling ball with arms and legs. Not yet. But it was strange to see her slender sister with a rounded stomach.

Jon grinned. "We're going to do the sonogram so we'll know what's happening, but if the daddy is a big man, it could be the baby is just taking after him."

Jennifer and Sarah exchanged a look, but neither spoke.

The nurse pushed in the portable sonogram machine. She handed the monitor to the doctor and plugged in the machine. Then she began to rub what looked like petroleum jelly on Jennifer's stomach.

"You're going to like this, Jen. I'll even give you a picture of your baby. And it doesn't even hurt."

"Did Tori have this done?" Sarah asked.

"Of course. Doc did it for us. I was so excited, he was afraid I'd break the machine if I tried to do it myself."

Jennifer gave him a tremulous smile but said nothing. Sarah took her sister's hand in hers and squeezed it for reassurance.

When the nurse had finished applying the jellylike substance, she nodded to Jon. He began rubbing the monitor over her stomach, pressing it into her flesh. Movement appeared on the screen, but the women weren't sure what they were seeing, never having seen this kind of image before.

The doctor and nurse, more experienced, watched closely. Suddenly, the nurse elbowed the doctor and he bent to look closer. Then he muttered, "Uh-oh!"

CHAPTER TEN

"WHAT'S WRONG?" Jennifer said with a gasp.

Sarah moved protectively toward her younger sister.

"Sorry. I didn't meant to scare you," Jon said hurriedly. "It's just that—are there any twins in your family history?"

Jennifer gasped again, turning her gaze to the monitor. "You're saying—"

"Yes." Jon watched the monitor a bit longer before he looked at Jennifer again. "I know you don't want to name the father, but do you know if twins run in his family?"

Jennifer looked away from Jon's gaze. "The father doesn't believe my baby—" she paused to correct herself, though disbelief was in her voice "—my babies are his, so there's no point in naming him. But there are twins in his family."

"Are they both all right?" Sarah asked. "There was a birth defect in the baby's father's family. His twin was born with a club foot. Is there any sign of—of a problem with either baby?"

Jennifer apparently hadn't thought of that. "Jon?" she added anxiously.

"We can't see that much detail now, but I don't see any problems with them. It appears they're very active."

"Yes, I can vouch for that." Jennifer took a deep breath. "Can I carry them all right? Is that the reason I look so big?"

"Actually, you're not overly large, Jennifer. But you will

get larger. I think you can carry them full term, but I want to keep a close watch on you. This is a first for me, too, you know? I've never delivered twins before," he said, excitement in his voice.

Jennifer smiled slightly and lay back down on the table. "Are you going to give me that picture of my babies that you promised me? Oh, and am I having boys or girls?"

"I'm pretty sure they're boys, don't you think?" he asked, looking at his nurse.

"Yes, Doctor, I concur."

"Jennifer, I don't want to interfere with your personal business, but I think you really should tell the father... whoever he is." Jon stood back from the table, fiddling with the machine.

Jennifer bit her bottom lip, unable to speak.

"She did tell him, Jon, but Gabe—"

"Gabe is the father?" Jon asked in surprise.

Sarah realized her mistake, but there was no point now denying who the father was. She cast an apologetic look at Jennifer, then said, "Yes. But Gabe didn't believe her. He—he accused her of trying to foist another man's baby on him." Sarah hated telling Jennifer's secrets, but she hoped Jon could help in some way.

Before Jon could ask any questions, Jennifer said, "I'll try again. When can paternity tests be done? He might believe science rather than me."

She sounded so weary, disillusioned, that Jon looked at her more closely. "You might consider getting a report once the babies are born. It's not worth the risk of piercing the placenta now."

Jennifer shuddered and looked at Sarah. She nodded her head in agreement with the doctor.

"Well, everything looks fine, but I'm going to up your vitamins' strength a little, and I want you to rest every afternoon. You don't have to sleep unless you want to, but

I want you flat on your back. And I'd like you to take a walk every morning to build your muscles. Can you do that?''

"Of course," Jon replied.

"Are you drinking milk?"

"I didn't at first, but I'm drinking it almost every meal now.''

"Good. Do you have any questions?"

"Don't twins usually come early?"

"Yeah. A normal pregnancy is forty weeks. We're going to hope for thirty-five. If you can carry them longer, all the better.'' He looked at Sarah. "She's going to need a good support system.''

"She's got one, Jon. I'll hire someone to help in the store.''

"No, Sarah! I can still help."

Sarah chuckled. "You don't understand how big you're going to get. You won't be able to get up and down the aisles, and you certainly can't lift anything heavy. I've been thinking about it for a while now, anyway.''

"You have? You didn't say anything."

"We'll talk about it when we get home," Sarah assured her sister.

"Don't forget to call Gabe," Jon said.

"He's not going to believe me until tests are done."

"Give it a try, okay?" he asked.

Jennifer nodded, but she didn't look happy about it.

GABE HADN'T PLANNED on coming back to the house that morning. But the man from the bank had come to see him, and Letty, knowing about Gabe having been turned down for the loan, called him on his cell phone. He'd headed for the house at once, wondering what the loan office wanted. His letter had been very clear.

Mr. Hobart looked overdressed sitting in the kitchen with

Letty. Gabe noted the man had a cup of coffee in front of him, so he grabbed a mug for himself before sitting down.

Letty got to her feet and excused herself.

Gabe broke the ice. "I got your letter. Is there anything to discuss?"

"Well, uh, yes." Mr. Hobart put down his cup of coffee and cleared his throat. "I've been thinking. I should have asked you about your expansion plans. I assumed you were moving too hastily when I turned you down for the loan."

Gabe stared at the nervous man. "Did my brother come see you?"

"Your brother?" the man asked, looking bewildered.

"Yeah. Looks just like me. Nick McMillan is his name."

"Why no. I hadn't heard…you have a brother?"

The man wasn't that good an actor, Gabe decided. "Okay, here's what I had in mind." He explained that he wasn't starting up a big herd now. No point in having to feed them through winter. He'd put money back to buy the nucleus of his herd next spring. And he hoped to buy from the Randall herd. "They're the best in the valley."

"That sounds like a good plan. No shipping costs."

"True." Gabe rubbed his chin. "I'm not sure what bull I'm going to buy. I'll have to see what's available between now and next spring."

"Of course. Of course. What's your brand?"

"Double Moon. That's the name of my ranch."

Hobart looked curious. Gabe wasn't surprised—it was an unusual name. He took pity on him and explained. "When the moon comes up and reaches a certain point in the sky, it's reflected in my lake. I expected to marry soon and I thought it sounded, uh, appropriate."

"You didn't include the information about your impending nuptials," Mr. Hobart said, beaming. "Married men are better risks, according to the statistics."

"I'm not going to be married. Things changed." He

didn't want to say she chose someone else. Someone whose baby she was carrying.

"Well, I'm sorry, of course, about the wedding, but I think I made a mistake when I turned you down. I would like to offer you the loan, Mr. Randall, at the rates we discussed. If you're still interested."

Gabe sat there, rubbing his eyebrow. Something wasn't quite right. Why would the man be willing to change his mind because Gabe told him his plans?

"You're sure my brother didn't come see you?"

"I'm positive. Mr. Randall didn't even tell me—" He closed his mouth and paled. "I mean—"

"Which Mr. Randall?"

"Um, Mr. Randall, Jake, that is, is president of the board of directors. I talk to him frequently."

"I see." And he did. Pete had told Jake about his being turned down, and Jake had applied the pressure. Gabe could turn the loan down, but he wasn't a fool. He had every intention of paying it off. He smiled at Mr. Hobart. "I'm still interested. I thank you for the second chance."

"Good, good," the man said with patent relief. "I brought the papers with me if your housekeeper would like to witness our signatures."

"I'll ask her," Gabe said calmly. He walked to the laundry room and explained to Letty. She hugged him with enthusiasm and came to be the witness.

Half an hour later, Gabe had the financing he needed to buy the place next door. As soon as the banker left, he called the real estate office's number and spoke to the agent, who promised to call him back as soon as he'd talked to the owner.

Gabe sat down at the table after warming up his coffee and had a couple of cookies in celebration. When the phone rang again, he jumped for the phone before Letty could even turn around.

"Gabe?"

He knew the soft, sweet voice. And hearing it, when everything else in his life was coming right, made him mad.

"What do you want?" he growled.

Silence followed his inhospitable answer.

"I wanted to tell you once more that there was no one else. You're the father of—"

He cut in. "Sure, now that I get the loan, you want me to forgive you! You want me to believe you *this* time. I'm no fool, Jennifer. I trusted you once, I won't make that mistake again."

He waited for her response. He heard her draw a deep breath, and he figured she was going to blast him, but all she did was quietly hang up the phone.

"Jen?" But she was gone.

Letty came into the room. "Was that the real estate agent?"

"No!"

"But I thought—"

"It was Jennifer."

"Oh! How is she?"

"I don't know. She hung up."

"Maybe she'll call back."

"No, I don't think so."

The phone rang again. This time it was the agent to tell him the owner had accepted his offer. He'd started with a low amount, figuring he'd need to negotiate. "But I didn't think he'd take my first offer."

"Frankly, I was surprised, as well, but he was anxious to sell." The man added the details of the closing and Gabe hung up the phone with the deal almost settled. All they had to do was transfer the money from the bank and sign the papers.

He told Letty the good news and she hugged him again. Blackie came in just then in time to hear his news, and he pumped his hand, congratulating him. Gabe was happy, too. But his happiness was seasoned with sorrow and anger. Jennifer was still trying to con him. And he still loved her.

NICK ARRIVED IN TOWN a little after nine. He entered the accounting office of Randall and Randall after having a cup of coffee at the café.

"Nick," Tori said as he entered. "How nice to see you. Come in and let me introduce you to my partner and cousin. Russ, this is Gabe's twin brother, Nick McMillan. Nick, this is Russ Randall."

The man standing beside her extended his hand and nodded, but Nick saw exactly what Gabe had described. While Russ may have appeared identical to his brother in earlier years, they were now easily distinguishable. He wondered if the same might happen to him and Gabe. A chilling thought.

"I'm going to be in town today and wondered if you would join me for lunch, you and Tori. I would like your advice on my business plans."

"I don't generally eat lunch," Russ said, as if weighing the invitation.

"Come on, Russ. You promised Aunt Janie you'd start getting out more," Tori urged.

Russ sighed, as if Tori's concern weighed heavily on his shoulders. "Fine, I'll be glad to join both of you, but I doubt I can offer much of an opinion."

"Maybe you can give me suggestions about being a twin. As you know, it's new territory for me and Gabe." Nick noticed a flicker of interest in Russ's eyes.

Nick told the two he had errands to run and would meet them at the restaurant at eleven. Then he headed for the general store.

Jennifer sat behind the counter, staring across the store, as if she were seeing ghosts.

"Jennifer, how are you today?"

"Fine, thank you. May I help you?"

"Where's Sarah?"

"She's not here."

Even as she said the words, the front door opened, the

bell attached to it jangling wildly. Nick was pleased to see Sarah coming toward him.

Sarah nodded at him but spoke to Jennifer. "I took care of it."

"I still think you're wrong," Jennifer replied.

"Don't be silly. There's plenty to do for all of us."

"I don't mean to intrude, but is anything wrong?" Nick asked.

Sarah turned to him. "No, of course not. How may I help you?"

"I don't really need anything. I wanted to make sure you accepted my apology."

She smiled, but it didn't have the usual warmth of her usual smiles. "Yes, the flowers were lovely."

He kept his eye on her. "I'm glad you liked them."

She said nothing else and he didn't know what to say. He'd never been tongue-tied in front of a woman before. It took him by surprise.

"Do you want to purchase the blanket this morning?"

"Sure. I guess the weather will get colder since we're approaching September."

"Are you looking at one of the electric ones?" Jennifer asked. "I love them. They keep you all toasty warm."

"Good idea, Jennifer," Nick said. He looked at Sarah. "Can you show me the electric blankets?"

"Follow me," she said, but not in a friendly way. "The electric ones come in two colors, blue and green, and three sizes, twin, full and king." She pulled one of the blankets off the shelf and partly unfolded it.

"This one will be fine. Uh, when would you be free for dinner? I'd like to take you out again." He smiled that charming grin that had worked effectively in Denver. In return, he received a frown.

"I don't think that would be a good idea."

"Why? And don't pull that bit about your sister."

"I beg your pardon!"

"You can't keep hiding behind her all your life."

He thought he was making a point that would win the game.

Instead, it appeared to cost him more than he realized.

Sarah carefully folded the blanket and placed it back on the shelf.

"Wait a minute. I'll take the blanket."

"No. I think you can find better in Denver."

He caught the reference to his statement the last time he'd been there. "Come on, Sarah, don't go all huffy on me. I was just pointing out—"

"You have no business telling me how to live my life. Please do your shopping elsewhere." She turned and walked away.

CHAPTER ELEVEN

GABE SLAMMED HIS TRUCK DOOR SHUT and headed for Red's kitchen. The housekeeper for the Randalls, even though he was a man, kept a good kitchen. Gabe knew he'd have a pot of coffee on and probably something good to eat.

Of course, these days, Red's wife Mildred was an able helper. They'd wed when Jake had married B.J. Gabe figured Red was the only man he'd find in the kitchen as it was the middle of the day and the Randall males would be at work. Gabe could've waited until evening to come over, but he was restless, unsettled. The men could check the fences without him for once.

He knocked on the back door. It swung open and Mildred greeted him. "Come in, Gabe."

"Thanks, Mildred. How are you?"

"Fine. Everything okay with you?"

"Yeah, but I quit work early to handle some business and thought I'd drop by in case any of the Randalls were here."

"Not yet, but they'll be here soon. They're coming in for lunch. Why don't you join us?"

"I don't want to add to your work."

"'Course not. There's hardly anyone here for lunch these days, what with the kids all off to college. Even Casey is gone these days."

"You've got Toby's kids here, don't you?"

She waved him to a chair and poured him a cup of coffee. "Sure do. They're great, but there's lots of women here wanting their turn to hold them. When are you gonna get you a passel of kids?"

Gabe wondered if there was anywhere he could go where the subject of marriage wouldn't come up. "I don't think anyone will have me, Mildred. After all, Red got to you before I could."

She laughed, but she kept watching him, as if she expected he would confess some deep, dark secret.

The kitchen door swung open. Gabe rose as Janie and Elizabeth came in, each one carrying a child. The one in Elizabeth's arms had to be a girl because the other one was definitely a little boy, about three years old. A boy who had the look of a Randall.

"'Morning, ladies," he greeted them.

"Gabe, what a nice treat," Janie said. "Sit down. What are you doing here? There's not anything wrong, is there?"

"No. I didn't know my visit would occasion such worry. Everything's fine."

"Oh, good. I know Jennifer was going in to the doctor this morning, so I—"

"That has nothing to do with me!" He drew a deep breath, trying to control himself. The little boy clung to Janie as if he'd scared him. "I'm sorry, I didn't mean to yell."

Mildred stepped in. "Gabe wanted to see the menfolk so he's going to join us for lunch."

"I don't think I should, Mildred," he said before all three women begged him to stay. He wanted to leave, but he'd already misbehaved, jumping down Janie's throat. No need to offend her a second time.

He talked about Nick awhile and asked questions about the children. Babies frightened him, but the little boy drew his attention. He guessed they all had to start out as a baby, but the boy was more fascinating. When he asked the boy if he had a horse, the child scooted closer to him and announced he did and his name was Mickey.

Surprised by his name choice, he looked at Elizabeth.

"I know. But we went to Disney World last year before Steffie was born and he met Mickey Mouse. So now we have our own Mickey."

"I see. Good choice. Did you like Disney World?" he asked him.

That question seemed to be the key to his shyness. He talked the rest of the time until they heard the men arriving. The boy jumped down from Gabe's knee and ran for the door, yelling "Daddy!"

"Sorry for his abrupt departure," Elizabeth said. "He adores his father."

Longing filled Gabe so much, he didn't know where to look. When Toby came in first, carting his son on his back, he headed straight for Elizabeth, kissing her and rubbing the baby's head. It was clear Toby loved his wife and children.

Gabe stood and greeted the men. They shook his hand and invited him to stay for lunch, as Mildred had already done. To Gabe's surprise, Red had ridden out with the men today, an unusual occurrence.

"Shouldn't have, neither," Red said. "I'm so sore I kin hardly walk."

The other men laughed and teased Red, but Mildred immediately had a cup of coffee for him and watched him anxiously.

"I really shouldn't stay for lunch," Gabe said suddenly. "I just wanted to have a word with the brothers. Then I'll be on my way."

"Nonsense," Jake commanded. "We don't see enough of you."

"You know why I'm here, don't you?" he asked, referring to the approved bank loan.

"I hope we have something to celebrate," Jake said as more ladies entered the kitchen, each greeting her husband.

"Well, yes, I do, thanks to you. I wanted to let you know I appreciate it."

All the men shook his hand again and the ladies congratulated him when the men explained that he'd gotten his loan. B.J., Jake's wife and also one of the local vets, asked him about the stock he intended to run. Gabe scarcely even noticed the food put before him, or the fact that he was eating, as he discussed his plans with people who understood him.

When the phone rang before the meal ended, Mildred got up to answer it, complaining that they never had a meal without it being interrupted. Then she came back to the table and looked at Janie. "Tori wants to talk to you."

Megan, Tori's mother, looked up, startled. "Didn't she ask for me?"

"Nope. Said she needed to talk to Janie," Mildred said calmly, but there was a hint of curiosity in her voice as she watched Janie speak softly into the phone.

A few minutes later, Janie hung up and started to leave the kitchen. Pete called her back. "You need to finish your lunch, Janie."

"I'm finished. I'm going into town."

"Why? What's wrong?" her husband asked.

Megan asked a question, too. "Is Tori all right? Is the baby okay?" Tori took her baby into work every day, since he still slept most of the time.

"They're fine. But the Randalls are having twins again!" Janie told them, clearly excited.

"What?" Megan screamed. "Tori's having twins and she told you first?"

"No, not Tori! Jennifer Waggoner is having twin boys. Jon thought it might help Jennifer if I talked to her a little. She just found out this morning and she's a little overwhelmed."

No one said anything as Janie ran out of the room.

Finally, Gabe pushed his chair away from the table. With a muttered "excuse me," he, too, left the kitchen. But he went out the back door.

The four brothers followed him.

"Gabe," Pete called, stopping him. "Janie forgot you were in the room or she wouldn't have announced it quite so—I mean, she was just excited."

"I know. But she shouldn't have called those babies Randalls. Jen was sleeping with someone else when I was on the road."

Chad frowned. "She was? We didn't hear anything about it. In fact, we talked about how faithful she was being. It took us by surprise. She used to have a date most nights of the week. Then, after you two started seeing each other, we never saw her out unless you were in town."

"Did you hear any rumors?" Jake asked Gabe.

"No. She told me."

"Did she name him?" Brett asked. "'Cause we'd act for her if we knew who left her pregnant and alone."

"And I'd help you, but I don't know who he was," Gabe replied.

"You sure you're not the daddy?" Pete asked.

Gabe's humiliation grew. "I can't think of any reason why she'd lied to me about such a thing."

The men all looked at one another and several of them shrugged their shoulders. But Brett finally said, "Unless you were having a fight." Everyone stared at him. "I mean, it wouldn't be right, but Jennifer is a proud little thing."

Gabe thought he was going to lose his lunch right there. "I've got to go," he muttered, and ran for his truck. It was bad enough that he'd been made a fool of by Jennifer. No need to completely humiliate himself at the same time.

"OFF TO BED WITH YOU, JEN," Sarah said as they finished their lunch at the consultation table. "You're supposed to rest in the afternoon."

"Don't you want me to watch out for everything down here while you take a few minutes for yourself?" Jennifer offered.

"No, I can manage. Besides, once we hire someone to help out, I'll have plenty of extra time. It will work out real well."

"I don't think there's that many people in town looking for jobs."

"Our newspaper has an exchange with all the other towns around here. My ad goes in all their papers for the price of one."

"You think some woman will drive a long way to work here? During winter that could be a problem," Jennifer reasoned.

"Could be a man who applies for the job. More muscles wouldn't be a bad thing."

"But we have Boyd."

"Yes, but I need someone to take over the store occasionally. When you were doing that, life was much easier for me."

"I know. I feel bad that I can't—"

The door opened and a man they'd never seen before came in. Sarah got up to offer to help him.

"My name's Jeff Fisher. I'm here about the ad," he said.

Sarah and Jennifer exchanged a look. Jennifer had been about to go up the stairs, as ordered, but she stood there, watching the man now.

Sarah said, "What ad?"

"Didn't you put an ad in the paper about needing some help in here?"

"Yes, I did, but that was only a couple of hours ago."

His face flamed. "I know I should've waited, but I was afraid someone else would get the job. You see, I went into the newspaper office to check the want ads. I've been doing that for a couple of weeks to get a head start. And the guy there has gotten to know me and he showed me your ad.

I'd do a good job if you'll give me a chance. I've got references.''

He was out of breath and eager. Sarah, with a smile, asked him to sit down at the table. ''I'll be up in a minute, Jennifer.''

Reluctantly, Jennifer went upstairs, conscious of the man's eyes on her. A room came with the job and Jen hoped Sarah would be careful about who she hired. The room she'd offered had been their father's bedroom downstairs. He'd moved downstairs when the girls were teenagers. He said he was too old to traipse up and down the stairs. He came up for his evening meal. Sarah brought lunch and breakfast down to him.

But this man was a stranger, and Jen wasn't certain about him living in her home.

When Sarah came up half an hour later, Jennifer was lying down, as instructed, but not asleep. ''Sarah? Is that you?''

''Who else would it be?'' she asked as she came into Jen's room.

''It could be that stranger. He could've killed you and be coming after me!''

''Jen! What a terrible thought.''

''Well? What do you think about him?''

''I think he'll do very well if his references check out. I've come up to call them while he tries his hand with the store.''

''But he could steal all our money and run away.''

''Honey, there's twenty dollars in the cash register. Everything else is locked in the safe. Besides, you know most of our customers pay monthly.''

''True. But I don't think I like the idea of him sleeping downstairs.''

''We'll throw the dead bolt each night. You'll be safe, Jen. You know I'd never do anything to hurt you,'' Sarah soothed, sitting down beside her sister.

"I know I'm being silly, but—everything seems so topsy-turvy right now. And for him to come the day we placed the ad is strange, you'll have to admit."

"Yes, it is, and my first call will be to the newspaper in Buffalo. But he's down on his luck, Jen, because his mother got sick. She died a month ago. He used what she left him to pay her hospital bills. Now he's got to move out of the house and find a job and a place to live."

"He could get a job on one of the ranches," Jennifer pointed out.

"He doesn't know how to ride a horse. But he does have a good head for numbers."

"What's he doing in Wyoming if he can't ride a horse?" Jennifer protested.

"His mother moved here after her husband died, two years ago. He came with her because he was worried about her being alone. He got a job at a store in Buffalo, but they recently laid people off because business was slow. Now, let me make my phone calls and get back down there. After all, he is new."

Jennifer lay back down and squeezed her eyes shut. Maybe she could think of something else. After all, Jennifer knew she could trust Sarah to do her best for them. She wondered how old the man was. He looked like a boy. Muscles, huh! She didn't think he had any.

Not like Gabe. Nope, not that subject. Her baby, perhaps? Oh, no. That would be babies! She was afraid to even consider what that would mean to her life. She sat up and looked around the room. Ah. Her baby book. She'd see what it had to say about twin babies.

NICK WAS ALREADY SEATED in the restaurant when Russ and Tori came in. "I hope we haven't kept you waiting," Tori said with a big smile.

"I just got here. Did you have a busy morning?" he

asked for an opener. Since his reason for talking to them had practically disappeared, he didn't know what else to say.

He wasn't certain he was staying in Rawhide. Not with Sarah's attitude. Not that she mattered to him, of course, but the negative vibes weren't pleasant. The only real reason to stay was to get to know Gabe better, but he was already closer to his brother than he'd ever imagined.

Tori chuckled. "You could say we had a hectic morning."

Nick looked up. "Something funny happened?"

"Not funny, but exciting."

Russ said, "Tori, I don't think you should—"

"It won't matter to Nick. I don't think it matters to Gabe, either. You'll have to admit he's being very cavalier about everything and it's not fair to Jennifer."

"You don't know the full story," Russ said.

"No, I don't. You wouldn't ignore a woman carrying your baby, would you, Russ?"

"No, but I wouldn't get a woman pregnant unless I was crazy about her." He grimaced, as if that were a foreign idea. "Right?"

"Right," Tori said softly.

The waitress arrived at their table, bringing their conversation to an end momentarily. After ordering, Nick didn't wait for them to speak. He'd put a few things together.

"This is about Jennifer's checkup with your husband this morning, isn't it? Is everything all right?"

"Yes," Tori said. "As long as you consider twins normal."

"Jennifer's having twins?" Nick asked, startled. "Are there twins in her family?"

Tori looked at him steadily. "No. Must be in the father's family."

"You're saying these are Gabe's babies? He doesn't think so."

"Well he'd better think again. Jen wasn't with anyone else while he was out of town. We even talked about it, Sarah and I, because it was so unlike Jennifer."

"But he swears she told him she'd been with someone else."

"Five months ago? I don't think so." Tori shrugged her shoulders. "Guess time will tell. Jon says he can't safely do the paternity test until after the babies are born."

"What if she doesn't have the test done?" Russ asked. "As it is, she can pick up and move away anytime. If Gabe doesn't claim those boys as his own, he might never see them."

Nick stared at Russ. "Why did you say that? I wouldn't think that would happen."

"The Waggoner sisters may not want to stay in Town after Jen had the babies. Might be too tough on Jen." Russ thanked the waitress as she brought their meal.

Nick's mind was racing. Having never known his father and losing his mother early, Gabe would never permit his children to be taken from him. But Gabe was so certain the babies weren't his. Yet Nick wasn't so certain now.

"Eat your steak, Nick, and tell us what you're doing in town," Tori ordered. "We shouldn't have discussed the news with you."

She was right. But someone should discuss it with Gabe. Someone who was on his side, wanted the best for him. Someone like his brother. Dear God, that was him.

What should he say? And what if he said the wrong thing and Gabe hated him?

CHAPTER TWELVE

JENNIFER DIDN'T GOT TO SLEEP.

Reading about carrying twins answered some of her questions, but she had trouble putting herself in that role. When a knock sounded on her bedroom door, which then opened, she tensed.

"Jen, you have a visitor," Sarah announced. Then she swung the door wider and Jennifer saw Janie Randall. The older woman stepped into the room and Sarah left, closing the door behind her.

"Hi, Jennifer. Dr. Wilson thought it might help you to talk to someone who's actually had twins."

Jennifer stared at her with her mouth open. She knew Janie, of course, but not enough to impose on her.

"Jennifer, if you want me to go, I will."

"No! It would be wonderful. But...I'm a little embarrassed."

"Why?"

"I'm not married and...and—"

"Your babies are Randalls, like mine."

Big tears spurted from Jennifer's eyes. "Gabe doesn't believe me!"

Janie gathered Jennifer to her in a motherly hug.

Jennifer decided to tell the truth. She was learning that that was the best way to go. "It's my fault."

"Really? Why do you say that?"

Jennifer told her sad story of her pride and anger. "It was wrong of me."

"Yes, it was, but you're not the first young lady to make a mistake in the love game. Have you told him the truth?"

"I tried, but he doesn't want to hear. First he accused me of trying to foist some other man's baby on him. Then I promised the doctor that I would call him again because of the twins. Gabe told me not to call him again, so I hung up."

"You poor dear, bearing all of this alone."

"It's my punishment, I guess. Did you have that experience?"

"No, though I did have my share of problems, but that's another story. Let's talk about you. First of all, do you have some good creams? I was told that if I rubbed my tummy with lotion every day, it was supposed to lessen stretch marks, and maybe it did. But it definitely made the boys happy. The next hour they rested. No kicking."

"Really? What kind of cream?"

"I'll get you some."

"Oh, no, I can—"

"These boys, and therefore you, as their mother, are Randalls, whether Gabe marries you or not."

There was a determined look in Janie's eyes that made Jennifer glad she wasn't mad at her.

"Also, you have to get used to the relationship between twins. My boys love me, but their closest friend has always been each other. Their wives had to accept that, too. Until Abby died. Russ has withdrawn from everyone, even Rich."

"I know. He's changed."

"Yes," Janie agreed. She sat there staring into space, a sadness in her eyes that made Jennifer want to cry.

With a sniff, Janie added, "And you're always emotional. Your husband will need— Oh, I'm sorry, Jennifer. I didn't think. Damn Gabe Randall. He's such a hardhead."

"No, it really isn't his fault. And—and Sarah is very supportive. I'll be fine."

"Of course you will. And I'll leave you my number. You can call me whenever you have questions. We can go out for lunch every week and you can ask me anything. Did you make a weekly appointment with the doctor?"

"Yes. Monday mornings."

"Okay. How about we do lunch every Friday? You can come with a whole bunch of questions. Maybe I can answer them so you'll have a calm weekend."

"Janie, you're being so good to me. Not having a mother—I mean, Sarah is great, but she doesn't know much about having a baby. This is wonderful!"

Janie leaned over to kiss Jennifer's cheek. "Don't worry. I'll enjoy it, too. We've taken Gabe in and become his family. You and the children have the same privilege. You may come to think there are too many Randalls."

"No. Sarah and I don't have enough family. We'll be delighted to be part of the Randall clan. Any way we can."

"Good. We'll have to talk to Jake about finding Sarah a husband. She's too pretty and smart to be alone."

"I agree. I thought Nick would be perfect, but something seems to have happened. They don't talk to each other anymore."

"Hmm. That's an idea. Then we could keep Nick here. Let me see what I can do."

"Janie, that's wonderful," Jennifer enthused. "I don't want Sarah to be alone. You know, an old-maid aunt."

"Don't worry. Matchmaking is a Randall tradition."

When Janie left an hour later, Jennifer felt much better. Even if Gabe continued to ignore her, she and her babies, and Sarah, were no longer alone. She had Janie's number and a date for lunch on Friday.

SARAH SAW JANIE COMING DOWN the stairs and met her at the bottom. "Janie, thank you so much for talking to Jennifer. I'm sure she feels much better now."

"She does. I'm telling you what I told her. You are part of the Randall family now. You call if you need something."

"That's wonderful for Jennifer, Janie. I know she feels better that someone in the Randall family is willing to accept her babies."

"I didn't say just Jennifer. You're her sister. You're part of our extended family. You've done a wonderful job carrying on since your dad died. But we're here for you, too."

Janie's words were firm, insistent, and Sarah smiled warmly. "Thank you, Janie, but I'm pretty independent."

Janie's firm look didn't change, though she said, "That's good, dear. I'm having lunch with Jennifer every Friday now so she can ask questions, and also because I love to do lunch,' as the important people say. It will help Jennifer to get out and dress up."

"Perfect. Thank you again, Janie."

"No problem. If you want, you can join us."

"I might, after a while. I've hired an assistant."

"Oh, really? Who is she?"

"*He* is from Buffalo. His name is Jeff Fisher and he'll start work tomorrow."

"Oh. Hiring extra help is a wonderful idea."

"Yes, I should've done this years ago, but I tried to do it the way Dad did, forgetting that he had me to help him. Boyd is good, but he can't run the store. I think Jeff can if it's necessary."

"That's wonderful. I hope he works out."

"Me, too," Sarah muttered under her breath after Janie left. She was nervous about what she'd done, though she'd never let Jennifer know that. She could see all the benefits of hiring someone to help out, but she knew a lot that could go wrong.

But the decision was made. Jeff was moving in this evening into the bedroom her father had used after her mother died. His bedroom and bath had access from outside and also a door into the hallway that led to the loading dock.

She shook her head and walked to the front of the store.

This was a quiet time of the day. Most of their customers came in the morning and late afternoon. She stood there, watching people pass on the sidewalk, looking in at their windows. Jen had done a good job.

Then Nick McMillan walked by. Sort of. He actually paused on the sidewalk, staring at their door. Sarah shifted so he couldn't see her. She'd been rude this morning. But she couldn't bear his pretending that they could have a relationship, if that was what he wanted, and ignore the problem facing Jennifer and Gabe. In Sarah's book, you didn't please yourself and ignore everyone around you. Maybe he felt that way because he'd never had any siblings until now.

Oh, well, it didn't matter anymore. He wouldn't speak to her again. Besides, he was used to more sophisticated women. She was sure of it.

With a sigh, she picked up the duster. She wanted to make sure everything was neat and tidy so Jeff would understand how she wanted to keep the store. She hoped he wasn't opposed to doing "women's work." She'd asked him, of course, and he'd given the right answer, but doing it was another matter.

WHEN NICK RETURNED to the ranch after lunch, he saw Gabe down by the lake. He drew a deep breath and headed for his brother's favorite place, a fact that hadn't taken him long to realize.

"Hi, Gabe," he called as he drew close. He wanted to give his brother time to pull himself together, in case he was upset.

Gabe waved back, which Nick took as a "come on over" signal. He paused to take another deep breath. He needed to be calm and logical, because he didn't think Gabe was going to like his news.

"How was your trip to town?" Gabe asked calmly, a good sign in Nick's opinion.

"Fine. I had lunch with Tori and Russ. There are obvious

similarities between him and his brother, but the gray hair makes it easy to tell them apart.''

"Yeah, that and his sad eyes.'' Gabe faced the lake, not looking at Nick.

"Yeah. Do you think that will happen to us?''

"What?'' Gabe asked, turning around.

"Do you think events in our lives will make us look different from each other?''

Gabe shrugged. "Probably not. Our lives haven't been similar.''

"True.'' Nick cleared his throat. "Uh, have you heard the news about Jennifer's doctor visit?''

"You mean the twin thing? Yeah, I heard.''

"Everyone thinks they're your babies.''

"Yeah. I guess that's your fault,'' Gabe said calmly.

Nick almost swallowed his tongue. "What?''

Gabe gave him a wry smile, more than he'd expected. "Just kidding. But the fact that I'm a twin, proved by your appearance, is what makes them think I'm the daddy.''

"Gabe, is there any chance you are the father?''

"I'm not sure how far along she is.''

"I asked Tori.'' Nick waited for Gabe to respond.

"Well?''

"Five months. When did you have your fight?''

Slowly, as if he were running memories through his head, Gabe said, "Four months ago.''

"So the babies could be yours.''

"Yeah,'' Gabe said in almost a whisper, sounding tired and defeated. Not himself.

"Now, Gabe, I'm not suggesting any specific behavior, but—Russ pointed out that she doesn't have to say anything to you, or have your permission to pack up and move. She could just take those babies with her wherever she wants. You might never see your sons again.''

"No, she wouldn't do that. She and Sarah are tied to the store.'' Gabe's voice was hard and sure.

"You said she's never been involved in running the store. I assume she gets some money from the place. If you've made her mad enough, she might leave."

Gabe put his hands on his hips and stared at the ground. Then he muttered, "Damn!"

"What are you thinking?" Nick asked.

"That I don't have a choice!" Gabe roared. "That she's managed to trick me into marriage even though she was with someone else!"

"You're still not sure the babies are yours?" Nick asked in surprise.

"Who knows? I could have that test done," he said slowly.

"The doc said it couldn't be done without risk to the babies until after they were born."

"And if I wait until they're born, she might be gone already," Gabe said. "It would be hard to be pregnant and single in Rawhide. It's a small town. I can see her deciding to go away."

A sudden ringing had Gabe pulling his cell phone out of his jeans pocket. "Yeah?"

Nick only caught Gabe's side of the conversation. "Uh-uh. I see. Thanks for letting me know." Then he hung up and returned the cell phone to his jeans.

"Who was that?" Nick asked.

"Pete. He wanted to tell me that Sarah has hired a man to help her run the store."

Slowly Nick said, "In case she needs to leave for a little while…"

"To take care of Jennifer," Gabe finished. "Jen's probably packing her bags right now! Damn, damn, damn!"

"Is it a Randall curse? To have boys raised without their father?" Nick asked.

"The four Randalls here had their dad until after they were all over twenty."

"True, but as I understand it, they didn't have their mother. Maybe the curse is to just have one parent."

Gabe turned around to stare at Nick. "I don't believe in curses!"

"Me, neither," Nick said sturdily. "Besides, you and Jennifer are both alive and well."

"But not together."

"You can change that, Gabe. You can marry Jennifer for the sake of your babies. It wouldn't be so bad. Jennifer is a beautiful woman."

"Yeah, but—I couldn't touch her."

Nick swallowed convulsively. That would be an impossible situation. Talk about being miserable. "Then I guess there's nothing—"

"All right. I'll marry her!"

That had been Nick's goal, to get Gabe to swallow his pride and salvage at least the right to raise his sons. But like this? It would drive his brother mad. "Gabe, you can't do that. That would be insane!"

"Don't you think I'd go insane, worrying over my boys? Wondering if Jen would marry some man like my stepfather? Have my boys think I didn't love them enough to take care of them? They'd hate me even if I found them. They'd blame me. They'd think I should've taken care of Jennifer, no matter what."

They both stared in silence at the shimmering lake. "Any fish in here?" Nick asked randomly, not knowing what else to say.

"Yeah. I stocked it so I could take my children fishing. My boys. Can't you see them, about the age of Toby's son, holding short poles I made for them?"

Nick stared at Gabe, at the dreamy look on his face.

"So you could be happy, having your boys, even if it meant living with Jennifer and not touching her?"

"Yeah. I can't live *without* my boys."

"But—"

"I have to marry Jennifer!"

Gabe seemed sure of his decision. Nick still wasn't sure it was the best option, but he could understand the reason for Gabe's choice.

"Okay, I guess that's a good decision," he agreed hesitantly.

"It is."

"Okay."

"But *you* have to do the asking," Gabe told him.

Nick almost passed out.

"Me? No, Gabe, that's impossible! I can't. That would be—"

"Not Jennifer. Sarah!"

Nick felt his blood leave his head and he was sure he was going to end up facedown on the grass. "Gabe!"

"No, no, I'm saying this wrong. I want you to ask Sarah to convince Jennifer to accept my proposal, with certain stipulations. You're a lawyer. I want you to represent me. Okay? Will you do that for me?"

Nick couldn't refuse. His own brother was asking a favor of him, asking him to use his skills to fix a bad situation. But with Sarah? When she didn't even want to talk to him? That wasn't going to work!

But when he opened his mouth to answer Gabe's question, "I can't" or "that's impossible" or even "Ask Jake or someone else" didn't come out.

Instead, he said, "I'll try."

God help him.

CHAPTER THIRTEEN

SARAH AND JENNIFER TOOK their usual walk after breakfast Tuesday morning.

"I had no idea your pregnancy would get me in shape," Sarah said as she accompanied Jennifer.

"I'm sorry," Jennifer muttered, trying to keep up with her sister, but not finding it easy.

"Don't be silly." Sarah linked her arm with Jennifer's and slowed down a bit, showing she'd noted her sister's struggle. "I'm going to be the best aunt your twins will ever have. And I'm going to have to move fast to keep up with them."

"It's a good thing they can't walk the first few months, so I can get back into shape," Jennifer said with a groan. "Sarah, I don't think I can go this fast."

"Why didn't you say something?"

"I didn't want to disappoint you."

"You can't disappoint me. Besides, I'm going to be a happy camper with help in the store today. It's going to make life much easier for both of us. Of course, paying Jeff's salary will cut down on profits."

Jennifer looked at Sarah. "Does that mean we need to cut back on expenses?"

"Nope. We both have good, healthy accounts, thanks to Tori. You know what a whiz she is with the stock market. In fact, I've been thinking that maybe we ought to build us a house. A single-story one. I'm not sure we can get it built before the twins are born, but we sure don't want them tumbling down the stairs as toddlers.''

Jennifer looked alarmed. ''I hadn't thought of that. Well, as long as it's built before they start to walk.''

Sarah sighed. ''The doctor may decide you can't go up and down the stairs. That's going to cause a problem.''

''Oh! I hadn't thought—I can take Daddy's bedroom. That would work.''

With a grimace, Sarah pointed out, ''I just put Jeff in there.''

''Could we trade—oh, no, he can't share the upstairs with you. Everyone would talk.''

''True. We'll be lucky if we aren't the subject of gossip when everyone finds out he's living downstairs.''

''I hadn't thought of that,'' Jennifer said with a gasp. ''And it's all my fault. They'll think you're going to turn up pregnant, too.''

''Not if I stay away from the Randalls,'' Sarah said, trying to turn things light.

Jennifer didn't say anything.

They got back to the store to find Jeff Fisher waiting on the sidewalk with several boxes and two suitcases beside him.

''Sorry to keep you waiting, Jeff,'' Sarah said as they approached. ''The doctor gave Jennifer orders to walk every morning and I went with her. Come on in.''

Jennifer unlocked the door while Sarah lifted one of the boxes. When Jennifer started to lift the other box, both Jeff and Sarah stopped her.

Sarah smiled at Jeff, feeling better about things since he seemed to be so nice. ''Follow me to your room,'' she added, leading the way through the store to the back hall.

''Why don't you take the morning to settle in. Jennifer will be able to help all morning. Then while she naps in the afternoon, you can learn how we do things.''

"It won't take me that long. I'll come out when I've finished," he said, smiling.

Sarah and Jennifer walked back into the store area together. When they were out of earshot, Sarah whispered, "I think our sales will go up if he smiles at the ladies like that."

"Are you interested in him?" Jennifer asked with concern.

"Me? No, not at all, but he seems nice."

"Just checking."

AFTER DINNER ON TUESDAY, Nick sat down at the table with Gabe and listened to his brother explain what stipulations he wanted in his marriage agreement with Jennifer. Nick was to present the agreement to Sarah so she could convince Jennifer to accept.

Nick figured Gabe might want a few things that Jennifer would object to, but negotiation was one of his specialties.

He had his legal pad in front of him, ready to write them down when Gabe pulled out a piece of white paper.

"What have you got there?" Nick asked.

"My list. I figured it would save time. You charge by the hour, don't you?"

Nick stared at Gabe, dressed in clean jeans and a shirt. For the first time since he'd found his brother, he wanted to punch him. "Are you trying to insult me? 'Cause you're doing a good job if you are."

"What do you mean?" Gabe demanded, sitting straight in his chair.

"You think you're going to pay me for helping you work out something as personal as this? Something so important?"

"I told you, I pay my own way!" Gabe snapped.

"So I need to pay you rent! How much?"

"You're already working for your lodging!"

Nick got up from the table. "If you have to be stubborn

and pay someone, go find another lawyer.'' He stalked out of the kitchen.

Gabe sat there with his mouth open.

Letty came in as Nick went out. ''Have you finished your talk already?'' she asked.

''No!'' Gabe shouted.

That got her attention. ''What's wrong with you, Gabe?''

''He won't help me with Jennifer.''

''What about Jennifer?'' Letty asked eagerly.

''I'm going to marry her, but I'm making conditions.''

''What kind of conditions?''

Gabe almost threw the list across the table. ''These.''

Letty had always been supportive, even when he'd not been on his best behavior. When she burst out laughing, he was stunned.

''I don't blame him,'' she said with a chuckle. ''I wouldn't offer these to Jennifer, either. She might shoot you.'' Then she tackled the other problem. ''Why won't Nick help you?''

''I have to pay him.''

''You mean he insists on charging? I don't think that's right.''

''No! *I* insist on paying,'' Gabe explained.

Nick appeared in the doorway. ''Did he explain it all to you, Letty? I think he's crazy.''

''So you must've looked at his list,'' Letty said with a grin.

Nick frowned and reached for the piece of paper in Letty's grasp. ''No, I haven't.''

Gabe reached for it first. ''No need for you to read it, since you're not going to represent me.''

''I was coming back to offer you a deal.''

Gabe looked at him suspiciously. ''What?''

''You got a dollar bill?''

''Of course I do.''

"Pay me a dollar. That's compensation. I'll be your legal representative then."

"You're being ridiculous!" Gabe shouted.

"No, you are," Nick returned.

Blackie stepped into the kitchen. "You know, I'm finally convinced you two are brothers. This is the first time you've argued. It was unnatural, you being so polite all the time."

They both turned on Blackie, glaring at him as they took in his meaning.

"That's because he's stubborn," Gabe complained, pointing at Nick.

"Me? Look who's talking."

Blackie rolled his eyes. "Shall we send them to bed without supper, Letty?"

"They've already had supper, but we could not let them have any of the cake that I made today," Letty suggested.

"Don't be ridi— What kind of cake?" Gabe asked.

"I made a carrot cake with that special icing you like," she said.

"Man, Letty, that's not fair," Gabe protested.

"It's that good?" Nick asked.

"Yeah. It's one of my favorites."

"Hmm, I'm willing to take two dollars instead of one. That's a one-hundred-percent increase."

"Make it five," Gabe responded.

"Three," Nick said sternly. "That's a real compromise."

Gabe hesitated. Then, after seeing Letty's pleading look and Blackie's stern one, he nodded and reached for his billfold. He took out three ones and handed them to Nick, who folded them carefully and stuffed them in his pocket.

Then he extended his hand to Gabe.

After they shook hands, Gabe asked for his cake.

"Before he looks at your specifications?" Letty asked.

"Yeah."

"Okay with you, Nick?" Letty asked.

"Sure. I'm sure he'll be reasonable."

Letty laughed and pulled out a glass cake stand. Then she cut four pieces of cake and served them, along with steaming cups of fresh coffee.

Nick took a bite of the cake and agreed with his brother that it was delicious. "What are you asking for that Letty thinks is so unusual?" he asked Nick.

"I don't know," Gabe said, but he didn't meet Nick's gaze.

"I happen to think that telling her she can only leave her room from eight to six is unreasonable," Letty stated firmly. "That means she has to eat dinner in her room alone. And what if she gets sick during the night?"

Nick stared first at Letty and then Gabe. "What's the purpose of that stipulation?"

"So I don't have to see her when I get in from work."

"And she can't go outside the house without Blackie going with her," Letty continued.

Nick looked at Gabe again.

"She might hurt herself," Gabe said pointedly. "Jennifer doesn't know anything about ranching."

"And she can only go shopping once a week," Letty added.

"Blackie can't go with her every day. He has work to do."

Letty sighed. "At least the allowance was generous—" she paused to stare at Gabe "—but I don't see how you'll stop her from taking money from Sarah. They both own the store. Jen is entitled to half the profits."

Nick shook his head. "You can't do that, Gabe. And why would you want to?"

"I don't want people saying I married her for her money."

"Do they really have that much?" Nick asked.

Gabe shrugged his shoulders.

"He even put in that she can't leave him. No time off for good behavior." Letty shook her head and tsked.

"She can leave once the babies are born. She just can't take them," Gabe said, as if he were being completely reasonable.

"Anything else?" Nick asked dryly.

"No intimacy between us. And none with anyone else."

"She's pregnant with twins, Gabe. I really don't think that's necessary," Letty stated.

"I mean after."

"After?" Nick questioned.

"After the babies are born."

Nick took a bite of cake and savored it. He was afraid if he spoke before he finished it, Letty would take it away. But he couldn't hold back from responding to Gabe's last stipulation. "You can't demand certain behavior without a time frame. Besides, are you going to remain celibate the rest of your life?"

"I didn't say me. I said her."

"You can't make demands on her that you're not willing to take for yourself," Nick stated reasonably.

"Well, hell! I don't like that!"

"Good, 'cause Sarah isn't going to go for anything like this. It won't even get to Jennifer. By the way, are you two going to share a room?"

"Hell, no!"

"Then you're throwing me out, I guess. Can I stay in the bunkhouse?"

"I'm not throwing you out. What are you talking about?" Gabe demanded.

"Pardon my math, but there are four bedrooms. There are the four of us who occupy them right now. How are you going to add Jennifer without someone sharing a room?"

Silence fell as they all realized Nick was right. But Blackie spoke before anyone else. "I have an idea. I've been thinking about buying one of those already-built homes. It just takes a little work to get 'em ready. We can put it near the barn and call it the manager's house.''

"Why would you do that? Aren't you happy here with us?" Gabe asked, frowning.

"Yeah, but Hazel is a little shy and would be uncomfortable sharing my room here.''

The silence was filled with astonishment this time. Then Letty said, ''My, you are a fast worker, Blackie. I didn't think Hazel was that kind of a woman.''

"What do you mean?" Blackie roared. "She's the sweetest woman I've ever met.''

"But to live with you without being married—" Letty said.

"We're getting married! What did you think I meant?''

"I guess it's obvious what we all thought," Gabe said. "Congratulations, Blackie. Is she willing to adopt me?''

"Of course. I told her we were family.''

Gabe blinked his eyes and looked away. "Good," he said gruffly.

Nick and Letty congratulated Blackie. Letty added that she would be glad to make a wedding cake and handle the reception.

"I might take you up on that, Letty," Blackie said. "I want everything to be nice for Hazel.''

"Where can you order these ready-made houses?" Gabe asked.

"I'm not sure, but there's one on the Bloomfields' ranch. You could call and ask them. I'll pay for it.''

"No, it'll be my wedding present to you," Gabe told him in a "no arguing" tone.

"And I'll do all the finishing work on the house," Nick added.

"Aw, you guys are great!" Blackie exclaimed. Then he stood. "I've got to go call Hazel. She'll be just tickled.'' Blackie left the room, all his thoughts on Hazel.

"Well, I guess things are changing," Gabe said with a sigh.

"For the better," Letty said firmly. "You and Blackie each have someone to complete your lives."

"And what about you and Bill Wilson? Are *you* going to leave me?"

Letty shook her head. "If anything should come of our friendship, I can move in with him and drive out every day."

"You wouldn't mind?"

"Of course not. I've worked all my life. There's no reason to stop now." She grinned. "Maybe Jennifer can handle breakfast so I don't have to come so early."

"No. Jennifer doesn't do things like that." Gabe looked away. "She—she's like a butterfly, pretty and delicate."

Letty and Nick exchanged glances but said nothing else.

"Do you really think I'm being difficult?" Gabe asked, waving toward his white sheet of paper.

"Not only difficult," Nick said. "Some of those things are illegal." He shook his head. "Besides, why marry her if you hate her that much?"

"The babies! I told you I couldn't stand my boys being abandoned by me. If they are my boys."

"I think they are, Gabe, don't you?"

"Yeah."

"Then why don't you marry Jennifer without any of this?" Nick asked. "Have a real marriage."

"Because I don't trust her. And I don't want to be weak. When she walks in the room, I forget what I'm doing. If she sees that, she'll take advantage of me. And I'll go crazy with wanting her."

"Look, I'll tell Sarah you're willing to marry Jennifer to provide for the babies and her, but it's a marriage of convenience, nothing more...unless the two of you want it to change."

Gabe sat silently, his head bowed. Finally he said, "If that's what you think is best, but it sounds like a marriage of *inconvenience,* if you ask me!"

CHAPTER FOURTEEN

"TODAY?"

Gabe's one-word question didn't faze Nick. Though they had only spoken about Gabe's marriage last night, he knew his brother was anxious to get things moving.

"Yeah, I'll talk to Sarah today. But you should wait until Blackie and Hazel are settled before Jennifer and you can marry. You know that, don't you?"

"Yeah," Gabe replied. "I called the Bloomfields this morning to see where they got their prebuilt home. Then I called the company, which is based in Minnesota. I've ordered a two-bedroom house. Once it's delivered, we'll need a plumber and electrician."

"I might be able to do that work," Nick interjected.

"Really? You sure know a lot. I'm impressed."

"So when will it be here?"

"I paid extra to put a rush on it. They promised delivery in eight to ten days. Two days to get it ready. Two weeks and we're set." Gabe swallowed. Two weeks and he'd have his dream...sort of.

"If Jennifer agrees."

Gabe drew himself up. "She's pregnant. Of course she'll agree."

Nick patted him on the shoulder. "I'll do my best."

"Hey, three dollars are at stake. Don't fail me," Gabe said with a grin.

Nick grinned back and saluted his brother. "You got it." Then he headed for town.

Gabe stood there. It was a strange feeling, letting some-one else handle his personal matters. It had never happened before. But he realized he trusted Nick. Maybe because they were so much alike.

He shrugged his shoulders. He had a lot to do and he wasn't used to standing around. He headed to the barn to saddle up his favorite mount. He had some more fence lines to ride until lunchtime. He decided to come back for lunch in case Nick returned by then.

He tried to put his thoughts away for another time, but they kept focusing on pictures of Jennifer big with his children. He'd never been around a pregnant woman. What did he know about having babies?

Should he go to Jon and ask for advice? That would be a good idea. And he could talk to Pete. He'd been through the birth of twins, and his boys were healthy and happy. Well, until Russ lost his wife. But that couldn't be helped.

He wanted his children to have a happy childhood. He wanted to give them what he'd never had. He wanted them to believe they could do anything and he would still love them. That his love wasn't conditional. He'd learned that from Blackie. But he'd gone through childhood believing he was a failure because his mother never smiled.

His thoughts turned to about Jennifer. Would she be happy with their marriage? He remembered her happiness the first time she told him she was pregnant. But the next time she called, he'd told her not to call again. Her voice had been quiet and timid. Not at all like Jennifer's.

Had he ruined her joy? Had he created a reincarnation of his mother? God help him, he hoped not. What could he do? He gave up trying to work and headed to the house. He needed to make plans.

JEFF WAS WORKING OUT WELL.

The three of them shared a lunch Jennifer had made. Fortunately it was one of her good days in the kitchen,

Sarah thought with a grin. Jennifer's adventures with new recipes had uneven results. She'd have to remember to warn Jeff.

He caught on quickly to her system and had been learning the location of all the items. When the bell over the door sounded the arrival of a new customer, he insisted Sarah stay at the "consultation" table and finish her lunch. She nodded and watched the effect of his smile on Mrs. Parker.

"Good afternoon, ma'am. How may I help you?"

"Who are you?" the lady demanded.

Sarah joined them. "Mrs. Parker, I'd like you to meet our new employee, Jeff Fisher. I think you'll find him well qualified to help you."

Mrs. Parker, a woman over sixty, stared at him from his head to his toes and suddenly broke into a smile. "I think you're right. Show me what you have in winter gloves, young man."

"Of course, Mrs. Parker. Right this way."

Sarah returned for her last few bites of the enchilada casserole Jennifer made.

"This casserole is really good, Jen."

"Thanks. It's one of Tori's recipes. She said Jon loves it."

"I can see why. You're going to be a great cook pretty soon."

"Yeah, right," Jennifer said with a grin. "But I'll have my hands full caring for the babies once they get here."

"Probably. Our dinners will go downhill if I have to go back to cooking. Your taking over that chore has made life easier. Now with Jeff here, I feel like I'm in semiretirement."

"He is good, isn't he?"

"So far. This afternoon, I intend to get caught up on paperwork while he tends to customers."

"Want me to help you? I could sit down and do the filing."

"Nope. You're under strict orders to lie down. That's your most important job these days. How's the knitting coming?"

"I think I have all thumbs. And I get lost trying to read what to do. It would be easier to have someone show me, but I don't know anyone who knits."

"Hmm. I'm trying to think who comes in and buys wool. Russ and Rich's grandmother and Mildred do. You know they teach those classes in the summer at the school, but they just finished. Oh, and a new lady, Mrs. Letty Dunlap. She works on a ranch near town, but I'm not sure which one. Next time she's in, I'll ask her."

"That would be great," Jennifer replied. "I've decided to dress one baby in blue and one in green. That way everyone can tell them apart. I want them each to feel like an individual."

"Good idea! I like that. Well, I've finished, so I'll help you carry the dishes up and—"

A loud voice interrupted them. "Well! I never!"

Across the store they saw Mrs. Parker heading out the door, her nose in the air.

"I'll get the dishes," Jennifer said. "You go put out the fire."

"Thanks, honey," Sarah said, and hurried across the store where Jeff stood like a statue, staring after the woman.

"Jeff? What's the problem?"

He turned to stare at Sarah. "I'm sorry, Sarah. I had no idea it would upset her."

"What would?"

"Everything was going fine, only she couldn't make up her mind which gloves she wanted, and she casually asked me where I was living. I told her you'd given me the downstairs room, which would make it easy during bad weather. And she demanded to know if you two were still living upstairs. She apparently thinks there's some hanky-panky going on.'' He shook his head, as if unable to believe what had just happened. "Don't worry, Sarah, I'll find somewhere else to live and get my things out of here as soon as I can."

"Don't move on my account, Jeff. Mrs. Parker is a terrible gossip, but I don't let her determine my behavior."

"Are you sure? Because I'd hate for you to lose business just because I'm living here."

"I should've warned you about Mrs. Parker. She comes in every day. She seldom buys anything, but it's her outing for the day. She loves to gather the news. I should tell her she can find out more by eating at the café, but I never have."

"If you're sure, I'd like to stay where I am. I like the work and I couldn't ask for a handier place to stay, or nicer people to be around."

"Good." She smiled and then added, "It wouldn't hurt if you found a nice young lady to date, though. And attended the local church. Then you can be forgiven your imagined sins," she added with a smile.

"Right. I know about small towns. We lived in one in Missouri. I can't promise to find a girl, but I'll definitely attend the local church."

"Good. Oh, Jeff, I forgot to ask you to spread out the sweatshirts I stacked up on the top shelf here. I'm afraid they'll fall down."

With perfect timing, as if planned, the stack of sweatshirts on the end came tumbling down to the floor one by one.

Jeff and Sarah looked at each other, startled. Then they burst into laughter. Sarah couldn't explain why it was so funny, but she reached down to pick them up while still laughing and lost her balance, sitting down on her bottom. Fortunately, her fall was cushioned by a couple of sweatshirts, and Sarah was still laughing as Jeff tried to help her up when the bell jangled.

Suddenly her eyes locked with a pair of very familiar brown ones. "Thanks, Jeff," she said as she struggled to her feet. "Um, good afternoon, Nick. Let me introduce Jeff Fisher, our new employee. Jeff, this is Nick McMillan. Why don't you help him?"

She turned to go, but Nick put out a hand and caught her arm. "No, I need to talk to you."

"I have work to do. Jeff can help you."

"No," Nick said again. "I need to talk to you about our sibling's problem."

Jeff moved closer to Sarah in a protective manner, which seemed to irritate Nick, if his expression was anything to judge by.

"It's all right, Jeff. I'll deal with Mr. McMillan." She turned and headed to the consultation table, where they'd eaten lunch.

"Why don't we go down to the café and talk. It's not busy in the afternoons. It will be more—private," Nick said, his eyes shooting daggers toward Jeff. "You don't want more rumors started, do you?"

"I really shouldn't—"

Jeff seemed to assume he was the reason she didn't want to go since he didn't know all the items in the store. "I can manage, Sarah. If I get into trouble, I'll call Jennifer."

With a sigh, Sarah agreed. "All right. I'll go up and get a sweater. Then I'll meet you at the café."

"I'll wait for you," Nick said firmly, as if daring her— or anyone else—to dislodge him.

"Fine. Suit yourself." In a huff, she hurried up the stairs.

NICK HAD LEFT FOR TOWN about nine o'clock, but he'd found several errands to postpone his visit with Sarah. He'd figured Gabe wouldn't come back to the house until the end of the day. So he'd looked at several properties on

Main Street with the real estate agent, just in case he should change his mind about settling in Rawhide. It was tempting.

And while he'd wandered the street with the agent, he'd been practicing his approach to Sarah. But he hadn't expected to find her on the floor, another man's arms around her, giggling like a schoolgirl.

She seemed so friendly with everyone but him. It irritated him. And that Jeff guy thought he needed to hover over Sarah to protect her from *him!*

Steps on the stairs drew his attention. Sarah ignored him and walked over to Jeff. "Here's the number for the café. If you need anything, call me instead of Jennifer. She's gone to sleep."

"Will they know you if I ask for you by name?" Jeff asked.

Sarah smiled at Jeff. "Yes, of course. Small town, remember?"

"Oh, yeah." Jeff nodded with a grin.

Then she turned around to face Nick, and her smile disappeared. "I'm ready."

He led the way out of the store, then complained, "You don't have to make it sound like you think you're being taken to the guillotine."

"I think you're exaggerating, Mr. McMillan."

"Hell! Sarah, why are you being so formal? And who the hell is that man? You got a crush on him?"

"I told you he's my new employee. I needed help running the store. Jennifer has been helping out, but she really can't anymore. And it's none of your business." Since she'd started walking faster as he questioned her, they quickly reached the café, and Nick still didn't have any answers he liked.

They took an empty booth in the back, away from everyone else. "Where's he from?" Nick asked, frowning.

"He's from Buffalo."

"Won't that make it difficult to get here in bad weather?"

Sarah sighed. "We don't do a lot of business in bad weather. Besides, he's moved to Rawhide."

She avoided his gaze, which made him think something was wrong. "Where? I didn't think there was anywhere to stay in town when I arrived."

"Did we come here to talk about my new employee or Jen and Gabe?"

"Hi there, Sarah, Nick. You want something to drink or a piece of pie?" the waitress asked.

Nick didn't wait for Sarah to answer. "Yeah, bring us both a piece of pie and I'll have coffee. Sarah, what do you want to drink?"

"I'll have iced tea and no pie."

"But Sarah," the waitress protested, "it's coconut pie, your favorite."

"Oh, okay, bring me some pie." She smiled at the waitress, but when she left, Sarah glared at Nick.

"Hey, it's not my fault it's coconut pie!" he protested with a grin.

"What about Gabe and Jen?"

He guessed he couldn't stall any longer. "Gabe wants to marry Jennifer." Getting straight to the point had been his decision. They could work out any details later.

Sarah looked surprise. She drew a deep breath and said slowly, "Why?"

Oh, yeah. Leave it to Sarah to take the same approach. Right to the heart of the matter. "Gabe believes Jennifer is having his babies."

"He knows she's having twins?"

"Yeah."

"He didn't learn it from Jen because he told her never to call him again when she tried."

Not only was Gabe his client, he was his brother. Nick

had to defend him. "Your sister lied to him. Don't you think you should cut him a little slack in that case?"

"My sister suffered almost four months with nausea every morning like clockwork. Don't you think he should cut *her* some slack?"

"Sarah, let's not argue. Gabe is an honorable man. He's willing to do his duty. You should be grateful for that."

Sarah stared at him, as if replaying his words over in her mind.

The waitress delivered the two pieces of pie and their drinks. "Let me know if you need anything else, okay?"

Nick dismissed her with a smile.

"Are you telling me Gabe isn't marrying her because he loves her?"

"Now, Sarah, he's willing to do the right thing. That's what counts."

"Give him a message. Tell him not to bother."

He grabbed her wrist, having read in her eyes her intention to stomp out of the café. "Whoa, lady! Eat some pie and cool off. You haven't thought this through."

"Oh, but I have!" Sarah told him as she tugged at her wrist. "My sister doesn't have to take his charity. We'll be just fine."

"You want to torture him? Make him pay for being so slow to offer marriage? I can understand that. But why do you want to hurt Jennifer?" He knew concern for Jennifer was his only hope of getting her to settle down.

"Hurt Jennifer? I'd never hurt Jennifer! It's Gabe who is wanting to tear her heart out. He wants the babies, but he doesn't want Jennifer. How do you think that will make her feel?"

"How do you think he felt when she told him there was someone else?" Nick had seen the torment in his brother's eyes every time Jennifer's name had come up.

"So it's tit for tat?" she demanded.

"Eat some pie and let me catch my breath. Please?"

She stared at him and finally nodded, much to his relief. He let go of her wrist, but watched her closely to make sure she didn't make a run for it.

He sat there watching her eat her pie and rubbed his eyebrow, trying to figure out how to get the results Gabe wanted. He took a bite or two of the pie also, discovering it could become his favorite very quickly. "Great pie."

"Yes, it is," she agreed stiffly.

"Look, Gabe is trying to do the right thing. I can't say how he feels about Jennifer. But he knows it's going to be hard for her to live in Rawhide as a pregnant, single woman. He wants to protect Jennifer from the gossip, and he's concerned about the babies, too. All he's suggesting is a marriage of convenience at the present time. If they feel differently at any time, they can renegotiate their agreement. I can't work that out. No lawyer worth his salt tries to negotiate emotions."

"So you're a lawyer today, not his brother?"

"I'm his brother always, but today I'm his lawyer, earning the whopping fee of—"

"You took payment from your own brother? You have no sense of family at all!"

Nick sighed. This was harder than running in waist-high water. "Sarah, that's neither here nor there. Will you discuss Gabe's proposal with Jennifer? That's all I'm asking."

"But, Nick, she'll want to know why, if Gabe wants to marry her, he hasn't come to see her. You expect me to tell her it's a marriage of convenience? That he doesn't love her? Do you think that won't hurt her?"

"I'm sure it will," he said softly, reaching across to catch her hand this time, to clasp it gently in his. "But Jennifer is a grown-up. You may find she prefers a marriage of convenience to her situation now."

"I'll talk to her. But I'm not promising anything!" Sarah snapped, then jerked her hand away from Nick's and got up to leave.

He didn't try to stop her. He'd known this would be a difficult conversation. At least she'd agreed to talk to Jennifer.

Damn! He'd forgotten to get her to agree to any time deadline. They could sit there waiting a week for their answer. Gabe was going to have his head.

CHAPTER FIFTEEN

NICK WORRIED ALL THE WAY home about his not setting a deadline. But he figured he had a couple of hours before Gabe showed up. He'd call Sarah. If she was still mad, she might hang up on him, but maybe not. She was a reasonable woman...most of the time.

He actually admired the way she'd stuck up for Jennifer. Too bad he hadn't managed to tell her that. What happened to his famous negotiating skills? It was because the situation was personal. He'd never faced such personal negotiating. Gabe wasn't going to think he was worth ever those three measly dollars.

Pulling up by the house, he was surprised to find Gabe coming toward the car. What was he doing home? By the time he got out of the car, Gabe was beside him.

"Well?" Gabe asked, grabbing him by the arm.

A man of few words. But Nick had no trouble determining what he wanted to know. Unfortunately, he didn't have an answer.

"I talked to Sarah. She—she was upset, worried about Jennifer. I explained that, uh, I wasn't trying to negotiate emotions. You and Jennifer will determine where the marriage goes, but you wanted to protect her from gossip and take care of her and the boys."

"Good. What did she say?"

"She agreed to talk to Jennifer."

"And?"

Nick rubbed his eyebrow. They were getting to the hard

part. And he had another one-word question to answer. "And we have to wait."

"But when is she going to talk to Jen? When do we get an answer?" Gabe asked, his face filled with anxiety.

"Gabe, I think maybe you should've asked Jennifer yourself if it means that much to you," Nick said, worried. His brother was still in love with the woman. He could tell by his reaction. And he'd just inferred to Sarah that Gabe didn't love Jennifer anymore.

Gabe immediately released Nick and took a step back. "I'm concerned about my sons, Nick, that's all."

He didn't believe Gabe's words. Oh, of course he was concerned about the babies. What man wouldn't be? But there was more. Gabe still loved Jennifer. "Look, I'll call Sarah when we get inside and see if she'll agree to a deadline. Will that help?"

"Yeah."

"What are you doing here? I thought you'd be out working."

"I couldn't work. My mind—I couldn't stay focused. Too dangerous to work like that. Especially with barbed wire."

"I guess so. I didn't think of that."

"Blackie's just as bad. He went to see Hazel to tell her about their house. He's excited."

"I'm glad he's the only one," Nick said, slanting a teasing look at Gabe.

Gabe's cheeks flushed, but he didn't say anything.

"You know, after your wedding, I'm going to need to find somewhere else to live." Actually, he'd just realized it when he saw the emotion on Gabe's face regarding Jennifer's decision.

"Why?"

"Newlyweds don't need a chaperone, and even if you did, you'll have Letty. I'd be in the way." He cleared his throat. "It's probably time for me to go back to Denver."

"I thought maybe you'd stay here. You've seemed happy."

"I have been, Gabe. But what am I going to do? Work as your handyman? I thought about practicing law here, but there doesn't seem much need."

"I don't think we have a lawyer in Rawhide," Gabe pointed out.

"I know. But I left Denver suddenly, and I'll need to go back there, anyway. Then I'll make a decision."

They entered the kitchen. Letty looked up from her cooking. "Need a cup of coffee?"

"Yes, please," Gabe said.

Nick thought of the half a piece of pie he'd left at the café. "You got anything to snack on?"

"Of course." She pulled out some cookies she'd made that morning and filled a plate, bringing it to the table.

"Call Sarah first," Gabe urged.

"One cookie, taskmaster. Then I'll call."

SARAH CHECKED WITH JEFF when she got back to the store, assuring herself that he was managing fine. Then she went to her office and settled in behind a pile of papers.

And stared into space.

Poor Jennifer. When she and Gabe had been together, her sister had been so happy. At times, Sarah had worried that Jennifer would never settle down with one man. But Jen hadn't dated anyone after Gabe. How sad that her silly lie had ruined her one truly satisfying relationship.

Sarah hated the thought of having to tell Jennifer what Gabe was offering. It was like a secondhand gift. Used, not new. Only half as good as she'd hoped for.

She made no progress with the paperwork. It couldn't hold her attention. When the phone rang, she picked it up at once. Anything to take her mind off Jennifer.

"Sarah, it's Nick."

"Yes?" She kept her voice emotionless, as if he were one of her suppliers.

"Listen, we forgot to discuss a—a deadline for when Jennifer would have an answer for Gabe. He's anxious to get things settled. Nothing can be done until Blackie's marriage, so—"

"What? Who's Blackie? And what does his marriage have to do with anything?"

Nick cleared his throat. "Blackie is Gabe's best friend and manager of the ranch. He lives in Gabe's house. And he's marrying Hazel someone. I can't remember her name. Once he moves out, there'll be a bedroom free for Jennifer."

"I see. I don't think you mentioned separate bedrooms when we talked."

"I assumed you would realize—a marriage of convenience doesn't usually—I'm sorry. I should've said so. My fault."

Okay, so he was being patient and charming. As charming as he could in the circumstances. It wasn't easy to represent the Prince when he rejects Cinderella and offers marriage to her at the same time!

"Have you talked to Jennifer?"

"No."

"When are you going—"

"I don't know!" Sarah snapped. It was difficult enough to tell Jennifer her dreams were gone without doing it according to a timetable.

"Look, I'm not trying to pressure you, but—it's Tuesday. Can we say she'll have an answer by Friday?"

Sarah knew she wouldn't be able to keep her conversation with Nick secret for long. And she figured Jennifer would know at once whether or not she'd agree to such terms. So she'd agree. "I will have talked to her before then. I can't promise when Jennifer will have an answer. That's her decision."

"Okay. You're right. But Blackie and Hazel are getting married in two weeks. And Gabe would like to take care of this situation immediately or—as soon as possible."

"You think we'll fool anyone at this late date? No one's going to believe Jen got pregnant on her wedding night!" she spat out.

Nick drew a deep breath. "Of course not. Gabe was thinking of Jennifer and the babies. The longer they put off the changes, the harder they'll be for Jennifer."

"How kind of him!" Sarah said, getting upset all over again.

"We'll look forward to hearing Jennifer's decision, hopefully by Friday."

"Fine."

"Thank you, Sarah," Nick said softly.

Sarah hung up the phone. Damn, she didn't want to talk to Jennifer. After staring at the walls for a few minutes, she shoved back her chair and headed for the stairs. When she reached their apartment, she discovered Jennifer still in bed. She tiptoed into the room and found her sister's eyes were open.

"Hi, there. I thought you were asleep."

"I was," Jennifer said, sitting up with a sigh. "I slept too long and now I don't want to get up."

"Are the babies kicking?"

"Yes, they sure are. I haven't started dinner. Sorry."

"Why don't we go to the café for dinner? They have coconut pie today."

Jennifer looked at her curiously. "How do you know?"

"Uh, one of the customers mentioned it," Sarah said hurriedly. "We can invite Jeff to come with us."

"If you want," Jennifer agreed, but she sounded discouraged.

"Jen, is anything wrong?"

"No, of course not. It's just hard to know what to do next."

"What do mean?" she asked cautiously.

"Oh, I mean about knitting or doing laundry. Things like that. They seem like such an effort some days," Jennifer said with a sigh.

"No laundry for you. It's too heavy. You're off the laundry detail for a few months. I guess you could fold clothes after they dry, but only if I carry them in here."

"But I don't have anything to do," Jen said, then paused. "I'm sorry. Never mind. I'm just spoiled."

"Yes, you are," Sarah agreed with a smile, and kissed Jennifer's cheek. "Oh! I forgot. We got something in the other day that I bet you'd like."

"What?"

"Some baby blankets with a cross-stitch pattern printed on them. You could do those for the babies." She jumped up and started for the door.

"But I don't know how to do that."

"It's really easy. Even I can do it. Let me show you. I'll be right back."

She hurried downstairs, glad she'd thought of the blankets. She'd have to look for other things for Jen to do, to keep her spirits up. And she certainly couldn't tell her about Gabe tonight. Not while Jen was so down.

"Did you get a lot of work done, Sarah?" Jeff asked when she entered the store.

"Not really. I had trouble concentrating. Jen needs something to do and I thought about those cross-stitch baby blankets." She'd reached the shelf where she'd put them, only to find they'd been beautifully displayed. "Oh, Jeff, did you do this? How nice."

"Thanks. I couldn't tell what they were with them lying flat. I thought the customers might have the same problem. I've already sold two of them this afternoon."

"Goodness, we'll be out soon." She found a blue blanket and a green one, as Jennifer had said she was going to use those colors. "Oh, Jeff, Jen and I are going to the café for dinner. Do you want to come with us?"

"Are you sure you don't mind?"

"Of course not. We'll introduce you to everyone, help you get acquainted."

"Sounds good."

Sarah went back upstairs. She opened the packages and spread out the directions for Jennifer. The two of them pored over them and Jennifer actually made several stitches before it was time to go to dinner.

GABE TRIED TO WORK the next day as he waited for Jennifer's response. It wasn't easy to wait and pretend everything was normal. He was short-tempered and distracted. Blackie fussed at him. Letty was incredibly patient with him, which irritated him all the more. Nick and the hands tried to avoid him altogether.

While they were eating that evening, the phone rang. Gabe jumped from the table, almost turning it over in his rush.

"Hello?" Gabe said anxiously.

"Gabe, it's Pete. Is everything okay?"

"Yeah, fine, Pete."

As if a switch had been thrown, Letty, Blackie and Nick went back to eating and all the tension rolled out of Gabe's body.

"Sorry to bother you. I bet you're sitting down to dinner."

"Yeah, but it's all right." He couldn't even remember what he'd been eating.

"Do you remember that young bull I told you about? We borrowed him for breeding last year and were real pleased with his offspring?"

"Yeah. Black Thunder, wasn't it?"

"That's him. He's for sale."

"What? Why?" Gabe's body stiffened, catching the attention of his companions.

"His owner passed away and they're selling everything," Pete told him. "His daughters didn't want to keep the ranch."

"How much?"

"There's going to be an auction. We were thinking we might phone in a bid, but I thought he sounded perfect for starting your herd. So I thought I'd let you know."

"Pete, you're the best friend a guy could have. I definitely want to try to buy him. Tell me where and when the auction is."

Nick was at his side, handing him pen and paper, and Gabe wrote down the information. When he hung up the phone, he told the others about the opportunity, excitement in his voice.

"This is the break I've been waiting for. You saw his calves, Blackie. Pete showed us some of them last spring when we were in town."

"Yep. They were fine. Black Thunder would be perfect."

"Do you have to go to Denver to get him?" Nick asked. "If so, I'll go with you and we can stay in my apartment. You did write Denver down, didn't you?"

"Yeah, it's just outside Denver. But we'll have to leave in the morning. The auction is Friday. I'll need to get there tomorrow in time to establish my credentials and get the details on the auction. I'll want to see him, too, to make sure nothing's happened to him, read the vet reports."

Letty, more calm than the men, cleared her throat. "Friday? You're going to go on Thursday and not get back until Friday or Saturday?"

"That's right, Letty. It's the chance of a lifetime. I don't think too many ranchers know about the auction. It's all happening in a hurry. It'll be great. We might even look over some of his equipment. There are a few more things I need. Depends on the price. I've got to do some figuring.''

He headed for his office, but came to a halt when his housekeeper asked, ''But what about Jennifer?''

CHAPTER SIXTEEN

DINNER AT THE CAFÉ cheered Jennifer up. That and the prospect of working on the baby blankets. She hadn't managed to do anything for her babies yet. Now she'd actually started a project.

"I love the blankets, Sarah. They're going to be so beautiful," she said as they walked back to the store with Jeff.

"Yes, they are. It's getting cooler earlier, don't you think? It's almost September, so I shouldn't be surprised, but summer is never long enough."

"That's true," Jeff agreed. "When we got here from Missouri, I didn't believe people when they told me they'd gotten snow in September."

"Not often, though," Sarah assured him.

"Last year, Buffalo got six inches on September twenty-first. I remember because that's my birthday."

"Oh, so your birthday is coming up. How old will you be?" Jennifer asked.

"Twenty-six."

"Well, I don't think we'll have snow that early this year."

"Yeah, and I won't have to drive far to get to work!" he added with a chuckle.

"It's nice, isn't it." She unlocked the door to the store. "Well, I'm glad you joined us, Jeff."

"I enjoyed it. The people here are nice."

"True. See you in the morning," she said as she and

Jennifer started up the stairs. Jennifer waved to him before she went into their apartment.

"I'm going to work on the blankets," she told Sarah.

"Why don't you come in the den and watch television while you work."

"That's a good idea."

Around eight o'clock, after they'd watched a comedy and Jennifer's stitching was going well, Sarah decided she couldn't wait any longer.

She got up and turned off the television. Jennifer looked up, surprised. "Why did you turn it off?"

"I need to talk to you. Put away the stitching. I don't want you to mess it up when it's going so well."

Jennifer did so, then she stared at Sarah. "Is something wrong?"

"It's about Gabe…"

"Something's wrong with Gabe? Has he hurt himself?" she asked, trying to get up to reach Sarah, but she fell back into the chair.

Sarah hurried to her side to take her hand. "No! No, Gabe is fine. He—he heard about the twins."

"I tried to tell him," Jennifer said, holding her head up, her mouth stubborn.

"I know you did, honey. But he had Nick come talk to me, to—to offer to marry you."

Surprise and excitement burst onto Jennifer's face. "Oh! How wonderful!"

Sarah said nothing, waiting for Jennifer to realize the implications of what she said.

"But why didn't he come—" As realization hit her, the color drained from her face. "Why didn't he come here? Why didn't he ask me himself?"

Sarah took her hands. "He believes you're having his babies, but—but what he's offering is a marriage of convenience."

"A marriage of convenience? What do you mean?"

"A legal agreement that binds him to the babies. A financial arrangement for you. Something that stops the gossips from hurting you. Separate bedrooms."

Jennifer had ducked her head in the middle of Sarah's reply. Now she raised it to stare at Sarah, big fat tears rolling down her face. "He doesn't want me anymore?"

Sarah couldn't bring herself to answer that question. "I think he's confused right now, and maybe still a little angry with you." She got up and fetched the box of tissues for Jennifer.

"I think he cares about you, Jen, or he wouldn't be worrying about the gossips."

"Yes, he would," Jennifer said, stopping to blow her nose before she continued. "He wouldn't want the boys to suffer because of our behavior. I don't either, but I tried!" she said as she broke into tears.

Sarah wrapped her arms around her little sister and rocked her against her. "Don't cry, Jen. It will be all right."

"No, it won't," she said, sobbing on Sarah's shoulder. "I thought he loved me. All my dreams are broken. I can't go on."

"You don't have any choice about that, Jen. You have to go on. For the babies' sakes." She tipped Jennifer's face up. "You haven't forgotten about the boys, have you?"

Jennifer hiccuped, tears still flowing. "No. You're right. I have to take care of *my* boys. But I can do that, Sarah, with your help. I don't need his money. What I need from him, money can't buy. But that's not what he's offering, is it?"

She sat up straighter and rubbed her cheeks with a tissue. "He thinks I can't manage, but I can."

"I know you can, Jen, and you know I'll help you. But are you sure that's what you want for your children?"

Jennifer looked at her in surprise. "You want me to marry him?"

"No! Not if you don't want to, but—I know, I'm surprising myself. But Gabe has put down roots here. He's not going to move on, as he used to do. Do you want your boys to grow up not knowing their dad? Or seeing him on the weekends?"

"Maybe I'll move. We could move to Denver or—or Butte, Montana. Couldn't we?"

"We could. I'd leave our life behind for you and the boys. But then the boys would never have a father. Is that what you want?"

"Maybe you'd marry, and their uncle could help raise them," Jennifer said, sniffing again.

"Maybe, but what if I don't marry? What about you? Would you marry someone else?"

Jennifer's bottom lip began trembling. Then she burst into full-blown tears. "I love Gabe. I couldn't imagine— never. I couldn't, Sarah. Never!"

"Oh, Jen, don't cry. You'll make yourself sick. You don't have to make up your mind right away. You have until Friday."

But Jennifer was beyond listening. After half an hour of sobs and strangled words, Sarah went to the kitchen and made some hot cocoa for them to drink. When she brought in the tray with the two cups on it, Jennifer had stopped crying. She took her cup silently.

"Jen? Are you all right? Do you want to talk some more?"

"No, Sarah. Thank you for trying to help me. I guess I brought this on myself. With my lies." She sank her teeth into her lips as they began trembling again.

"Oh, honey," Sarah began, but Jennifer held up a hand to stop her.

Jennifer drained her cup and returned it to the tray. "I'm going to bed," she whispered. "I have to think."

"Okay. Call me if you need me," Sarah offered. Many

a time after their mother's death, Jennifer had crawled in bed with her big sister to be comforted.

"I'm going to be a mother, Sarah. I have to learn how to take care of others. But thank you for being there."

Sarah watched Jennifer leave the room, her cheeks wet, her head down. She'd hated having to break the news to Jennifer. She'd known Jennifer was still hoping Gabe would come to his senses and come back to claim her and their babies.

If the man were anywhere nearby, she'd slap him so hard he'd fall over. Then she'd tell him to get on his knees and be thankful for Jennifer's love. To have found such a gift, and then reject it was unpardonable in her book.

Of course, she knew Jennifer's behavior had a part in this sad story, but that didn't make it any easier. What would happen? What would Jennifer decide? She'd surprised herself, urging Jennifer to consider her answer. It wasn't that she wanted Jennifer to be unhappy. But the babies hadn't asked to be born to fighting parents. They were innocent and defenseless. She had to urge Jennifer to think of them.

Should she tell Jennifer to reject Gabe's cold offer and help her move away? But then it wasn't her decision to make.

She went to bed, too, and spent a restless night, trying to see into the future, hoping it wasn't as bleak as it looked right now.

GABE SLUMPED AGAINST the front seat. "Are you sure we made the right decision?"

Nick, whose eyes had been on the road, looked over at his brother. "You said this was a chance in a lifetime. He's the perfect bull for you, right?"

"Yeah, but Jennifer—"

"I left a message on Sarah's answering machine. They'll understand. I'm sure they will." Nick was dealing with a few things himself, finding himself on the road back to Denver. But he heard Gabe's worry.

"You're right. If Jen's going to be a rancher's wife, she has to realize the importance of— Damn it! Who am I trying to fool. Jen won't stand being passed up for a bull."

"You're not passing her up, Gabe. You're delaying receiving her answer. Letty will explain if she calls."

"Yeah." Gabe slumped against the seat again.

Nick was feeling edgy about his return to Denver. They'd agreed to go straight to his apartment. They'd have to park the truck and trailer out on the street. It wouldn't be allowed in the garage.

His apartment. It had been decorated by a very expensive decorator. But he'd added a few personal touches. He should be glad to return to the luxury he'd grown up with. After all, he'd been sleeping in a narrow bed with a thin mattress.

Gabe's spare room had bare walls, little comfort. Yet, it had come to feel like home. Strangely enough, his apartment was what seemed foreign. But maybe those feelings would disappear once he was there.

Maybe.

They switched drivers when they stopped for lunch so it was Gabe who was driving when they reached the outskirts of Denver.

"Almost there," he pointed out to Nick.

"Yeah, I know. Take the next exit."

"Okay," Gabe agreed, moving the truck and trailer to his right. "I hate the traffic here."

"It's not the evening rush hour yet. It gets worse in a couple of hours."

"How do you stand it?"

"Once I got out of law school, I got an apartment downtown, so I didn't have to go far. I'd go home a couple of times a month, enough to satisfy Mother, so it wasn't bad."

"A couple of times a month? That's all she wanted to see you?"

"Mother had a very busy social life. In fact, the only times she called was when she needed an escort and Dad wasn't available."

"An escort? You mean you went to things that required you to wear a tux?"

"I'm afraid so."

"Renting those can be expensive," Gabe pointed out.

"I didn't rent, Gabe. I own several tuxes." Nick chuckled when Gabe stared at him. "Watch the road."

"Sorry."

"See that high-rise two blocks ahead? That's where my apartment is. Anyplace you can park close by will be fine."

Gabe didn't talk anymore. He found a close parking place and shut off the motor. "Nick, I think it might be best if I found a hotel for the night. I don't fit in a fancy place like that."

"Yes, you do. I want you to see it. I may decide to give it up. But it was part of my life for a while. It might make you appreciate what you've got."

Gabe looked doubtful, but he grabbed his small suitcase out of the back, as did Nick, and followed him across the sidewalk to two large glass doors.

A uniformed doorman immediately held the doors open. "Welcome back, Mr. McMillan. You've been missed. And this is—" he began until his gaze reached Gabe's face. His mouth hung open.

Nick smiled. "Thompson, this is my brother, Gabe Randall. He's going to stay with me a couple of days. I don't think you'll have any trouble recognizing him."

"N-no, sir. Hello, Mr. Randall." He let the door swing to and hurried past them to press the button to summon an elevator. "Mr. McMillan, he looks just like you!"

"I know, Thompson," Nick said softly. "We're twins."

Nick got in the elevator and Gabe followed. The doorman stared at them until the door closed.

Gabe let out a pent-up breath. "Well, that was fun."

"Thompson's very efficient."

"Does he do anything but open doors and elevators all day?"

"Yeah, he screens guests, receives packages, does errands. A good doorman can save you a lot of time. It's almost like living in New York."

"And that's a good thing?"

Nick chuckled. "Some people think so."

Nick's apartment was on the twenty-fourth floor. When the elevators opened to a quiet hallway, Gabe followed Nick to one of two doors. "Just two people live on this floor?"

"That's right." Nick slid his key into the lock. It suddenly occurred to him that he hadn't seen a key used in a while. Well, that wasn't true. The real estate agent had used a key on one of the properties. But Gabe never used a key at his house.

Nick threw open the door, but there was no rush of homecoming. No sense that the world had righted itself.

He stepped onto the Oriental rug in the entryway, his image reflected in a huge gilt mirror underneath which sat a marble table with wrought-iron legs. Overhead was a chandelier.

"Holy cow! You lived like a damned prince!" Gabe exclaimed after glancing into the living room and dining room. They both had floor-to-ceiling windows with elegant drapery and beautiful antiques.

"I told you I had more money than I could spend." Nick led the way through the apartment. "Here's the guest room," he said, pushing open a door and stepping aside for Gabe to enter. "That door over there is your private bath."

"Just for me?" Gabe asked.

"Yeah," Nick said, grinning.

"I don't want to mess anything up."

"Don't worry. The maid will clean it up if you do. She'll be here tomorrow."

Nick went on into his bedroom, pausing at the door. It was a spacious room with floor-to-ceiling windows and drapery to offer him privacy. The furniture was grand and elegant.

Nothing. He still felt nothing. He pictured his room at Gabe's house. It symbolized home. Not that he wouldn't appreciate a bigger bed, more comfort, but...but this room didn't welcome him.

A knock on the door had him turning around. "Yeah? You're not lost, are you?" he teased to hide the fact that *he* was, in a sense.

"Nope." Gabe put his hands on his hips and stared at him. "Were you happy here?"

Nick wanted to tell him he was, but when he tried, he couldn't. "I thought I was, but...no. This place was a status symbol. My mother helped me pick it out."

"Well, that's a relief. I was just thinking my house must've been a shock to your senses."

"Nope. I've been happy there."

"Then why are you thinking about moving out?"

"I don't want to be in your way."

"You're not."

"We'll talk about it later. I'm going to grab a quick shower and change clothes before we go see what's what with the auction."

"Can I take a shower at the same time? Is there enough water pressure for both showers to be running?"

"Yeah, Gabe. Help yourself."

Fifteen minutes later, Gabe was wandering the living room, looking at the items on the wall, when the doorbell rang. At least he assumed it was the doorbell. Nick hadn't emerged from his room. When it sounded a second time, he walked into the entryway and swung open the heavy door.

"Nick, darling, you're back. I've missed you so much!" a voluptuous blonde in a red dress said as she threw herself into Gabe's arms and pressed her lips to his.

When he finally peeled her off his body, Gabe was relieved to hear a discreet cough. Gabe kept his eyes on the woman but said to the man behind him, "Brother, I believe I've found something you left behind."

The blonde looked at him and then at Nick, gave a refined scream and fainted gracefully on the Oriental carpet.

CHAPTER SEVENTEEN

SARAH TOOK ONE LOOK at herself in the mirror and then avoided it as much as possible. Her restless night was showing. She hadn't heard a peep out of Jennifer. Hopefully she was catching up on some missed sleep. She'd check on her midmorning.

Downstairs, Jeff was cheerfully waiting for her instructions.

"I need to introduce you to Boyd," Sarah said. "He was off yesterday. He does our heavy work." Since it was getting toward the end of the week, business picked up a bit and the two of them stayed busy with customers when they opened the store.

Sarah was showing a lady some new corduroy fabric that had just come in when the phone rang. Jeff looked at her.

"Don't worry. The machine will pick it up." She continued to wait on her customer, but she did notice the phone only rang twice before the machine clicked on. That meant there'd been an earlier call. Maybe when they were on the dock talking to Boyd. She'd check the messages when business slowed down.

A few minutes later, the opportunity came and Sarah headed for her office. Sure enough, the machine showed two calls. She pushed the play button and reached for pen and paper. Sometimes people placed orders and she had to get the information down.

"Sarah? It's Nick. Gabe has to go to Denver for an emergency. We'll be back either Friday night or Saturday. Sorry about this, but I'm sure you and Jennifer will understand. Gabe is anxious to know Jen's answer, so she can call Letty, the housekeeper, and talk to her if she wants. Thanks for talking to her. Bye.''

Sarah couldn't believe that after all she and Jennifer had suffered, those two had gone off to Denver. Denver. Maybe Nick wasn't even coming back. After all, Denver was his home.

Why should that matter? Sarah wasn't involved with Nick. Where he lived didn't affect anything. She'd probably be happier if he did stay in Denver. She knew he was too sophisticated for her.

She didn't bother to listen to the second message.

Instead, she left the office and climbed the stairs. Time to check on Jennifer. She marched up to the apartment and found Jennifer at the kitchen table drinking a cup of tea.

''Jen, how are you this morning?''

''Fine,'' she said listlessly.

''Did you sleep late?''

''I just got up a few minutes ago.''

Sarah wanted to ask if she'd made a decision about Gabe, but she couldn't bring herself to come right out with the question, so instead she said, ''There was a message on the answering machine. I guess Nick called last night. It seems Nick and Gabe went to Denver. They'll be back late Friday or Saturday. Nick said he hoped you'd understand.'' She couldn't keep a certain bitterness from her voice.

Jennifer only said, ''I see.''

''Jen, aren't you angry with them? Have you made your decision?''

''No, Sarah, I haven't, but it doesn't matter. It won't change the fact that he's offering marriage without love.''

''Well at least you don't have to make up your mind by tomorrow. You can wait until Saturday.''

''Yes. I'm going to go work on the blankets.'' She stood and began to walk away.

"Uh, Jennifer," Sarah called.

Jennifer stopped. "Yes?"

"Could you make some sandwiches for lunch? We're pretty busy today."

"Sure. I'll bring them down in an hour."

Sarah smiled and waved before heading back downstairs. Last year, she wouldn't have asked as much of Jennifer even in the best circumstances. But Jennifer had changed. And she thought it best to give her something to do.

When Jennifer came downstairs carrying a tray of food, Sarah rushed over to help her.

"Aren't you going to join us?" she asked when Jennifer turned to go back upstairs.

"Yes, but there's more."

"I'll go get it. You don't need to make too many trips up and down," Sarah hurriedly said. When she came back down, the store was empty of customers and Jeff had joined Jennifer.

"Jen, you did a great job with lunch," Sarah said as she set the cans of soda and a bowl of potato chips on the table. "Jeff, there's a folding chair in that closet if you'll get it, please."

He did so, and they began their lunch.

"We were pretty busy today," Jeff said after taking a sip of soda.

"Wait until tomorrow and Saturday," Jennifer said. "Until recently, Sarah managed the store all by herself. It must have been murder for her."

"You didn't work in the store?" Jeff asked, surprised.

"No. I didn't realize she needed help. I'm not the best sister."

"Nonsense," Sarah said. "It's a long story, Jeff. But eat up. You'll need the energy. That's why I can afford to eat potato chips." She grinned at the other two.

"Tomorrow, I'm going to lunch with Janie, remember.

But I can make sandwiches and bring them down before I leave,'' Jennifer reminded her.

"I'm glad you're still going. And it would be great if you could make us lunch before you go.''

"I can. I know you'll be busy.''

"Are you going to talk to Janie about, uh, your decision?''

"It won't hurt your feelings, will it? She's had more experience with marriage than both of us put together.''

"No, I'm glad you are.''

Jennifer smiled back, looking almost cheerful and Sarah felt a lot better. Jeff said nothing, eating his sandwich. Sarah decided he was a good hire since he knew when to keep his mouth closed.

THE AUCTIONEER RAPPED his gavel. "Sold to number twenty-eight.''

"We're next,'' Gabe whispered to Nick.

"Right,'' Nick returned while waving at another blonde two rows down.

"You do that during the bidding and you're going to buy something pretty expensive,'' Gabe reminded him.

"That's why I waited,'' Nick said with a grin.

"Next up is the best little old Charolais bull you ever did see,'' the auctioneer said. "Really makin' a name for himself. Vet's reports are on file. Hope you had a chance to look at them. Who'll start the bidding? Let's open at a thousand.''

"Aren't you going to bid?'' Nick asked.

"In a minute.''

Suddenly the auctioneer pointed to an older man on the first row of bleachers. "Thank you, sir. A thousand dollars! Who'll bid two?''

Another man, dressed like everyone else in jeans and a cowboy hat, raised the bid.

Nick looked at Gabe. "Do you need some money?''

Gabe shook his head no. The bidding continued, until it reached ten thousand. Then Gabe raised his hand, two fingers up.

"Twelve thousand! I've got a bid of twelve thousand. Anyone willing to go thirteen? Thirteen? Twelve-five?" There was no movement from the previous bidders. "Twelve going once, twice and sold to bidder number fifteen."

Gabe got up and climbed down the bleachers and Nick followed him. They went over to a table where Gabe wrote a check for the bull.

"You got a buy," one of the men said.

"I know."

Nick waited until they'd turned away from the table. "Why did you wait until the last to make your move?"

"It's a psychological thing. The other bidders think they've already won and then someone starts it again with more money. The original bidder hesitates and suddenly, it's too late."

"Glad to know I've got a smart brother."

"And I'd like to know about my brother, too."

"What do you mean?" Nick asked.

"I've never seen so many interested women. At least half the females in Denver seem to want you."

"Only half?" Nick asked with a teasing grin.

"Maybe more. But in Rawhide, I thought you were interested in Sarah. Was I wrong?"

Nick followed Gabe over to a nearby barn where some of the equipment up for auction had been stored. Finally, when Gabe stopped to examine a tractor, he answered. "You weren't wrong. But I don't know…. Sarah's a nice girl. But I didn't want to mislead her. I don't know where I'm going to settle. It's tough to ask someone to have a relationship if you don't know where you're going to live."

"Well, you certainly have your choice of ladies."

"You think I'm a woman magnet because of my body?

My mind? Wake up and smell the coffee, bro. They all know about my money. It's always been that way. Except for Sarah. She was furious when I hinted it wouldn't be wise to reject me because of my wealth.''

"You didn't!"

"I'm ashamed to say I did."

"Do I need to punch your lights out for insulting my future sister-in-law?"

Nick held up both hands. "I didn't touch her, if that's what you're implying."

"I may love Jennifer. But I know Sarah is a good woman. Don't mess with her unless you're serious," Gabe said before swinging up into the tractor seat.

"Come on, Gabe, get serious."

"I'm as serious as a heart attack. It's not just me. I'll be joined by all the Randall men. They protect their women."

"Sarah's not a Randall," Nick was quick to point out.

"She'll be related to us if I marry Jennifer."

"Then it's a wonder you didn't get knocked out for messing with Jennifer. I haven't ever gotten anyone pregnant."

Gabe's cheeks flushed. "She didn't have any brothers or I would have been beaten to a pulp. At least I'm giving you fair warning."

"So maybe I'd better stay in Denver, where I'm wanted."

Nick turned to walk away from Gabe. He pretended interest in a machine he couldn't identify until he felt a hand on his shoulder.

"Yeah?" Nick said.

"I didn't mean I didn't want you to come back to Rawhide. You know I do. But after seeing all these women falling all over you, willing to do anything you want, I got worried about Sarah. She doesn't have much experience."

"I know that. But I outgrew easy women a long time ago."

"I'm glad. I'm not sure how long it took me to realize I wanted a real relationship. We have these buckle bunnies on the rodeo circuit. I enjoyed a few when I was younger." He laughed at Nick's consternation.

"You rat! You were acting like a saint and you're as bad as me!"

"Naw, not as bad as you," Gabe protested, ducking his brother's right hook. "Come on, let's grab some lunch. I think I'm going to bid on the tractor this afternoon."

THE NEXT AFTERNOON, Jennifer brought down the sandwiches she'd made, carefully covered in plastic wrap. She set the food on the table just as the door opened again.

Janie and Megan Randall came in together. Jennifer waved to them and they came over.

"Hi, Jennifer. I asked Megan to join us for lunch. She's working in her store today. Is that all right?"

"Of course," Jennifer said, though she wasn't sure she could talk to Janie with Megan there. She didn't know her very well.

"We thought we'd try a new sandwich shop that opened. It reminds me of one that used to be in town." She shot a teasing glance at Janie, who giggled.

Janie leaned closer to Jen and whispered, "I almost started a fight in the old sandwich shop. But I'll be on better behavior today."

"Sure, because Pete won't be there," Megan added, laughing with her.

Jennifer's smile wobbled. "Good. I'll just get my purse."

When she came back downstairs, they escorted her a couple of blocks away from the café to the new sandwich shop. It was decorated for the female customer, though there were one or two men in it. Jennifer couldn't imagine Gabe in there.

"They offer quiche, too, with fruit," Megan said.

"Oh. It goes with the decor," Jennifer said.

Janie laughed. "That's what Megan and I thought, too. See, Megan, I told you she was a Randall woman."

Jennifer looked at the two women and burst into tears.

The hostess came over to seat them, but Megan told her to hold a table in the corner for them. Then she and Janie took Jennifer to the ladies' room.

Once inside, they gave her tissues and asked her what was wrong.

Jennifer shook her head, wiping the tears. "It's nothing. Just hormones," she said, hoping they would believe her.

Whether they did or not, they took her out to the corner table and discussed food for several minutes while she composed herself.

When the waitress came they all ordered the quiche and fruit. Then the two Randall wives focused on Jennifer.

"You might as well tell us what's wrong, honey. We won't give up until we know. And we might be able to help you."

"It's true. No one can resist us," Megan added. "And if the two of us don't do the trick, we bring in B.J. and Anna."

"Yeah," Janie continued. "B.J. is very firm, you know, like a teacher or principal. But it's usually Anna who does a job on the tough cases. She's so gentle and sweet, no one can help giving in to her."

Jennifer didn't fight. She confessed at once. "Gabe has offered to marry me."

Both women sat back in their chairs and stared at her. Finally Janie asked, "And this isn't a good thing? I thought you loved him."

"I do! But he doesn't want me. He's offering a marriage of convenience. Separate bedrooms," Jennifer finished in a whisper.

"Good Lord! Are we sure he's a Randall?" Megan asked, still staring at Jennifer.

"Is she pregnant?" Janie pointed out with a droll look.

"I wasn't pregnant when I got married," Megan said.

"I'm sorry. I shouldn't have—" Jen began.

"Of course you should have," Janie said, patting her hand. "You poor dear. How terrible of him to put you through this."

Jennifer wiped her eyes again as the waitress set down their iced tea. "Is anything wrong?" the waitress asked.

"Her allergies are acting up," Megan politely explained.

"Oh, you poor dear. Maybe food will help. I'll hurry your order." With a nod, the lady rushed to the kitchen.

"Well, if we ever want fast service, we know what to do now," Megan said with a grin. "Jen, honey, how do you know that's what Gabe wants? The last time I saw you together, he was crazy about you."

"I lied to him."

Janie raised an eyebrow.

Jennifer explained about how serious her lie was. She even told them about Gabe's reaction to the news of her pregnancy. And his last response when she called to tell him about the twins.

"The beast!" Janie said, which made Jennifer feel better.

"But I deserved it. I shouldn't have lied."

"No, you shouldn't have," Megan agreed with a smile. "But when you're pregnant, you act differently. Those hormones are killers."

Jennifer didn't want to tell Megan she hadn't known she was pregnant at the time, so she simply nodded in agreement.

The waitress delivered their food. Jennifer discovered she was hungry, much to her surprise. She hadn't eaten breakfast, she'd felt so miserable.

"You skipped breakfast, didn't you?" Janie asked. "You mustn't do that. And you mustn't worry, either. It's not good for the babies."

"It's...been difficult."

"Of course it has. Men never seem to understand," Megan added. "They act like they've done nothing at all. What did Gabe say when he proposed to you? It must have been awkward."

"He didn't."

"But you said—" Janie started, looking confused.

"He had Nick ask Sarah to ask me." Jen sighed. "I'm supposed to give him my answer today. But then, Nick left a message on our answering machine that said they had to go to Denver for an emergency and they'd be back either later today or tomorrow. Just as if my answer didn't matter. It could wait."

"But I thought they went to Denver to buy a bull," Janie said. Jennifer looked horrified, and she added, "I guess that's something I should've kept to myself."

"Probably," Megan said. "Now we'll have to order dessert."

By the time lunch ended, Jennifer hadn't made her decision, but she wasn't feeling as desperate as she had. Her two companions suggested they go back to the store and talk to Sarah, too.

When they reached the store, the traffic had died down a little. Janie and Jennifer went straight upstairs, leaving Megan to talk to Sarah about joining them.

Sarah didn't hesitate. "Jeff, I have to go upstairs. People will wait. Do the best you can," she said, and hurried up the stairs with Megan. It was time for a powwow, and she wasn't going to miss it.

CHAPTER EIGHTEEN

NICK HAD MADE HIS DECISION. He was leaving Denver. Even if he found someone to marry here, would he want to raise his children where everyone knew of his wealth? Not only would his children be spoiled, they could be in danger.

Besides, Rawhide had really started to feel like home.

As he went through some of his mail he found a bill for fur storage and groaned.

Gabe, sitting at the table finishing breakfast, looked up. "What's wrong?"

"My mother's been dead three years and we're still storing her furs. Dad just paid the bill rather than deal with it. But this is ridiculous."

"So sell them."

"Couldn't get even a tenth of what Dad paid for them. Just like her jewelry." He stopped to stare at Gabe.

"What? I didn't say anything."

"Yes, you did. I'm going to make some calls."

When Nick came back into the kitchen, Gabe was finishing his coffee. "Gabe, will you do me a favor?"

"Sure."

"Run this check down to Thompson so he can pay the fur storage people. Give him this to tip the men who deliver them, and this is for him." He handed Gabe two twenties.

"Hmm, if I ever get too crippled to be a rancher, I'm gonna get a job as a doorman." Gabe grinned at his brother and headed for the elevator.

Nick smiled. His banker should be here soon, he decided, looking at his watch. He'd had a great idea. If Sarah would cooperate, he'd take his mother's furs and jewelry and put them in Sarah's store. He'd dedicate the proceeds from whatever sold to a fund for something in Rawhide. He didn't know what yet. He didn't know what the town needed.

He hadn't mentioned it to Gabe yet. He was afraid he'd tell him he couldn't do that. But it was becoming terribly important that he do so.

When the doorbell rang, he figured it was the banker. He'd called and asked him to deliver the contents of the safe-deposit box to him. It wasn't normal service, but then he wasn't a normal customer.

Instead, it was Gabe.

"You didn't take the spare key," Nick said, shaking his head.

"Nope. Never need one at home."

"I know. I noticed that. It's one of my favorite things about Rawhide. Gabe, listen, I've got an idea."

"Okay." Gabe settled down on the couch, giving him his full attention.

"I'm going to take all the things I have that I don't want or need and sell them."

"Good idea."

Nick drew a deep breath and added, "In Rawhide."

One eyebrow went up. "You're going to open a store?"

"No, I'm going to give some to Sarah, and some to Megan Randall for her store. Mark them with special tags, and the money they make will go to Rawhide to build a, uh, I don't know what. Child-care center, pay for more deputies. You tell me what Rawhide needs."

"Will it raise that much?" Gabe asked.

"Even at a fourth of what it's worth, it will bring in a lot of money. You see, I stored all the furniture from Dad's house. I didn't know what to do with it."

Gabe frowned. "How big was his house?"

"I don't know in square feet, but it had eight bedrooms, twelve baths, living room, parlor, library, den…"

"I get the picture. Did he have books in the library?"

"Of course."

"Well, then, I know what you can give Rawhide. The townsfolk have been wanting one for a long time."

"What's that?" Nick asked, leaning forward.

"A library. And you can put those books in there. You can even name it after your mom and dad."

Nick was more excited about this project than he'd been about anything in a long time. "I need to make some more calls. I think I have the name of the company that moved everything for me. Maybe they'll do a long-haul move to Rawhide."

"Whoa! Winter's coming. Where you going to put everything for the time being?"

"Oh, right. Glad I've got you here," Nick said. "I'll call the real estate agent and buy the space across from the general store and just down the block from Megan's store. It's large and empty. I'm going to turn it into a law office with its own legal library, so I'll need the space eventually, but not for a while. How's that?"

"Works for me," Gabe agreed with a smile.

The doorbell rang again. Nick swung it open. Thompson pushed in two long racks of furs in plastic bags. Behind him stood several men in suits carrying large steel boxes. They were from the bank.

"Come in, gentlemen," Nick said to them after thanking Thompson for bringing up the furs. He closed the door behind him and then asked the men to put the boxes on the dining table.

"I'm afraid the metal might scratch the wood, Mr. Mc-Millan."

"I'll get a couple of towels," Gabe offered, and Nick smiled.

"That will solve the problem nicely, Gabe." Nick's smile widened as the two men stared at Gabe.

"We're identical twins," he said quietly as Gabe left the room. "We've just discovered each other."

When Gabe came back into the room, Nick invited him to watch as they unloaded each large box. As he'd known, Gabe got bored with it soon. He asked if Nick would mind if he called home. "Just to check in," he said, his voice edgy.

"Of course I don't mind. There's an extension in your bedroom. Dial direct."

In a few minutes, Gabe returned to the room, his face downcast.

"No word from Jen?" Nick asked.

"Nope."

"Don't give up, Gabe. It's a big decision."

"We've come to the pearl section, Mr. McMillan," one of the bakers said.

Nick sighed. His mother had loved jewelry. She'd inherited a lot of it, but her husband had bought her jewelry instead of spending time with her. She'd been satisfied, which now struck Nick as bizarre. The marriages he'd seen in Rawhide didn't work that way. He knew which kind of marriage he preferred. But he hadn't actually realized that until he went to Rawhide.

When he'd signed some papers and escorted the men out, he turned to Gabe. "Okay. I'm not going to bore you by asking you to look at all the jewelry, but you should be interested in wedding rings."

Gabe frowned. "'Course I am, but I don't want to spend more on a ring than I did on my bull."

"You're not going to spend any money. Mother has at least six wedding ring sets."

"She was married that many times?"

"No. But she liked to change rings. I'm going to pick my favorite set for the future. You will, too. Then maybe a string of pearls for each future bride and anything else you think Jennifer would like. Then I'll turn all this over to Sarah to sell.''

Gabe whistled. ''That ought to build a library right there.''

''Close. Come on over here.''

''No, Nick, there's no reason for you to give me—''

''Get the hell over here before I come beat you up. The markup on jewelry is huge and you never get as much back as you paid. Don't be stupid.''

Gabe got up and leisurely crossed the room. ''You know, Nick, you're kind of getting into this brother thing.''

''You bet I am. It's the best thing that's ever happened to me.'' He grinned at his mirror image, liking what he saw. ''Do you want a Rolex?''

''Why would I?'' Gabe asked. ''I bought this watch with my own money ten years ago. It's good enough for me.''

''Okay. I was going to wear my dad's, but a gold watch looks a little pretentious in Rawhide. I'll sell it here.''

He began unwrapping jewelry and Gabe shook his head, overwhelmed.

SHE WAS GOING TO ACCEPT. Jennifer was going to become Mrs. Gabe Randall any way she could. And if it didn't work out, at least she'd know she'd given it her best shot. She could tell her boys she'd tried.

That was her decision. She'd still debated it back and forth, but when push came to shove, Jen realized she had to be with Gabe. She'd hold back. Give him time to get used to having her around. And she could show him that she'd learned to take care of herself, to be of some benefit to the household. That would surprise him, she thought with a smile. That in itself surprised her.

She had come up with one stipulation about their marriage. It had to appear to be a normal marriage in public. And he had to attend her doctor's appointment Monday morning. If he wouldn't make that effort, she'd change her answer to no.

Chuckling, she realized what a difference yesterday had made. *She* felt confident enough to make stipulations. She wasn't going to go into this marriage like a prisoner, under the heel of her husband.

Jennifer had everything organized for lunch. She opened the door to take the tray downstairs and saw Jeff on the stairs.

"Sarah asked me to take the tray down to you," he said with a smile.

"Thanks, Jeff. The tray is a little heavy."

"My pleasure. Having lunch here sure saves us a lot of time. Saturdays must make your business."

"I think so," she said, smiling.

Once they got downstairs, she set things out on the table. When Sarah came over, the store still had shoppers. "Sarah, I ate upstairs. While you and Jeff eat, I'll wait on people. When you're back working, I'll run the cash register until two. Then I'll go up and lie down. Okay?"

"That's two hours, Jen. Can you manage it?"

"If I can't, I'll let you know," she said with a sassy smile, and headed over to the nearest customer.

"Seems like your sister has her spirits back," Jeff said to Sarah.

"Yes, and I'm so thankful. The Randall ladies' visit did the trick." Sarah smiled and sighed, biting into her sandwich. She'd slept last night as if she hadn't slept in weeks. She could finally believe everything was going to be all right, thanks to Megan and Janie.

Jeff finished first and immediately returned to work. He hadn't taken much rest. Only fifteen minutes. But they were really busy. A lot of people were here to stock up for winter. No one in Rawhide took the upcoming season lightly. They knew how dangerous the weather could be.

Sarah had ordered large amounts of certain items, like

the canned goods. Everyone kept a good stock of food that didn't spoil that they could rely on when they couldn't get to town.

She finished her food, too, and set the tray of leftovers in her office. They could carry it up later. Now, if Nick, or even better, Gabe, would call, life would straighten out. Her sister would be happy and she would be—alone. She hadn't really thought about that. She'd lived too many years through Jennifer, raising her, helping her, trying to guide her. Her life revolved around Jennifer, and it wasn't Jennifer's fault.

It was the circumstances. Her mother's death and then her father's. The store. And above all, protecting Jennifer. Well, at least she could feel good about doing that. Not without help, and most especially not without Jen's courage since she'd become pregnant. Her parents would be proud of her.

But Sarah would be left alone.

She threw back her shoulders. She'd deal with it somehow. She'd find a way. If Jennifer could go forward with her babies and face Gabe in a convenient marriage, well, she could manage her own life.

"Sarah? Can you help me? The others are busy," a customer asked.

"Of course I can," Sarah said with a smile, and moved to the cash register. In a few minutes, she sent Jennifer to the cash register where there was a stool and took her place on the floor.

But she didn't forget to remind Jennifer when the clock showed two o'clock. "Okay, Jen, nap time for you. I'll ring up Mrs. Albers."

"Oh, yes, dear, you must get your rest. I heard it's twins?" Mrs. Albers commented.

"Yes, it is. Twin boys," Jen replied.

"Oh, my! How fortunate you are. God has certainly blessed you."

Little Mrs. Albers, a widow living all alone, meant nothing but exactly what she said, and Sarah was relieved that Jennifer could smile and thank her for her words. Yesterday, she would've burst into tears and run up the stairs.

She slid behind the cash register as Jen went upstairs and began checking out the customers.

At the end of the day, she and Jeff fell into the chairs at the table. "You know, Sarah, it wouldn't cost a lot to hire a couple of high school boys or girls to work part-time. I'm not complaining, but Jen filling in a little helped a lot. When she has the babies, what are you going to do?"

"You're right. Today was particularly heavy. And I think Jen will be moving out in a couple of weeks. She's marrying the father of her babies. But keep it under your hat because I'm not sure yet."

"You mean, don't tell Mrs. Parker?" Jeff teased.

"Exactly." She grinned, enjoying the exchange. "And I'll ask around about any kids who want some work. I could have them come a couple of afternoons and all day Saturday."

"I could probably manage most afternoons by myself during winter. Everyone was stocking up today."

"I know. I ordered a lot of disposable diapers, but I may need another order before Christmas. It seems everyone is using them now."

"Jen may want her own truckload with twins," he said with a chuckle. "Will she be moving far away?"

"Just to a local ranch." She still felt a little uneasy talking about Jen's marriage. It wasn't a sure thing yet. She'd urged Jen to call Letty, the housekeeper, and leave a message, but she hadn't. Jen was standing up for herself, which was a good thing. She was making demands. Not bad ones, but she'd surprised Sarah.

"Sarah?" Jeff asked. "I'm going to the café. Want to come?"

"I need to check with Jennifer. If she hasn't prepared

any dinner, we'll both join you. But I'm really tired. If she's got something ready to eat, I'll eat at home and fall into bed."

"I don't blame you. Let me know."

"Thanks, Jeff. I will."

When she got upstairs, she found Jen had made a casserole and salad. She called down to Jeff that she was eating in and fell into her chair at the table. "Thank you so much, Jen. Today was tough."

"I know. How are you going to manage without me?"

Sarah almost burst out laughing, but she didn't. It was true that Jen had helped a lot in the past month. Before that, however, Sarah not only worked the store by herself, but did all the cooking and cleaning, too. She wasn't sure how she managed. But the town of Rawhide had been growing lately. Even if she didn't count the Randalls, who always seemed to have a baby on the way.

"I don't know. But Jeff suggested hiring a couple of teenagers to work Saturdays and maybe an afternoon or two a week. That would help a lot."

"Yes, it would. I wouldn't worry about you so much."

Sarah smiled and touched her sister's hand. "No need to worry. We're both going to be fine, aren't we?"

"Definitely," Jen agreed, as if she'd swallowed *The Power of Positive Thinking* book whole, which wasn't a bad thing.

The phone rang.

"I'll get it," Sarah said softly, knowing if it was Nick, she needed to give Jennifer time to compose herself.

"Hello?"

"Sarah? It's Nick. Is everything okay?"

"Everything's fine. Why wouldn't it be?"

"We hadn't heard from you."

"No. You weren't there to hear anything."

"You got my message, didn't you?"

"Yes, and we heard your big emergency was a bull."

Her tone of voice told him what she thought about putting a bull in front of her sister.

"Now, Sarah, it was a special bull, at a low price, perfect for Gabe's ranch. You can't be mad about him providing for his future."

"You'll have to talk to Jennifer about that. It affects her more than me."

"Wait! Before you go, I've got lots to tell you, and a favor to ask, but we're still on the road and Gabe wants to know if Jen has her answer."

"Yes, she does." She handed the phone to Jennifer. But in spite of herself, she was intrigued with Nick's words. And suddenly she didn't feel quite so lonely.

CHAPTER NINETEEN

GABE HAD A LOT OF CHORES awaiting him when they reached the ranch. Number one was getting Black Thunder settled. His name made him sound ferocious, but he was the most docile bull he'd ever been around. It made him wonder if he'd made a mistake in purchasing him.

"Do you think I made a good decision, Blackie? There doesn't seem to be much thunder in him," Gabe asked his friend.

"That's good. You don't want a mean bull around little ones."

He'd told Blackie about Jennifer saying yes, but he hadn't mentioned the conditions. He'd been astounded that Jennifer thought she was in any position to make demands. But she had. And he'd agreed to them.

They made sense, but they created problems for him.

He had to act like a real husband in public. It hadn't occurred to him that they would appear together in public. Somehow he'd thought she'd stay in her room most of the time.

The whole idea, for Gabe, was not to touch her. Not to get too close. He had to preserve his sanity, and he wasn't sure he could if he touched Jen. And she expected him to go to the doctor's office with her? That idea blew him away. He'd only visited a doctor when he broke his arm in a fall off a bull. After they put him in a cast, he left it on as long as the doctor said, then he got Blackie to cut it off.

What was he supposed to do at the doctor's office? Watch?

He kept debating what his role would be. He asked Nick several questions, but he'd never been married or had a child, so he wasn't much good at answering. Finally he suggested Gabe should call Jon Wilson and ask him. He *was* Jen's doctor, after all.

Sunday night, Gabe called Jon.

He answered on the first ring. "Dr. Wilson here."

"Uh, Jon? It's Gabe Randall."

"Yeah, Gabe. Is this a medical emergency?"

"No! I mean, I need help but—no. It's not an emergency. I mean, I had to call tonight. I couldn't wait until tomorrow morning, but it's not an emergency."

The tension in Jon's voice eased. "Okay. I'm not too clear on why you called, so why don't you just tell me."

"I'm supposed to come to your office in the morning."

There was silence, but when Gabe didn't say anything else, figuring he'd stated his problem succinctly, Jon said, "You don't have an appointment, Gabe."

"No, not me. It's Jennifer."

"What about Jennifer?"

"She has an appointment."

"Yes, she does."

"Well, I'm coming with her."

"Why?"

"That's what I wanted to know!" Gabe exclaimed.

More silence. Finally, Jon said, "Who said you were to come to see me in the morning?"

"Jennifer."

"Oh. Have you—do you believe she's having your babies?"

"Yes. I'm marrying her in two weeks."

"So you're coming to my office in the role of the expectant father."

"I guess so. Do you know why Jen wants me there?"

"Fathers play an important role in the health of the mother and the baby. In the case of twins, it's even more important. One of those ways is talking to the doctor, staying informed about the mother's needs and keeping an eye on her progress. I imagine Jennifer thought you might like to hear how the babies are doing. Don't you?"

"I guess. So all I have to do is listen?"

"That and reassure the mother, help her get on the examining table, things like that."

"You mean I'm going to be there when you examine her? Won't that be kind of embarrassing?" Gabe asked, holding his breath.

"I suppose it could be, but if you stand up by her head, you won't see anything, Gabe. But you'll be there to hold her hand and make her feel better."

"Oh."

"Any more questions?"

"No, I guess not."

"You'll do fine, Gabe. And congratulations."

"Uh, yeah, thanks."

"I'll see you tomorrow."

Gabe hung up the phone. Lord have mercy, tomorrow was going to be difficult. He'd thought he could ease into this marriage thing. Occasionally sit across from her for a meal. Smell her perfume in the air. See her from a distance. But he was going to see her up close and personal, the first thing.

This wasn't working out the way he'd thought.

THE FOLLOWING MORNING, Sarah was in the store working when Jennifer came down, ready to go to the doctor.

"Is Gabe meeting you here?" she asked. Her sister had been jittery all morning, scarcely able to eat her breakfast.

"Yes," Jennifer said a little shakily.

"Did you finally get your breakfast down?"

"Some of it," Jennifer said with a slight smile. "Where's Jeff? I thought he'd be here to help you."

"He is. He's unloading a shipment with Boyd on the dock."

There was a knock on the front door. Jennifer froze, so Sarah said she'd get it. She prayed this morning went well. Jennifer had worried herself to death ever since she said she'd marry Gabe.

It surprised Sarah to see Nick and Gabe at the door. After Nick's intriguing statement, she'd heard nothing from him the rest of the weekend. Strangely enough, they each had a rack of clothes and packages in their hands. She unlocked the door and swung it open.

"Good morning. Uh, come in."

To her surprise, they rolled the racks in. Though everything was in plastic, Sarah thought at least some of the articles on hangers were furs.

Jennifer stared at them. Whatever was going on appeared to ease the awkwardness of the moment for her. "What in the world is all this?" she asked.

"It's a surprise for Sarah. I'm sure she'll explain it to you when you get back," Nick said.

"Yeah. We'd better go or we'll be late," Gabe said, not meeting her gaze.

"All right. Shall we walk?"

"No. I'll drive."

He didn't want anyone to see them, Sarah realized. Not a good sign.

Jennifer pressed her lips together, but she said nothing as she turned and walked to the door. Gabe hurried after.

"See you later, Sarah," Jen called before she stepped outside. Sarah hurried over to lock the door behind them. She didn't want any customers for another hour.

She came back to where Nick stood. "Do I get to know what all this is?"

"Of course. Gabe said you want a library here in Raw
hide."

"Well, yes. But I don't see—"

"I'm donating the proceeds of the sale of my parents
things to a fund to build a library."

He gave her a sexy smile and she took a step back
"That's very nice of you, but I don't see how—I mean
unless their estate is very large—a building and books are
very expensive."

"I know that. It might not pay for all of it, but I thin
it will get us started. If the men pitch in the labor, w
should be able to put up a building next spring."

"That would be wonderful. It's very generous of you
Nick. But what is all this?"

"Well, I brought this along to get us started." He bega
opening the packages he'd carried in. But he looked up an
asked, "Where is the man you hired?"

"He's working on the dock with Boyd."

"Maybe we should go in your office."

Sarah frowned and said stiffly, "I don't see why."

"You will."

Though she was irritated, she gave in to his suggestion
At least she would have her desk between them. Sh
opened the door and went in. Nick followed and put th
obviously heavy packages on the desk and returned to clos
the door.

Sarah was about to oppose closing the door, but h
reached for the first package and brought out a handful o
gold. At that point, she lost interest in the door.

"What in heaven's name is—"

"Part of my mother's jewelry collection."

There must've been twenty to twenty-five gold chains
several bracelets made from large chunks of gold and ear
rings of every shape and size.

"I thought if you could sell some of this here in the store

at prices below its value, of course, the citizens of Rawhide would get a good deal and we'd start the library fund.''

Sarah was stunned. "I'm not sure how we would price it. I don't know anything about fine jewelry.''

"You can form a committee. I'm going to ask Megan to take some of the furniture.''

"You brought furniture with you?''

"No. I hired a mover to bring it to Rawhide. After all, there's a large collection.''

"How much?'' Sarah asked faintly, beginning to get an intimation of what she was facing.

"I don't remember exactly, but the house was large. Eight bedrooms, twelve baths, living room, library, den—''

She held up a hand to stop him. "And what are on the racks you pushed in?''

"Mom's furs. She was particularly fond of furs.'' He walked out of the office, but Sarah's legs were shaking too much to follow him.

He was back quickly with a hanger in his hand. He was pushing up the plastic to reveal a luxurious mink jacket.

"It's gorgeous,'' she said in a strangled voice. "How—how many furs are there?''

"About twenty-five.''

Sarah plopped down in her chair. "And you think the people in Rawhide will want to buy them?''

"If we price them right. You know, like five hundred for this jacket.''

"It must have cost ten times that much.''

"Oh, more than that.''

"But why are you pricing it so cheaply?''

"I want to help the town. If we sell these items here, the folks in Rawhide can get something nice at an affordable price and help the library.''

"Nick, I'm out of my league. I sell overalls, for heaven's sake. What do I know about furs? Or gold?''

"Diamonds?" he asked hopefully.

She groaned and covered her face.

"Come on, Sarah, don't take it so seriously. I'm going to be relieved to get rid of all this. I've been paying storage on the furs for three years because I didn't know what to do with them. This will be a relief to me."

She lifted her head to stare at his laughing brown eyes. She couldn't believe what he was saying.

"I—may I call Megan and—and the other Randall wives for help?"

"If you think you need it. Why them, by the way?"

"They're the most sophisticated in the valley."

"Okay. I can work things out with Megan about the furniture then, too."

"Excuse me," she said, and reached for the phone. He shoved his hands in the pockets of his jeans and walked out of her office, whistling, to wander the store.

Sarah called Megan and learned the woman had planned to come in today, anyway. When Sarah explained the magnitude of Nick's offer, however, she promised to bring her sisters-in-law with her.

Sarah figured they wouldn't get there until after the store was open. She stepped out of the office. "I think we should move everything upstairs, because they won't be here until people start coming in. I don't want to leave this stuff out in the open."

"Good idea. I'll start with the furs. Will you get the door?"

Sarah hurried up the stairs to open the door. The living room was tidy and she instructed him to take everything there. Then she went back down to her office and put all the gold back into the paper bag. It was quite heavy. But the fact that there were five more large bags overwhelmed her. She made three trips to bring the jewelry upstairs, but Nick had to make about ten trips. On the last trip, he brought the two racks and hung the furs back on them.

In the meantime, Sarah called Tori. When she explained the situation and invited Tori to join them, she immediately agreed.

Next, Sarah went into the kitchen and mixed up some muffins to serve with the coffee and tea for them all.

"I've never seen you in a kitchen before," Nick said, leaning against the door to the living room. "You look right at home."

"Well, of course. We didn't exist on frozen dinners, Nick."

"I guess not. I may have to, though. I'm used to ordering food in already prepared. There's a restaurant in my apartment building in Denver. I put my apartment up for sale, too. It should bring a goodly sum."

"You *owned* it?" Sarah asked.

"Yeah. At the time, I thought I'd be in Denver all my life."

"Are you saying you're going to move to Rawhide? Are you sure? Life here isn't anything like it is in Denver."

He grinned and sat down at the kitchen table without asking. "I think I've figured that out, Sarah. After all, I've been here for a couple of weeks, you know."

The coffeepot signaled its readiness with a red light and she got a mug and filled it with coffee for him. "I know you've been here, but that's not the same as living here. You haven't experienced a Wyoming winter yet."

"We get snow in Denver," he said, almost defensively.

"Yeah, but we get more. In winter, you don't see your neighbors all that much. It can get very lonesome. And there are no movie houses or theaters, no sports teams."

"But with cable television, you can watch games like most of the people in Denver," he added with a grin. "Do you like sports?"

"Sometimes." The buzzer on the stove signaled the muffins were ready. She pulled them out and quickly filled the pan again with the rest of the muffin mix.

After she'd finished that task, she asked, "How did Gabe take Jen's demands?"

"He was shocked. I don't think it occurred to him that Jennifer would have any say in anything. He was extremely nervous about this morning."

"They should be back soon."

"Sarah?" Jeff called from downstairs.

"Excuse me a minute."

Nick scowled at her, but she ignored him. Hurrying outside the door, she answered, "Yes, Jeff?"

"Is there anything special you want me to work on before we open?"

"No, except to see if we need to restock anything. I'm afraid I'll be tied up this morning. If things get too busy, give me a call, but if you can manage, I'd really appreciate it."

"I'll do my best," he promised with a cheerful smile.

"Oh, and when the Randall ladies come, just tell them to come on up. And Tori, too. You met her, didn't you?"

"Sure did. I'll send them up."

"Thanks, Jeff."

When she went back in the kitchen, Nick was eating a muffin.

"Those are for when the ladies arrive!" she protested.

"They won't miss one. So the guy is working out?" Nick asked.

"The guy has a name. It's Jeff, and he's doing great. It takes a lot of stress off me."

"Good. It gives you more time to do other things."

"Well, yes, but—"

"How about going to dinner with me tonight?"

GABE WAS IN A STATE of shock. He'd known, of course, that Jennifer was bigger, but to actually see her stomach, to watch it move as his children kicked her, was amazing.

He wanted to put his hands on her, to feel that movement, like Jon did, but he didn't dare.

"Okay, Jennifer, looks like things are going well. Get dressed and come to my office. Gabe, you come with me while Jennifer dresses."

Relieved, Gabe moved toward the door. He glanced back to see Jennifer awkwardly struggling to sit up. He stopped and turned to help her. It was the first time he'd touched her in a long while, and he did so without thinking.

Then he couldn't turn her loose. It had been too long.

"Gabe, you coming?" Jon asked from the door.

"Uh, yeah, I was just helping Jen."

"Good." Jon stood holding the door.

Gabe forced himself to turn her loose. He walked out the door and took a deep breath when Jon closed it. "Now what?"

"I want to tell you a few things about Jennifer's care before she joins us."

Gabe frowned. "Uh, okay."

Jon sat down behind his desk and indicated that Gabe should sit in either of the two chairs in front of the desk. "I usually have this talk the first visit, at the beginning of the pregnancy. First of all, having a baby plays havoc with a woman's hormones. Tears can be frequent. Men want to solve the problem, but you really can't. If she gets upset, hold her, reassure her. If she hurts anywhere, call me at once. If she asks you if she looks fat, or ugly, or anything like that, you know to tell her she's beautiful, don't you?"

"Yeah," Gabe agreed with a grin, but inside, he was thinking he'd be spending a lot of time in the barn.

"Normally, I tell the husbands that intimacy is okay until the eighth month, unless the lady doesn't want it. But with twins, I would prefer that you not do so after the seventh month. She may be close to delivery by then. Before that time, play it by ear. See what she wants to do."

Gabe was red-faced and avoided looking at Jon.

Thankfully, the door opened and Jennifer walked in. He'd prefer her presence to Jon's instructions. He couldn't tell the doctor there would be no intimacy ever. Not when he promised Jen he'd pretend that their marriage was real. Crazy idea!

Jennifer looked a little apprehensive, too. It suddenly struck Gabe that she might be frightened.

"All right, Jennifer. Any problems you've had this week? Anything you want to ask?" Jon questioned.

"No, but I want to thank you for sending Janie to me. We've already had one lunch, and she was a lot of help."

"Why are you having lunch with Janie?" Gabe demanded. He didn't like the sound of that.

"Because she's had twins. She can tell me if what I'm feeling is normal."

"Oh."

"I'm glad you're going to be there to support her, Gabe," Jon said before turning to Jen. "And remember, any pain, no matter how small, call me. Okay?"

"Okay," she agreed, smiling.

"Oh, and keep your trips up and down the stairs to a minimum. Gabe, does your place have stairs?"

"No. Are they bad for her?"

"Yes, but she'll be moving in with you, right? When?"

"We thought in a couple of weeks, but we can move it up if we need to." He watched Jon intently.

"That might be best," Jon said in a considering manner. "I think she'll be able to carry the babies longer that way."

Without even consulting Jennifer, Gabe said, "Right. We'll take care of that this week."

Since Jon stood and escorted them out at that point, Jennifer didn't have time to respond to his decision. But when they got in his truck, she turned to face him.

"Just who do you think you are, telling the doctor we'd get married at once?"

CHAPTER TWENTY

GABE WAITED UNTIL THEY WERE in the truck before he answered her question. "*You said* I was the daddy."

"You are, but that doesn't give you the right to just make a decision like that without asking me!"

"You mean you'd rather continue going up and down those stairs and maybe have the babies too early?"

"No, of course no! But—"

Then, just like the doctor predicted, she burst into tears.

Fortunately, he only had to drive two blocks. He parked his truck and turned to her. "Jen, don't cry. I spoke without thinking 'cause I was worried about the babies. What do you want to do?"

She drew a deep breath and wiped the tears from her face. "I'm sorry. I cry sometimes even when I'm not upset. I—I guess we could get married this week. But you said there was no room for me until Blackie moved out."

"Blackie will understand. He can sleep in the bunkhouse for a week. He won't mind when he knows it will keep the babies safe."

"Are you sure? Oh, and Gabe, I want my bedroom furniture. Sarah said I could have it. Can you move it for me?"

"Sure, Nick and I can do that. How long will it take you to pack?"

She licked her lips and Gabe almost bent over to do the same. Whoa! He'd almost forgotten their agreement already. "Maybe we'd better go in and talk to Sarah," he suggested. At least then he wouldn't be alone with her.

"Okay," Jennifer said, wiping her cheeks one more time. "Do I look all right?"

Ah, the doctor's words came out automatically. "You look beautiful."

She blushed and smiled at him, and he wanted to tell her he didn't mean anything by it, but he couldn't. Instead, he got out of the truck and came around to assist her to the ground. He hurried her inside and immediately released her.

There were a couple of shoppers, but only Jeff was in sight. "Sarah must be upstairs," Jennifer said with a frown. "Usually she stays down here with Jeff." She waved to the man across the store.

"Who is he?" Gabe asked with a frown.

"He works for us, and he's living in Daddy's old room."

"He lives here?"

"Yes. It's very convenient."

"It certainly is. I'll have to talk to Sarah." Gabe's lips firmed and he looked grim.

"Is something wrong?"

"We'll see. Come on." He reached out for her arm again without thinking.

When they got to the stairs, he asked, "Do you want me to carry you up?"

"No, that's not necessary."

They climbed to the top and Gabe opened the door to the kitchen, to discover his brother there, talking to Sarah.

Gabe immediately asked, "Sarah, have you lost your mind?"

SARAH HAD A LOT ON HER MIND. She'd avoided answering Nick's question about going to dinner by staying busy this past hour. She'd made far too many muffins and had talked about inconsequential things to keep Nick off the subject of dinner. But she couldn't ask him to leave before the

Randall women arrived. She'd just taken out yet another batch of muffins and was expecting the ladies any moment.

"What are you talking about, Gabe?" she asked.

"You're letting that man sleep here. What are you going to do when Jen moves in with me?"

"Why should I do anything?"

"Because there will be all kinds of gossip. You know that!"

"Wait a minute, what are you talking about?" Nick asked.

"That man downstairs is sleeping here," Gabe informed his brother.

"Here? In the apartment? No, Sarah wouldn't be that dumb!"

"Gee, thanks for your vote of confidence," Sarah said.

"But Sarah, that wouldn't be smart, and you are smart," Nick stated.

"Jeff, who has worked here for almost a week, is using the downstairs bedroom that has its own outside entrance and a private bath. I see no problem with that."

"But what about when Jen comes home with me?" Gabe asked.

Nick frowned. "That could be a problem."

"No. It's not a problem."

"By the way, Jen and I are getting married at once so she can move in with me. That way, she won't have to go up and down the stairs. The doctor said it's not good for the babies."

Sarah wanted to get back into bed and start the day over. "Immediately? Like today?"

"Actually, I was thinking Wednesday. We've got to go to Buffalo to get a license. We could do that this afternoon."

"Jen takes a nap in the afternoon, doctor's orders," Sarah said, just to be difficult. Too much was happening all at once.

"Could you sleep in the truck, honey, if we went this afternoon?" Gabe asked Jen.

"I suppose so," she replied.

"Then we can stop by the church and ask the preacher to marry us tomorrow. What do you think?"

"But what about Blackie?" Nick asked.

"He can move into the bunkhouse."

"But you need to paint that bedroom before Jennifer moves in," Nick pointed out.

"You mustn't paint it with her in the house. Paint fumes are bad for a pregnant woman. After painting you'll have to air it out at least twenty-four hours," Sarah pointed out.

"Okay, so we're back to Wednesday."

"I'm moving out right away. I'm going to hire some painters. They could do the bedroom first," Nick said.

"Are there any painters in town?" Gabe asked as the front door opened and five Randall women stood there looking at them.

"Are we interrupting something?" Megan asked.

"No, of course not," Sarah said. "Come on in. We've got things set up in the living room." Everyone went through the kitchen to the living room. Sarah brought in the muffins and coffee. She returned for everything necessary for tea.

Gabe asked everyone about painters.

"Paul Wilton did some painting as an extra job," B.J. said. As one of the local vets, she saw a lot of people in the county.

"I'll call him," Nick said at once. He looked at Sarah. "Is that okay?"

"Yes, but call from the kitchen. We have too much going on in here." When he and Gabe left the room, she repeated what Nick had told her about his plans to build a library in Rawhide. Then she opened the sack of gold jewelry and they all admired the beautiful pieces. Almost with trepidation, she opened a second bag. It appeared to hold a sapphire collection that was magnificent.

Sarah couldn't believe the amount of jewelry. Nor the value of it. Clearly Nick lived in a completely different world. Everyone stared at the sapphires.

"I hate to ask," Janie said slowly, "but I see there are four more bags. Are they also jewelry?"

They opened them up and, sure enough, they were filled with more jewels, including rubies, diamonds, emeralds and pearls.

Sarah swallowed, trying to figure out what she should say or do. "And—and those racks hold the furs."

AN HOUR LATER, Sarah felt better. The Randall women, as she had hoped, took charge. Megan had a friend with a shop in Denver who could handle most of the furs. The larger pieces of jewelry had been separated and would be shipped to one of the auction houses in New York as they were too impractical in town to even consider purchasing— no matter what the price.

"Even after they take out their fees, we should have a wonderful return on them," B.J. said.

"Can't you just see Mrs. Wainscot wearing that huge emerald out to milk the cows?" Janie said, chuckling. "But you'll have to admit, Nick's mother had exquisite taste in jewels and furs."

"Jake said Nick was wealthy, but I had no idea it was to this extent," B.J. said, staring at the jewelry.

Sarah nodded. She'd known Nick was more sophisticated, but this much wealth was scary. And a big responsibility.

"So we're going to sell some of the simpler pieces of jewelry here in the store? And two furs? Will you be able to do that, Sarah?" Megan asked.

"Yes, I suppose I can."

"I think you should put up a sign asking for donations

for the library right by the cash register, too," Janie said. "The nice thing about Nick's plan is it will make the community think they're helping contribute to the library when they purchase these things."

"Yes, that will be nice," Sarah agreed.

"I can't wait for all the furniture to arrive. Did he describe any of it to you, Sarah?"

"No. He probably didn't think I'd understand, anyway. I'm not as knowledgeable as you all."

"Sarah, don't put yourself down just because you don't normally sell jewels and furs. You do a great job of running this big store," Anna assured her.

"Yes, but I wouldn't have any idea about calling an auction house and asking them to come look at the jewels."

"Neither did Nick. A lot of rich people don't understand how to dispose of what they've bought. Did he say when the furniture would arrive? If they have paintings, the auction house might be interested in those, too. And what's he going to do with that big space across the street?"

"He said it would be his law office, but he'll also have a legal library there."

"Wow! That's expensive."

"Maybe he'll need some of the money back to buy the books for that."

"I don't know," Sarah said with a sigh. "We're going to get all the books his father had in his library. I doubt he has a lot of children's books, though."

"It's lunch time. Why don't we go to that little sandwich shop," Janie suggested. "We went Friday, didn't we, Jennifer. I thought the food was good."

"Oh, I've left Jeff on his own all morning. I'd better fix some sandwiches here. But thank you for helping me out," Sarah said.

"No problem," B.J. said. "We're delighted to be on the library committee. It's going to be great to have one here in Rawhide."

"Yes," Sarah agreed, but she actually felt like crying. She didn't say so to her friends, however. She didn't want to explain why. "Uh, Jen, maybe you'd better take my place on the committee. I'll be busy with the store and—"

"No," Megan protested. "You're the one he brought these things to. I think Nick wants you to be involved."

"He just did so because I own the store," Sarah replied.

"But Sarah, I'll have twins by Christmas. I won't have time for anything." Jennifer patted her stomach. "Jon said they could come as early as October."

A knock on the door signaled Gabe and Nick's return.

"What color do you want your room, Jen?" Gabe asked.

Jennifer turned a bright red, knowing the ladies would know they were talking about a separate bedroom for her.

Sarah jumped in. "You'd probably better go look at the paint we have in stock, Jen. Otherwise they'd have to go to Buffalo for it."

"Thanks, Sarah, I hadn't thought of that," Gabe said. "Come on, Jen, I'll take you downstairs. Oh, and we're going to Buffalo today to get the license, Sarah. Is that okay?"

"Of course," she agreed, as if she had a choice. Jen excused herself for a minute upstairs. All the ladies understood. But Gabe had a questioning look on his face.

Anna, a midwife, said, "Pregnant women have to go to the bathroom often. Get used to it."

Gabe turned a bright red. "There's lots to learn."

"Yes, there is, but we'll help you," Anna assured him.

Nick said, "I'm going to stay in town until they get back. Want to go over to my new home and help me plan things, Sarah?"

"Thanks, but I can't. I haven't worked all morning. I need to get busy." The words were fine, but she sounded stiff and unfriendly.

"Did everything go all right this morning?" Nick asked.

B.J. began to explain about their decisions, and Sarah sank back against her chair. She'd always thought Nick was more sophisticated than her. But she'd had no idea he'd lived such a privileged life. He needed to marry a woman who cared about jewels and furs. Sarah didn't.

She loved her life in Rawhide, while everyone knew everyone else. Where people helped one another out. She didn't want to live in a high-rise apartment. She didn't want to dine in ritzy restaurants with snobby people. She—

"Have you also figured out what Sarah is going to do about that guy downstairs?" Nick asked suddenly.

"What are you talking about?" Tori asked.

"I don't think she should let him live downstairs when she's alone up here."

Sarah stood and glared at him. "That's my business and none of yours."

SARAH SILENTLY CHASTISED herself all afternoon. She'd known she'd never have a chance with Nick. What was wrong with her? Nothing had changed. It wasn't as if she'd lost anything she'd ever had.

She decided to keep her mind on work and gave Jeff an entire hour for lunch to make up for his working all morning alone. He took the sandwich she'd made for him and went to his room, remarking on how convenient it was.

Sarah said nothing. If Nick had his way, it wouldn't be convenient anymore. But Sarah wasn't going to ask Jeff to move out. Nick was being ridiculous. The Randall women had questioned it a little, but she pointed out it was part of Jeff's salary. And she trusted him.

Janie had said it was her decision, but if she needed any help convincing the man to stay at the bottom of the stairs, she only had to call. Sarah assured her she wouldn't need to make that call.

They'd all gone to the sandwich shop, offering to bring back some lunch for Sarah, but she told them no. She needed to get used to managing on her own again. But she was going to look for a couple of high school kids to help out. Jeff's idea was a good one.

But her life was going to change. Jen was marrying Gabe on Wednesday. She'd called the florist to arrange for a bridal bouquet. She wanted Jen to have as nice a wedding as she could manage in two days. The ladies promised to ask Mildred to make a wedding cake.

While Sarah worked, she tried to think of what else she needed to do for Jennifer. It kept her thoughts off her being alone once Wednesday came. A dress! She hurried to see if she had anything that would do. She did keep a couple of wedding dresses on hand, but they wouldn't fit a woman five months pregnant with twins. But when she looked at one of them, she realized the style might work. It had a high waistline and was a couple of sizes larger than Jen normally wore.

When Jeff came back to work, she carried that dress and a veil upstairs. She wanted Jen to take a look at it. While she was upstairs, she also called the preacher.

Gabe had forgotten that chore before he and Jen had left for Buffalo. But, much to Sarah's satisfaction, Gabe had seemed more concerned with Jen's comfort. Maybe the marriage would work out, she thought as she came back downstairs.

Which brought her back to her own situation. Maybe she'd start going to the bar down the street where all the young people went on Saturday nights. The problem was she was almost too old for that crowd.

Maybe she should just give up and accept her old-maid status. At least she would have two adorable nephews.

"Sarah?"

She turned around to find Nick staring at her. "Is everything all right? You haven't moved the past five minutes," he said.

"I was thinking. Is there something you want help with?"

"Yeah, what time shall I pick you up for dinner?"

She'd forgotten about his asking her to dinner this morning. She hadn't actually agreed to go. "Oh, sorry, Nick, but I can't go tonight. I—I have some work to do."

"But the store closes at six."

"And I can't leave the jewels and furs here without someone to protect them."

"Damn it! I didn't bring that stuff to you to cause problems. You don't have to guard it. No one knows it's here."

"Yes, they do."

"Sarah, what's the matter? You've acted funny ever since this morning."

"Nothing's wrong. But I'm busy."

"Fine! Be busy! I'll find someone else to eat with!"

He left the store, not looking back.

CHAPTER TWENTY-ONE

NICK CAUGHT A RIDE to the ranch with Gabe after he and Jennifer got back from Buffalo. Instead of eating with Sarah, he ate at the ranch with Gabe, Blackie and Letty.

When Gabe told Blackie about marrying Jennifer on Wednesday, the older man immediately agreed to move into the bunkhouse.

"Good," Nick added, "because I've hired a local guy to paint that room first thing in the morning. Hey, do you want him to paint my room, too, for a nursery?"

"That's a good idea," Letty said. "Jennifer will want it nice for the babies, and you need to get it done before she moves in. Or it could be done while she's in the hospital. She'll have to stay several days and the babies may have to stay longer."

"What? Why?" Gabe asked. "No one said anything about that."

"Twins usually come early, Gabe. You should know that. So sometimes they're underweight and they haven't developed as well as they should have."

"And they send the mother home without them?" Gabe asked.

"Yes. It's hard on mothers. You'll have to be very supportive, of course."

"Of course," Gabe said dryly. "I tried that today when she cried, and I think it gave her the wrong idea."

"What do you mean?" Nick asked.

"She wanted to know how she looked after crying. Doc

said if she asks about her looks, always say she looks beautiful. I did, and she smiled at me like she used to.''

"Did she mention anything about Sarah?" Nick asked.

"No, not a word."

"I don't like the idea of that man living there with her." Nick frowned at his dinner as if it had offended him.

"What? Jennifer's sister is living with a man? Who?" Letty asked.

"No, not exactly. She's letting her new employee use the bedroom and bath downstairs where her father lived after their mother died," Gabe explained.

"Oh. I guess it would be handy in the winter," Letty said thoughtfully. "Sarah is a nice girl."

"Yes, she is, but she obviously doesn't think I'm a nice man," Nick said bitterly. "I was taking her to dinner tonight and she suddenly canceled on me. She's upset about something, and I don't know what."

"Have you decided you're really interested?" Gabe asked.

"Yeah. It's like I've been chasing fool's gold. Now that I've seen the real stuff, it's all I want."

"That's wonderful," Letty said enthusiastically. "So you'll settle down here?"

"Yeah. I bought a large space in town. I'm going to open my law practice there and live upstairs."

"But who will cook and clean for you?" Letty asked, apparently worried about Nick's well being.

"I'll hire someone," Nick said, seemingly not concerned. "Do you know of anyone?"

"Not right offhand, but I'll look around for someone. When are you moving in?"

"Tomorrow. I'm going to buy a bedroll until I get a proper bed. The furniture should be here on Thursday."

"The furniture from your home in Denver?" Blackie asked.

"That and the furniture I've had stored from my parents'

house. I'm giving it to the town of Rawhide. What they make from the sale of it will go toward a library.''

Both Letty and Blackie praised his generosity.

"I'm happy to get rid of the stuff. And Sarah's in charge of it. I thought it would please her, but she seems unhappy with it.''

Gabe chuckled. "She might be a little overwhelmed. She's also not used to all that wealth.''

"Why would that bother her?''

"It bothered me when we went to your apartment,'' Gabe told him. "You should have seen it, Letty. The floor was covered with Oriental rugs. The furniture was big and carved and gleaming. There were paintings all over the walls. Lots of books. Fancy lamps and crystal things. I was afraid to move in case I bumped into something expensive.''

"I thought the only thing that bothered you was the blonde,'' Nick teased, but he frowned, too, thinking about Sarah and her attitude. Could his plan to give them more time together be too much? If so, he'd better fix the situation before his furniture came. And his folks' house had been huge and stuffed with items. He and Sarah would be forced to spend a lot of time together sorting through everything.

Maybe he should take Sarah and Megan to Denver and let them decide what they could sell and what should go to an auction somewhere before it was moved.

After dinner, he called Megan Randall and asked her about that. "If you can put off the movers for a few days, that might be a good idea,'' she responded. "But with Jennifer getting married Wednesday, we couldn't go until Thursday. And it would take several days for us to make arrangements and go through everything.''

"Of course I can make arrangements. Would Chad want to come along? Then we'd have an even number for dinner out in the evenings. We could maybe even take in a play.

There are a couple of good theaters there. And I could get tickets for a Broncos game on Sunday. We could drive back afterward."

"That sounds wonderful. I'll ask Chad. Will Sarah agree to go?"

"I think so—if you and Chad come. She's a little shy, you know."

"True, but I think it will be good for her to have something to do after Jennifer moves out. She's going to miss her sister a lot."

"Good thinking. I'll talk to her in the morning," Nick offered, a grin on his face that Megan couldn't see. "Can I tell her you'll be coming with us?"

"Definitely. It's the least I can do for a library."

"Wonderful."

AFTER SARAH WENT DOWN to the store the next morning, Jennifer got a phone call from Janie. "Do you mind if we come to your wedding?"

"Of course not," she said, "but we're just keeping it simple. We'll say the vows and then…well, I guess that's it. Not much to see."

"But Mildred's making a cake. We thought we'd give you a little reception here. Would you mind that?"

"Of course I wouldn't mind, but—remember that we're just getting married because I'm pregnant."

"Well, I was pregnant, too, when I got married. That didn't stop me from having a church wedding and a reception. You'll make a beautiful bride. So all the family is invited! It will be wonderful."

After Janie hung up, Jennifer went downstairs. The store hadn't opened yet and she found Sarah in her office. "Uh, Sarah, Janie called. They're all coming to the wedding and giving a reception at their house afterward. Is that all right?"

"Of course, Jen. I should have thought of that. The Randalls are wonderful."

"But, Sarah, what will I wear? Nothing's going to fit me!" Jennifer wailed.

"I forgot. I took up a dress yesterday in case you wanted to wear it. I'll come up with you now and you can try it on."

"But I'm so fat," Jennifer said faintly.

Sarah jumped up and put her arms around her. "You're not fat. You're pregnant. And you'll look beautiful. Come on."

Upstairs, Jennifer slipped the white gown over her head. It was true that she still looked pregnant, but she also looked beautiful.

"Wait. Here's the veil," Sarah said as Jen moved to the mirror. Once the veil was added, Jennifer started crying.

"Don't you like it?" Sarah asked, concern in her voice.

Still crying, Jen managed to say, "I love it! I didn't think I'd get to wear a wedding dress."

"Goodness, we'd better get you out of it before you get tears all over it." After she'd hung the dress back up, she asked, "Did Janie say Mildred was making a cake for you?"

"Yes, Sarah. Thank you so much for making it a nice ceremony for me. I thought it would just be Gabe and me, and I don't think he's very enthusiastic about it."

"It's going to be a lovely wedding. Which reminds me— I need to get some rolls of film for my camera. It sure is handy having a store."

"Yes, thank you."

The phone rang again. This time it was B.J., saying Jake was offering to give her away since her father wasn't alive. Jennifer accepted again, tears of gratitude filling her eyes. Sarah kissed her cheek, then said she had to open the store and had to go downstairs. Jen managed to tell her about Jake's offer before she went.

Several old family friends called during the day, asking to attend. The first time, Jennifer called the Randalls to see if they'd mind. Mildred told her she was making a big cake and a groom's cake. There would also be hors d'oeuvres, so she could invite anyone she wanted.

Then Jennifer called Gabe's ranch. When a female voice answered, she said, "Is this Letty?"

"Yes, it is."

"Letty, this is Jennifer. Gabe and I are getting married tomorrow. I assume you know."

"Well, yes, he said you were."

"I wanted to ask if you and Blackie wanted to come to the ceremony. Some friends are coming, and I'm sure Gabe would like you to be there. We're having a reception afterward at the Randall house. Mildred is making a cake."

"Oh, we'd love to. Thank you so much for thinking of us. I'll call Mildred right away and see what I can bring."

"That's so nice of you, Letty," Jennifer said, fighting back tears. "I'm sure Mildred would appreciate it. And…and I'll try not to be too much trouble."

"I'm sure we'll manage fine, Jennifer. I can call you that, can't I?"

"Of course. Oh! Are you the Letty who comes into the store to buy knitting yarn?"

"Why, yes, I am."

"Could you teach me how to knit? I've been trying, but I'm having difficulties with it."

"Of course I can. I'd love to."

"Thank you. I'll be able to help some with the cooking. I've been learning how."

"Bless you, child. I'll teach you that, too. This is going to be fun."

"Thank you again, Letty. You make me feel much better."

"I'm looking forward to having you here."

"Then we'll see you tomorrow."

SARAH HAD BEEN BUSY this morning, mostly in the housewares. A lot of the Randalls, including Tori, had been in to buy her sister a wedding present. She'd been sworn to secrecy, of course. But she knew she'd have to warn Jennifer.

She ate with Jennifer while Jeff continued to wait on customers. "Uh, Jen, you need to be prepared. There are going to be presents tomorrow."

"Presents? Sarah, you've done too much. You don't need to buy something for us."

"It's not me, Jen. Oh, I'll get you something. But we've had a bunch of Randalls in to get you a present. And several old family friends. They said they'd invited themselves to the wedding, too."

"Yes, I checked with Mildred and she said to invite anyone I wanted. She's making a groom's cake, too. And I called Letty, Gabe's housekeeper. She's wonderful. I invited her and Blackie to the wedding. She said Blackie would invite Hazel, his fiancée. She'll be living on the ranch as soon as their new house is ready. Anyway, Letty is going to teach me to knit!"

With tears building in Jen's eyes, Sarah took her hand and squeezed it. "It's great, but don't start crying again. We don't want you with red eyes tomorrow."

Jennifer laughed. "You're right. I thought tomorrow was going to be so grim, but it's going to be wonderful!"

"Yes, it is. Oh! Gabe will be so surprised."

That gave Sarah pause. "Uh, Jennifer, don't you need to warn him? He should dress up, you know, or he'll be embarrassed."

"Well, of course, he'll dress up for a wedding. My goodness, he wouldn't—oh, no, you're right. He'll probably come in his jeans." The tears flowed in earnest then.

"I'll take care of it, Jen. I'll warn him to put on a suit, or slacks and a nice shirt. It will be all right. Have you finished lunch? Why don't you go upstairs and lie down. You didn't get much sleep yesterday.''

Jennifer sniffed her agreement. She hurried up the stairs and Sarah prayed she'd go right to sleep. Then she sat thinking how she'd get hold of Gabe. Maybe she should go through Letty. She got up, about to go to the phone, when Nick came into the store. When he saw her, he made a beeline toward her. Normally, she would've tried to avoid him. At least, since yesterday, that had been her plan. But she could warn Nick about tomorrow and he could take care of the situation.

"Nick, I'm glad you came in."

He looked surprised and pleased. "Good. I like it when you're glad to see me."

Sarah continued as if he hadn't spoken. "A lot of people are pitching in to make tomorrow a special day for Jennifer, which I really appreciate. I found her a wedding gown and veil. The Randalls are throwing a reception. And there are going to be other guests at the wedding. I've arranged for a bouquet for her. But Gabe doesn't know of any of this. I think he'll probably come wearing his jeans, and that won't do."

"Do you think so?"

"Yes, I do. We don't want him to be embarrassed. Letty and Blackie, along with Hazel, are coming, too. Can you let Gabe know? Hopefully he'll find something nice to wear."

"Sure. I'll take care of it. I have just the thing. Now can you help me? I need to get a bedroll. I'm going to sleep across the street tomorrow night."

Sarah stared at him. He had all this money and he was going to sleep on the floor? "Why?"

"Because it's Jen and Gabe's wedding night. I don't want to be in the way."

"But you know what kind of a marriage it is. There's no point in you being uncomfortable."

"I'll be okay. Has Megan talked to you about Thursday?"

"No. Isn't that when the furniture is going to be delivered?"

"No, we've changed that. I thought it would be better if you and Megan went through all the furniture at my parents' home and decided what should be sold here and what should be sent to auctions. It would save moving it twice."

"That's a good idea, but Megan won't need me. She knows much more about it than I do."

"Maybe, but I thought it would be rude to make her do all the work by herself. Chad and I are coming along. We can move things and help any way we can. And we'll reward you for your hard work with good meals, and maybe a trip to the theater. We'll try to wrap it all up on Sunday with a trip to see the Broncos. Then we'll drive home."

"Good heavens. You want me to leave the store in Jeff's hands for four days, including a weekend? I can't do that."

"Sure you can." Without asking her, he waved Jeff over as he finished with a customer. "Jeff, Sarah needs to go to Denver for four days, starting this Thursday. Can you hold down the fort here for her?"

Sarah met Jeff's gaze. "I know it won't be easy, but I have a lead on the teenagers I wanted to hire. If I have them here on Saturday and maybe one each afternoon, would that make it better?"

"Yeah, it would, but you used to manage on your own. I can probably do it, even without help," Jeff replied.

"That's wonderful, Jeff. I'll give you an extra day off next week," Sarah promised. After Jeff moved away, she glared at Nick. "You had no business making that request. He's my employee!"

"I know he is, but I didn't think it was fair to put all the burden on Megan. I was just trying to help."

"Well, I didn't find it helpful."

"Sorry," he said cheerfully. "Now, don't forget to take

warm clothes for the football game Sunday, and several nice outfits for dinner and the theater.''

''Where will we stay? I don't know—''

''I'll take care of all that, and it's all on me. After all, you're doing me a favor.''

''But I know several women who would do a better job than me.''

''Sarah, you can leave the hard decisions to Megan, but she'll need you to write things down or put markers on the things to be moved. You'll be a lot of help, and in the evenings, we'll have fun.''

Sarah didn't know what to say. But she'd think of some way to get out of the trip. She had to! She couldn't be around Nick so long. ''Don't forget to tell Gabe about the wedding, okay?''

''I'll take care of it. I suppose if I asked you for dinner tonight you'd turn me down?''

''Yes. It's the last night Jennifer and I will have together for a long time.''

''That's what I thought. I'll see you at the wedding.'' Then he leaned over and kissed her briefly on the lips.

It wasn't a brief, friendly peck. But a kiss that warned of more to come. A kiss that had Sarah's body tingling all over and left her standing in the middle of the store, staring at the door where he had just left. Speechless.

CHAPTER TWENTY-TWO

SARAH STARED ACROSS the table as she sipped the last of her morning coffee. Jennifer was still asleep. They'd stayed up too late last night packing her belongings.

It was going to be strange not to have to worry about Jennifer, to keep an eye on her. That was going to be Gabe's job now.

She hoped and prayed the marriage would be a happy one. She'd warned Jennifer to have patience. Jennifer had asked if she didn't think Gabe was coming around as he was being so considerate of Jen lately. Reluctantly, Sarah told her no. She thought Gabe was trying to ensure the babies' safety.

Jennifer had been disappointed.

A loud banging on the store's front door jerked her from her thoughts. What was going on?

Sarah hurried down the stairs, wrapping her robe around her. Normally she was dressed by this time of the morning, but today was a special day.

She unlocked the front door to Gabe and Nick. "What is it?" she asked.

"We're here to move the bedroom furniture Jen asked for," Gabe said. He didn't appear to be in a good mood.

"Jennifer's not awake yet."

"Well, can you wake her?"

"Gabe, I think she needs more sleep. We were up late last night because of all the packing."

"Do you want us to wait until this afternoon after the

wedding and announce to the entire town that Jennifer wants her own bedroom furniture in her room?''

''All right. I get the picture,'' she assured him crisply. She may have understood his point, but she didn't like his attitude. ''I'll get her to move to my bed.''

She led the way upstairs, asking them to wait in the living room, but Gabe followed her into Jen's bedroom. ''I'll carry her so she won't wake up.''

Sarah reluctantly agreed. ''Okay.''

She hurried ahead of him to turn down the covers on her bed. She'd already made it up.

When he slipped his arms around Jen's warm body, he paused, staring down at her, holding her close.

''Gabe,'' Sarah whispered, ''this way.''

Jennifer never woke up, which told Sarah how badly her sister needed the sleep. The wedding had been set for eleven, so she could sleep a couple of more hours.

Gabe and Sarah met Nick in Jennifer's bedroom. ''Okay, we're going to load all of this in the back of my truck. I assume we're taking all the suitcases, too?''

''Yes, please. And I have new sheets and a bedspread for the bed, too. If I pack it up, can you get Letty to put it on the bed as a surprise for Jennifer?''

''Yeah, I suppose.''

''And Nick explained to you about the wedding? Did you find something to wear?''

Gabe's displeasure doubled. ''Yeah, but I don't like it.''

Nick grinned at his twin. ''Brother, what happened to your gratitude? I expected you to be thrilled.''

It was clear Nick was teasing his twin, but Sarah had no idea what was going on.

''Just pick up your side of the chest, brother, and get moving. We've got a lot to do before eleven.''

Sarah left them to it. She dressed and went downstairs and gave the store a final check before she went into her office to do paperwork. Poor Jeff would be on his own today, also. But she'd close the store before she'd miss her sister's wedding.

After a while, Nick stuck his head in the door. "We're off. I think we've gotten everything."

"Oh, good, thank you. Why is Gabe upset?" she asked.

"I'm making him wear a tux."

Nick's smile told her he was enjoying Gabe's irritation.

"Where did you get a tux around here?"

"I had a couple and we wear the same size. I brought one from Denver on my last visit so Gabe would have it on his wedding day."

"Well, thank you. Jen will be thrilled."

Nick waved to her with a smile and disappeared.

After checking the time, she went upstairs to fix a special breakfast for Jennifer. Her favorite was pancakes with bacon. When Sarah fixed the breakfast tray, it was perfect. She carried it into her room and wakened Jennifer.

"Oh, what time is it?" Jennifer asked as she stretched beneath the covers.

"It's ten o'clock. You have forty-five minutes to get dressed for your wedding, so eat up and hit the shower. I'm going down to open the store."

"Why am I in your room?"

"Gabe and Nick moved your furniture this morning. It was early and I thought you should sleep late."

"But how did you get me in here without waking me up?"

"Your future husband volunteered to carry you."

"Oh."

"I'll be back up in fifteen minutes to get dressed myself, so get a move on."

"Yes, ma'am!" Jen agreed with a mock salute.

JENNIFER HAD ALWAYS DREAMED of an elaborate wedding in a big church, a glistening chandelier on the ceiling, flowers everywhere. But she wouldn't complain about anything today. Her sister had worked fast to arrange everything. There was a large floral piece at the front of the church that framed the preacher. And Jen held a beautiful bouquet. She was wearing the lace-trimmed white gown that flowed gently over the swell in her stomach. She supposed, technically, she shouldn't even be wearing white, but she didn't think anyone would object.

The church organist was even there, playing beautiful music before the wedding started. She'd actually get to walk down the aisle to the wedding march.

"Sarah, thank you. Everything is beautiful."

"I'm glad. I didn't think to hire the organist. I suspect one of the Randalls did that."

"Well, it's all beautiful. I couldn't ask for more."

Sarah kissed her cheek. "I'm glad. Be happy." Then she snapped one more picture of her beautiful sister and entered the church.

When Jake knocked on the dressing-room door, Jen proudly took his arm. His presence was a sign of approval from Gabe's family, whether Gabe wanted her or not. "Thank you, Jake," she whispered softly.

"My pleasure, Jennifer," Jake assured her in his deep voice.

Then that famous song she'd imagined started and they were moving down the aisle. The church was almost full. She was startled to see so many people. But she forgot all about them when her gaze traveled to the front of the church where Gabe stood waiting for her.

Gabe was dressed in a tux!

He looked elegant and sophisticated, like the groom on a wedding cake. Jennifer couldn't believe it. Her dreams had come true down to the last detail! Tears shimmered in her eyes, but she fought valiantly to hold them back.

Gabe turned to look at her. She saw surprise in his eyes though he tried to hide it. Did he think she'd be wearing maternity clothes? She held herself proudly. Well, he had surprised her. She was glad she had returned the favor.

When they reached the pastor and Gabe, accompanied by Nick, also in a tux, Jake kissed her cheek, shook Gabe's hand and sat down beside his wife.

Gabe stepped closer to her.

The ceremony began.

After the pastor had pronounced them man and wife and told Gabe he could kiss his bride, Jennifer looked into Gabe's eyes, hoping he could see the love she felt for him. But he brushed her lips gently with his, keeping contact to a minimum, which told her that her hopes were futile.

Then he turned her to face their audience. Jennifer smiled brilliantly while tears ran down her face. She wasn't going to let anyone know how unhappy she was. She'd let everyone think she was crying tears of joy.

GABE HAD ASKED NICK to drive Jen and him to the Randalls not because he'd be too excited to drive but because he didn't want to be alone with Jennifer. When she'd lifted her lips to his after the ceremony, it had been all he could do not to grab her in his arms and head for the nearest bed. But then she'd know she'd won. Then he would be at her mercy. It was important she not know how much he wanted their marriage to be real.

He had to remember that he couldn't trust her.

"It was a beautiful wedding, wasn't it?" Nick tossed the words over his shoulder after several minutes of silence as they headed to the Randall ranch.

"Yes. Everyone was so sweet to arrange everything," Jen said brightly.

"Yeah. They sure were, weren't they, Gabe?"

"Yeah."

"Too bad you can't have a honeymoon right now. But maybe after the babies are born," Nick said.

Neither one responded to that suggestion.

Gabe didn't look at Jennifer, and he kept a little distance between the flowing white skirts and the black tux he wore.

"We're almost there. You ready to face everyone?" Nick asked, a subtle warning in his voice.

Gabe straightened his shoulders, which looked magnificent in the tux, and nodded. "Right. Jen? Are you ready?"

"Yes, of course. And Gabe, I appreciate you wearing the tux. You look…very nice."

Nick stopped the car and came around to open Jennifer's door. Gabe sat there, wishing he'd taken the time to tell Jen how beautiful she looked. But he was afraid it would give his emotions away.

WHEN THE RANDALLS THREW a party, they did it up right. Their huge living room was filled with people, and the dining room table was loaded with food. There were delicate sandwiches with the crusts cut off, as well as a huge roast from which Brett, one of Pete's brothers, was slicing off big slabs of beef. There were numerous hors d'oeuvres and a big bowl of potato salad. Something for every taste.

Sarah made it a point to thank all the Randalls. She wasn't sure Jennifer would remember, as her sister had a glassy-eyed look. Sarah hoped she at least remembered the reception, because it was a wonderful one. The bride and groom had circled the room, greeting their guests like pros. She noticed Nick at Gabe's elbow frequently, seemingly directing him in his duties.

Then he led the pair to stand in front of the big fireplace, each with a glass filled with sparkling wine, or, in Jennifer's case, sparkling cider.

"I only found my brother a few weeks ago, but today I'm willingly giving him to the prettiest bride I've ever seen. Lift your glasses in a toast to Gabe and Jennifer. May your days together be happy and your marriage prosper. I would say 'may it produce children,' but we all know it's doing that," he said with a grin. Then he lifted his glass a little higher, and said, "To Gabe and Jennifer." Everyone repeated the toast, then took a sip of their drinks. They applauded the couple.

Nick whispered in Gabe's ear. Gabe looked at him as if to complain, but he finally nodded. "Folks, Jen and I want to thank you for helping us celebrate this special day." Then he leaned down and whispered something to Jennifer before he gave her a light kiss again. Everyone cheered.

Jennifer gave a gallant smile, but Sarah was worried about her. She seemed a little strained. Gabe again whispered in her ear. Then the couple moved into the dining room, where they cut the cake. Sarah took more pictures. She'd already gone through three rolls, but she wanted Jennifer to have all the pictures she wanted. After the beautiful wedding cake, they also cut the groom's cake, chocolate with thick chocolate icing and decorated with green and blue, the colors Jennifer had picked out for her boys. Gabe fed Jennifer a small piece of each cake and she returned the favor, but Sarah thought she was fading fast. As they moved away from the table, Sarah eased her way to Jennifer's side.

"Honey, have you eaten any lunch?"

She shook her head.

Sarah looked at Gabe. "Get us to the kitchen."

He managed to get them through the surging people seeking a piece of cake. Once the door had closed behind them, Sarah urged Jennifer to sit down. "How are you doing?"

"Fine, Sarah, really," Jen said, blinking her eyes rapidly.

"Relax, honey. It's okay if you cry a little. We'll tell them it's your hormones. Gabe, could you get her some food?"

"Sure." He hurried out of the kitchen just as Megan and Janie came in.

"Are you doing okay, Jen?" Janie asked. "These things can be ordeals, especially when you're pregnant."

Jennifer nodded.

"I sent Gabe for food," Sarah said.

"Oh, good. You need something solid," Megan said to Jennifer. "Not just wedding cake."

Anna peeked in. "Everything okay?"

"We're getting Jen some food," Janie told her. "You might come check her pulse."

"I will, but Jon is in the next room if you need him, Jennifer."

"Oh, no, Anna, I'm fine. And I had a big breakfast. I'm not really that hungry." She leaned a little against Sarah.

"The thing is, honey, everyone's brought gifts and they'd love for you to open them before you leave. This is a wedding and a shower combined."

"Sarah's right," Anna said. "The back bedroom is full of gifts. Once you eat something, we'll find you a seat in the living room and start bringing them in. With Gabe to help you, maybe it won't take too long. I'm sure he has his pocketknife with him."

They all laughed, but Sarah wasn't so sure. Nick might not have let him put his knife in his pocket, but someone would loan him one.

Gabe came in with a plate piled high.

"Why don't you explain what's going to happen to Gabe, while Jen eats a little bit," Sarah asked the Randall women. "Gabe might want a plate of food, too." Sarah knew the ladies would take him under their wing. Sure enough, the four of them surrounded him and led him back to the food in the dining room.

Sarah sat beside her sister. "Glad to have it quiet for a while?"

"Yes."

"My gift to you is a new bedspread and sheets on your bed tonight to match the new paint job. I hope you like them."

"Oh, Sarah," Jen said softly, throwing her arms around her sister. "I'll love them! But you've already given me the perfect wedding."

"It was beautiful, wasn't it? But I didn't do that all by myself."

"Thank you so much."

"You're welcome. Now, eat some more."

A few minutes later, Gabe, followed by Nick, came to collect Jennifer. "Feeling better? We need to start unwrapping the gifts," Gabe asked.

"Yes, I'm ready." Jennifer took a deep breath and stood. Gabe took her arm and led her to the door.

Nick looked at Sarah and she caught her breath.

"I don't know if anyone's taken the time to tell you, but you look beautiful today, too."

"Thank you."

"They're getting paper and a pen to make a list of the gift-givers. Tori's going to keep track if you don't mind."

"I'm delighted. I'll get some food to eat now. I don't want to faint," she said with a chuckle.

"Good idea. Mind if I join you?"

"Uh, there are a lot of beautiful women in the living room, Nick. You might want to meet a few more."

"But I might faint. And that would embarrass my twin, don't you think? So we'll sit down and enjoy the meal while they open lots of presents, and hope they don't get embarrassed."

"They probably will. People seem to enjoy that."

"Because it reminds them of their own wedding day. They're being mighty generous to the two of them. Gabe's only been here a few months."

"Yes, but they've known him for a few years, ever since he first came here with Blackie."

"Well, let's go celebrate today with them."

Sarah told herself she had no choice, but she knew she was lying. She wanted to celebrate with Nick. As long as she remembered it was her sister's wedding they were celebrating, not her own.

CHAPTER TWENTY-THREE

JENNIFER LAY BACK AGAINST the pillow in her new room. Sarah had done a good job of picking out a bedspread and sheets to match the pale green walls.

The reception had gone on until three. When she'd gotten to Gabe's house, she'd unpacked her suitcases. She wanted to feel at home. So she'd filled the drawers and hung up her clothes in the closet. But she still didn't feel comfortable.

She'd changed into loose-fitting pants and a long shirt and hung her wedding dress at the back of the closet. She'd caught a glimpse of Gabe back in a plaid shirt and his worn jeans, heading outside. But he didn't stop to speak to her.

He was definitely making it clear he didn't intend to have much to do with her.

Okay, fine. Letty had been kind, coming in to help her unpack. She said the Randalls had sent enough food home with them that she didn't even need to cook dinner, so she might as well help Jen get settled. She was cheerful and welcoming, and Jennifer decided she was lucky to have her there since Gabe wasn't going to be any of those things.

She was settled in by six o'clock. Letty told Jennifer to change into a nightgown and crawl into her bed. She deserved dinner on a tray tonight. She also brought in one of the presents. It was a small color television that fit well on the top of her dresser near the head of the bed. "I'll get Gabe to hook it up to the cable so you can get a good picture."

"Thank you, Letty. You've been very thoughtful."

"My pleasure. After you eat, you go on to sleep. And sleep as late as you want in the morning."

Jen actually dozed a little, but she was hungry. When the door finally opened, it was Gabe who brought the tray. "I didn't expect to see you," she said coolly.

"Letty insisted." He didn't bother to say anything else. He set the bed tray over her lap, shoved another pillow behind her without asking, and immediately moved to connect the television.

She began eating to keep from crying. He couldn't have made his attitude more obvious. When he had a clear picture on the television, he asked, "Is this all right?"

She would've agreed if it had been a blank screen. Fortunately, the picture was bright and clear. "Yes, thank you."

"Good. No need to get up in the morning."

"Letty told me."

"Oh. Okay. Good night." He closed the door behind him.

Jen ate a little more, finishing with a piece of wedding cake and the last of her milk. She crawled out of bed and put her tray on the floor by the door. Then she visited the bathroom.

Snuggling down under the covers, she thought about her beautiful wedding. At least she had those memories. And she'd have pictures. Sarah had taken a lot of pictures. And now she had Letty. She'd be her friend. She'd concentrate on Sarah, Letty and her beautiful wedding. She closed her eyes, determined not to cry. But all that filled her head were pictures of Gabe in his handsome tux.

NICK GOT AN EARLY CALL on his cell phone. It was Megan. "Nick, Chad is going to come, but he'll have to drive down this afternoon. So may I catch a ride with you and Sarah? I think we'll need every hour we can get."

"I'm afraid you're right. That will be fine." He gave Megan the name of the hotel in Denver to pass on to Chad.

"We can meet him in the hotel after we finish working and have dinner together."

"Perfect. And B.J. will drop me off in half an hour."

"I can come get you."

"No, she's coming that way. See you in half an hour."

He'd already showered and dressed. All he needed was breakfast. He called Sarah and asked her to meet him at the café. It was a few minutes after seven, but he knew it would be open.

"I'm making breakfast now if you want to come join me," she told him over the phone.

"I'm on my way," he said, a big grin on his face. Breakfast with just the two of them. He'd hoped for that. He hadn't made much progress with Sarah, but this trip would give him a lot of opportunities.

When he got to the store, she let him in and he followed her up the stairs into the kitchen. "Can I do something to help?" he asked.

"I think the coffee is ready. Mugs are on that second shelf. Why don't you pour us each a cup."

He did so and sat down at the table. "Megan should be here in half an hour."

"What about Chad?" she quickly asked.

"He's coming this afternoon. But we're going to need all the time we can get. There's a lot of furniture." Nick told her just how large his parents' house was. She stared at him.

"Will we be able to get through all of it in three days?" she asked.

"I hope so. I have a pretty good idea about the paintings. Dad purchased some of them in Denver and some from the very same New York City auction house that we're going to be selling them through. So we can get through those pretty quickly."

"Good, because I don't know much about art, I just know what I like."

"Me, too."

"Surely your father taught you, since he was such a collector...."

"He tried. But he gave up on me after a while."

She put a plate of scrambled eggs and bacon in front of him. Then she brought a plate of biscuits to the table along with her own breakfast.

"Mmm, this looks good," he said.

"I like breakfast. But we don't have much time if Megan is going to be here at seven-thirty."

Actually, Megan got there a little early. B.J. came in with her and both enjoyed a cup of coffee.

"Well, I'd best go so you three can get on the road," B.J. finally said, standing up. "Be careful, though. They think the weather might turn bad around noon. There's a front coming through."

"How cold is it supposed to get?" Nick asked.

"Below freezing, and there may be sleet or snow."

"Don't let Chad leave until tomorrow if it gets bad, B.J."

"I'll try, but you know how hardheaded he is, like all the Randalls, right, Nick?" B.J. said with a grin.

"I've heard that," he said with a charming smile. Everyone laughed.

After doing the few dishes, Nick carried Sarah's bag down and put it in the back of his Lexus. Megan got in the back seat, insisting Sarah take the front passenger seat. "I may nap a little. We were up late last night."

Nick wanted to thank her, but he didn't dare.

"Was everything all right?" Sarah asked. "I hope you weren't still cleaning up that late. I could've stayed."

"Don't be silly. Weddings bring back a lot of memories. We've had a lot of them...and hope to have more."

"I guess you do still have some prospects," Sarah said with a grin.

"Yes. I still have two boys to marry off. But Janie, well, she's hoping Russ will find someone else. She worries about him so much."

Sarah nodded.

Nick kept an eye on her as he drove. "No prospects in town?"

"There doesn't seem to be. Once we thought maybe Sarah." She grinned when Sarah turned around, surprise on her face, to look at her. "I know, Sarah, neither of you have shown any sign."

"Russ is a wonderful guy, but he hasn't gotten over Abby."

"But will he ever?" Megan settled her head against the back of the seat. "Anyway, we were just talking, hoping. The wedding made for an enjoyable evening."

"Well, Jennifer and I really appreciate all you did for us."

"It was our pleasure. And now, I think I may just close my eyes."

They rode in silence until they heard a consistent, delicate snore. "I think that means she's asleep," Nick said softly. "How about you? Do you need a nap?"

"No, I was so tired last night I fell right to sleep. I thought I'd have a hard time going to sleep with Jen gone, but I didn't."

"I'm glad. I assume you left the keys for Jeff."

"Yes, of course. I think he's very trustworthy."

"I hope so. Does he have a girlfriend?"

Sarah looked at Nick. "He hasn't said so, but he's mentioned a friend in Buffalo a number of times. Her name is Susan. He says she works for a law firm. He's gone back to Buffalo the last two weekends, so I suspect there's something going on."

"Good," Nick said quietly but enthusiastically.

"Why does that please you?" she asked, raising her eyebrows.

"Because it means he's not interested in you."

He waited for her to ask why he wanted that, but she didn't. Her cheeks burned and she said nothing else.

"Hey! Do you think he'd like his friend Susan to have a job in Rawhide?"

"I don't know."

"Remind me to ask him when we get back. I'll be needing a legal secretary for the law firm when I get set up."

"Are you sure you'll be happy practicing law in Rawhide? It's a very quiet town. Not much going on."

"Yeah, I do. I like Rawhide very much." Without saying anything, he reached over and caught her left hand in his as he drove. She pulled on her hand at first, but he kept his hold firm yet gentle. Finally she stopped tugging and they headed for Denver hand in hand.

GABE WAS UNSETTLED. Nick was in Denver. Blackie's every spare minute was spent with Hazel, and Letty had become Jen's best friend. For the past three mornings, Letty had accompanied Jen on her morning walk. According to Letty, it was the doctor's orders. And Jen always chose to walk down to the lake.

Jen never joined them for breakfast. Letty assured him she ate a good breakfast when she got up. He'd stopped going in for lunch, so he only had to face her at dinner. During both dinners, she'd talked to Blackie and Letty, but never directly addressed him.

That was what he wanted, wasn't it? He should be grateful she was accepting his rules so easily. Yet it bothered him.

Yesterday, though, he'd come in early. Letty and Jen were standing in the kitchen. Letty had her hands on Jen's stomach.

"My goodness, they're strong," she said.

"Who's strong?" Gabe asked with a growl.

Jen started, stepping back, but Letty just smiled at him and said, "The babies, of course. Come here, Gabe, and feel how hard they kick Jen. No wonder she needs to rest."

He couldn't resist. He stepped into Letty's place and,

after a quick look at Jen, put his hands on her protruding stomach. Immediately, he felt a bump.

"That's the babies kicking?" he asked, astounded.

"Yes," Jennifer said calmly.

He put his hand back on her stomach and felt several more bumps. Then he didn't feel anything. "What happened?"

"I don't know." Jen had a surprised look on her face. "I guess they like your touch and calmed down for you."

"Well, my goodness, isn't that something?" Letty said. "They must know you're their daddy," she said with a beaming smile. "You'll need to call Gabe when they won't let you go to sleep at night."

If Jen had agreed with Letty, he would've protested at once. But she didn't. Instead, her cheeks red, she backed away from his touch. "No, I won't do that. I'm sure Gabe needs his rest, too."

Then last night, calling himself all kinds of a fool, he stopped beside her door before he went to bed. The television was still on and he thought she might have fallen asleep. He knocked, then opened the door. She was rubbing her stomach.

"What's wrong?" he asked.

"I think the babies are playing a game of soccer."

"Hard to sleep if you're the soccer ball," he said.

She nodded.

"Let's see if they recognize me this time."

He sat down on the edge of her bed and put his hands on her warm stomach. The movement stopped. Jen's eyes rounded. "I didn't think—"

Gabe took his hands away—and to his surprise, the kicking started up again. They tried it several times. Finally Gabe took his boots off. Jen stared at him. "You're not going to get any sleep and neither am I unless we settle these guys down. I'll scoot into bed with you until you all go to sleep."

He didn't give her an opportunity to protest. He snuggled

up to her, putting his hands on her stomach. The boys settled down again. "Close your eyes, Jen. You need to get to sleep."

They both fell asleep until early the next morning. It had been the best night's sleep he'd had since the last time he'd shared a bed with Jen. He slipped away to his room and dressed, hoping no one else knew what had happened. Because nothing had changed, of course. He still couldn't trust her. He was just making sure they all got a good night's sleep.

NICK AND CHAD MANAGED to pull Sarah and Megan away from the storage rooms early enough Friday night to see a play. But Sarah had fallen asleep on his shoulder almost immediately and Nick hadn't had the heart to wake her.

They worked straight through Saturday, until almost one in the morning. Chad had gotten them burgers and they had eaten them as they worked. When they finally finished, everyone was exhausted and headed back to the hotel.

"I vote we all sleep in tomorrow. The football game starts at noon, but I don't care if we don't get there until halftime," Nick said.

"I'm for that. I think Megan and I will have breakfast in bed. It's been a long time since we've done that." Chad looked at his wife with a roguish grin and she blushed.

Nick laughed. "I don't think I'll ask for details."

"Good thinking," Chad said.

"All right. We'll call your room when we're ready to go," Nick said, catching Sarah's hand in his to lead her to the set of elevators that would take them to their wing of the hotel.

He and Sarah had worked together every day and spent every evening together since arriving in Denver. Each night, he'd held her hand and kissed her goodbye at her hotel room door. And he'd felt he'd made progress in getting closer to Sarah. Last night, their kiss had turned into a marathon make-out session that ended much too soon in

his mind. Nick figured when he and Sarah finally made
love, the results would be cataclysmic.

In the elevator, where it was just the two of them, he
pulled her against him and her eyes closed at once. She
leaned against him, her body warm and relaxed. When the
elevator stopped, the only way to get her out was to pick
her up or drag her. He swept her into his arms. She settled
against him with no protest.

He had to stand her on the floor, leaning against him, to
get her key and insert it in the lock. Then he carried her
into her room. He lay her on the freshly made bed and
slipped her shoes off. She was wearing jeans and a knit
shirt. He wondered what he should do.

He decided to give her a kiss and leave her in her clothes.
Otherwise, things would be awkward in the morning. He
bent to touch her lips.

Sarah linked her arms around his neck and responded
passionately. She opened to him, giving as good as she got.
Nick felt his control slipping. Either he was going to strip
her naked and make love to her, or he had to get out of
there. He knew what *he* wanted, but he had to discover
what Sarah wanted.

"Sarah, wake up. I want to make love to you, sweetheart."

"Okay," she said, in a startlingly cheerful voice.

"Sarah, are you sure you're awake?"

"What?"

Nick tried again. After a long kiss, he shook her gently.
"Sarah, do you want me to leave? Or do you want to make
love?"

She suddenly sat up, shoving him off her. "What did
you say? What are you doing?"

CHAPTER TWENTY-FOUR

SARAH STARED UP INTO NICK'S brown eyes as he bent over her.

"Sarah, I want to make love to you. I've been wanting to for days. But I'm not going to unless you want it, too. So, it's up to you whether I go back to my room...or spend the rest of the night with you."

Sarah knew what her decision was. She wanted him, too. She wanted him even if he walked away afterward. She figured she was the world's oldest virgin, having spent all her life taking care of her sister.

She wanted to experience what everyone said was so wonderful. And she figured with Nick, it would be just that. She realized for him, making love might be a casual thing. But then, she hadn't ever expected anything permanent from Nick. At least if they had tonight, she'd have an experience to remember all her life.

With a slow smile, she nodded yes.

"Are you sure? I want you, Sarah, but only if you want it, too. We'll be together, in every sense of the word."

She slid her arms around his neck and pulled his mouth to hers. She loved his kisses.

Nick obliged her at once, his mouth joining with hers. His body came down on Sarah's, a satisfying pressure to which she responded.

When he began unbuttoning her jeans, pulling up her shirt, she did the same to him. She'd already felt the difference in his body. Though she hadn't experienced love-making before, she had a pretty good idea of what went on. In no time, they were both naked, their flesh responding to the touch of eager, hot fingers. She wanted to touch all of him and he seemed to feel the same way.

"Oh, Nick," she whispered.

"You're wonderful, sweetheart." Then his lips returned to hers and she was lost.

She suspected he was taking it slow because he thought she wasn't very experienced. Should she have told him it was her first time? She didn't think it mattered, and she was embarrassed. When he touched her between her legs she experienced surprising panic. Then she calmed herself looking for ways to encourage him. She found some he really liked.

"I've got to put on a condom," he whispered.

That hadn't occurred to her, and considering her sister's situation, she should be ashamed of herself. "I don't have any," she said, her voice tight.

"I do. Let me find my jeans."

She felt exposed, lying there, her flesh cooling without his touch. She began to wonder if she was making a mistake. But she wanted to know what it was like. And Nick was the one she wanted to teach her. "Nick!" she called softly, an unspoken plea in her voice.

"I'm coming, baby. There, I'm ready." His mouth plundered her lips, and instantly she was warm again, willing, eager. She rubbed her hands over his back. She felt his firm hips, their strength obvious.

When he parted her legs and began to enter her, she took a deep breath, trying to quell the natural urge to retreat. But he moved quickly, and when she felt the pain, she couldn't hold back a gasp.

"Sarah? Sarah, why didn't you tell me?" he asked, frustration in his voice.

"I—couldn't!" she exclaimed.

"Calm down, honey, it's going to be all right." He lay

still on top of her, but his hands stroked her, as she'd earlier enjoyed, until she scarcely noticed the movement he began, rocking slowly against her.

Suddenly, she was caught up in a torrent of all-consuming sensations. When Nick found his own release and collapsed against her, she felt exhausted. Gently, he kissed her even as he rolled to her side.

"Are you all right? Sarah, did I hurt you?"

"No! Yes, a little, but—" She closed her eyes, exhausted. She intended to say something else, but she couldn't remember what. Then she fell asleep in his arms.

NICK WAS TIRED, TOO. Making love to Sarah was the best thing that had ever happened to him. He adored her. Not only because she was beautiful but because she was strong, determined, a complete person.

Women had chased him for his money, or for his body. But what they offered had no value. He'd wanted, needed more. But he hadn't understood exactly what. Now he knew. He'd needed Sarah.

He was her first lover…and her last, he determined. They were destined to be together. He'd felt sure he'd gone to Rawhide to find his brother. But now he believed he'd gone to find his destiny, and that destiny was Sarah.

He covered them both and cuddled her against him. Then he let the weariness overtake him and he fell asleep with his lover in his arms.

GABE WOKE UP SUNDAY MORNING in Jen's bed again. Her room was very feminine, of course. The bedspread was green with flowers all over it. But it didn't bother him like he'd thought it would. In fact, he felt damn comfortable.

She was lying with her back to him and his arms were wrapped around her so he could keep his hands on her stomach. He pulled the cover down to her waist, exposing her cotton nightgown which showed enough cleavage to make his body tighten. As if it would take much.

Her breasts were larger than they'd been before. Not that he'd ever complained. Jennifer had always been exactly what he wanted from the first moment he'd seen her, last year at the Randalls' Fourth of July party.

He'd never stopped wanting her, even after she told him there was someone else. He'd told himself he should hate her. But he couldn't. He never would be able to.

He cupped her breasts with one hand. So beautiful, so soft. He shouldn't be touching her like this. He'd give himself away if she woke up.

She stirred, pushing herself into his warm hands, moaning just a little. Did she want his touch? Mercy, he wanted her. Every minute of every day. He rubbed the nub of her breast through the material. She began to move again. As if trying to wake her, he moved above her and lowered his mouth to suck on her breast through the material.

That did it. "Gabe!" Jennifer gasped. Without a word, his lips leaped to hers and he pressed into her. He couldn't help himself. She, too, seemed eager for him. He had to accommodate the babies, and he tried to be gentle, but he couldn't hold back.

When her clothes and his had been thrown to the floor, they found completion. For several minutes he held her against him. Then his doubts came back to haunt him.

"This doesn't mean anything, Jen," he told her gruffly. "I still don't know if I can trust you. Not after all the lies you told."

He'd expected tears and pleadings. Instead, all he received in response was silence.

Finally she said, "Then you'd better fall asleep in your own bed. I'll manage without you."

She pulled the cover over her and said nothing else. He got out of the bed and found his underwear and his jeans.

"Fine. It doesn't matter where I sleep. I was just trying to help."

He hoped she believed him, because he didn't. But what could a man expect? Months before he'd been ready to offer everything he had to her and she'd lied to him. He'd be a fool to let her wrap him around her little finger again.

"YOU'D BETTER GET IN the shower, sweetheart. Breakfast will be here in fifteen minutes. I'm going to my room and dress."

At Nick's words, Sarah opened one eye and was immediately cognizant of the changes last night had made in her life. Nick kissed her briefly and left the room. Sarah was glad for the privacy as she wasn't sure she'd have the nerve to get out of bed completely naked and waltz to the bathroom in front of him.

When she realized someone, either a waiter or Nick, would be back in less than fifteen minutes, she raced to the shower. Under the hot water, she discovered some stiffness, as if she'd found new muscles last night.

She actually blushed in the shower, and it had nothing to do with the water's temperature. Now what? she asked herself. She knew she wasn't someone Nick would marry. Would he let her down gently? She hoped so.

Stepping out of the shower, she pulled on her underwear, added clean jeans and a white turtleneck. She planned to wear her insulated overalls and a matching jacket over her clothes for the football game.

As she began to braid her long brown hair, someone knocked on the door. Praying it was the waiter, she swung the door open. She was rewarded with a large cart pushed by one of the waiters. She moved back for him to enter and saw the elevator doors open. Nick stepped out and hurried toward them.

She occupied herself with directing the waiter. Nick had

ordered a lot of food. "You must be hungry," she said with her back to him.

"Oh, I am," he assured her. She didn't even have to look at him to know he wasn't talking about food.

Nick took the bill from the waiter and signed it. Sarah had sat on the edge of the bed and taken a plate of food from the cart. She hoped eating would buy her some time before Nick started discussing their future—or lack of one.

It didn't work. He took her plate out of her lap and put it on the small table. Then he pulled her into his arms and thoroughly kissed her. "Why are we strangers this morning, Sarah?" he asked when she didn't kiss him back.

"I'm hungry," she replied, not meeting his eyes.

She knew he was staring at her but she kept her gaze down. When the phone rang she felt relieved.

Nick answered and Sarah could tell he was speaking with Chad. "We just ordered breakfast. We'll be ready to go in half an hour."

She surreptitiously looked at her watch. It was eleven-thirty. They would only miss a few minutes of the football game.

He'd caught her movement. "Anxious to get to the game?" he asked, surprise in his voice.

Of course she was, because at the game she wouldn't be alone with him. But she couldn't tell him that. "I just wondered what time it was."

"Are you all right this morning?"

"I'm fine." Then she took a big bite of Belgian waffle.

"I hoped you'd like those. They seemed self-indulgent and I don't think you give in to temptation often."

"No, I don't." Except for last night. That had been rather self-indulgent. She'd wanted to know what sex was like, and she'd found out. Now she desperately wanted to do it again. But she couldn't. Nick was out of her league. She was certain they could never have a future together.

Letting herself fall into his arms once more would only lead to further heartbreak.

He served himself and sat down across from her. "Sarah, I'm glad you like your breakfast, but you're going to have to tell me what's wrong."

She looked up, ready to tell him nothing was wrong, but he stopped her. "Don't even try to lie. You're not very good at it."

Her response was only silence.

"Do you regret last night?"

"No! Yes! I mean—"

"What? What do you mean?"

"Nothing. I mean nothing. We did it, and there's nothing to say. We won't do it again, of course, but—"

"We won't?" His voice held surprise and laughter.

"No. I know I'm not your type."

"What if I say you are my type?"

"But I'm not."

"You don't think you'll like making love with me for the rest of your life? Having my babies? We'll raise our children in Rawhide with Gabe's and Jen's boys. And every once in a while, we'll take an exotic vacation."

He was smiling at her.

Sarah felt numb. Was this a proposal? Rather than deal with the enormity of his words, she blurted out, "I won't be able to simply take off on vacation."

"What are you talking about?"

"I'll have the responsibility of the store."

"No, you won't. We'll sell the store. After all, you won't need the money. I'm rich, remember."

Now she was mad and had no difficulty looking him in the eye. "You expect me to sell the store? To strangers?"

"It doesn't matter if you sell it to strangers or friends, as long as you don't have to mess with it anymore. I plan on keeping you busy." He chuckled, apparently picturing the future as he saw it.

''Did you know that my great-grandfather started that store at the turn of the century? It's been in my family more than a hundred years. But that doesn't matter to you. You think *you'll* toss it aside. Who made it your decision? What were you thinking? 'Sleep with her once and she'll bow down to me forever after'? You've got no control over my life, mister, and you can't make decisions for me!''

She stood and went to the window that looked out over Denver, staring at nothing, waiting in silence for Megan and Chad.

Nick was watching her. He cleared his throat. She didn't turn around. ''Look, honey, maybe I jumped a few stages. We'll talk things out. It hadn't occurred to me that you'd want to continue working. Most women are delighted when they don't have to hold down a job.''

''I'm not most women!''

''I know that. You're special. That's why I—''

''Don't even bother!'' she yelled. A knock on the door kept her from saying more. Still, she didn't move.

She heard Nick open the door, and Megan ask, ''Are we too early?''

Nick responded. ''Nope. I think breakfast is a lost cause. Maybe football will fit Sarah's mood better.''

Maybe it would. She certainly felt the need for a little violence.

CHAPTER TWENTY-FIVE

SARAH COULDN'T AVOID being alone with Nick in his car as they drove to the football game. Chad and Megan had taken his pickup to the stadium as they intended to leave for Wyoming right after the game.

Sarah would be facing a six-hour drive home with Nick. Just the two of them. How could she avoid conversation for that long? He seemed content to leave her alone now. Would she be so lucky on the way home?

"You think you'll be warm enough?" he asked as she slid on her jacket.

"Yes."

"I brought along a blanket."

She said nothing. Snuggling under a blanket with him would be far too close for comfort. She kept reminding herself their relationship had no future. She'd indulged herself last night. Today she needed to be strong and keep her distance.

At the stadium they joined Megan and Chad. Megan walked with Sarah while Chad and Nick discussed the Broncos' chances against Kansas City.

"Are you all right?" Megan asked softly.

Sarah nodded. She couldn't tell her what had happened last night.

"You seemed a little upset. Did you and Nick have a fight?"

She appreciated Megan's concern, really she did, but she didn't want to discuss her problem. She shrugged.

"Anything I can do?"

"Wanna trade places on the way home?" Sarah asked, managing a slight chuckle.

"I don't think Chad will go for that. We don't get to spend a lot of time together."

"I was just joking," Sarah assured her.

Once they found their seats, good ones, of course, Nick offered to spread the blanket over the four of them. As she was seated next to Nick, Sarah made a suggestion. "Why don't you move and sit next to Chad so you two guys can discuss football?"

But Nick wouldn't budge. "I like my seat just fine," he said with a wink.

Nick spread out the blanket and then put his arm around Sarah. She jumped up immediately. "I need to go to the ladies' room."

He stared at her. "Planning on beating the halftime rush?" There was more than a touch of sarcasm in his voice.

"Yes," she said calmly, already inching her way past Megan and Chad to the aisle.

In the rest room, she stood in front of the mirror a couple of minutes, wondering how she was going to get through the game. Then a young woman tapped her on the shoulder.

"Are you here with Nick McMillan?" she asked.

"No! I mean, uh, yes."

"Are you *sure* it's Nick? 'Cause there's someone who looks just like him around somewhere. I jumped into his arms and kissed him last time I saw him, only to discover it wasn't Nick at all."

"Was his name Gabe?"

"I think that was it. But it was Nick I wanted."

Sarah took a good look at the woman. She was definitely Nick's type. The woman wore a fur jacket over very tight pants and her jewelry looked very expensive. Her hair was long and blond. Her makeup was exquisite.

"So you're involved with Nick?" Sarah couldn't help but ask.

"I'm trying, honey, but he's not easy to catch."

"He's been out of town."

"Yes, and I can't even find out where."

"He's living in Rawhide, Wyoming."

"Where's that?"

"A couple of hours past Casper," Sarah responded, though the town's name didn't seem to ring a bell for the blonde.

"Is he going back there again?" the woman asked.

"As soon as the game's over."

"Damn! So how do you know Nick?"

"Uh...his brother just married my sister."

"Is his brother as rich as Nick?"

"No."

"So you're trying to catch Nick?"

"No. I'm not right for him. Not like you are."

The woman looked past Sarah into the mirror. "I am, aren't I?" she asked, pleased with herself.

"Do you want to come to Rawhide with us? We're driving back this afternoon. I have an empty bedroom. You could stay with me."

"Well, aren't you the sweetest thing!" The blonde giggled and then looked at Sarah again. "You're serious?"

"Yes, I am." Inside her, a little voice was calling her crazy, but she couldn't face the long drive with just her and Nick. "Um, I'm not sure how you'll get home."

"Oh, don't worry about that. Nick will take me if my plans work out. I'll go pack my bag and get back here before the game ends. Is that all right?"

"Yes, of course," Sarah agreed, thinking the lady wasn't quite sane, either. "Um, I'm Sarah Waggoner. What's your name?"

"Oh, I forgot," she said, giggling again. "I'm Brandy, my daddy's favorite drink."

"Ah, I see. Brandy what?"

"Brandy Williams."

"All right. Will you be able to get back into the stadium?"

"Sure. So, I'll see you in an hour."

"Fine."

Brandy sashayed out of the rest room and Sarah called herself all kinds of a fool. But she'd done it now. At least she wouldn't be riding alone all the way to Rawhide.

Megan entered the ladies' room. "Sarah, are you all right? You've been gone so long."

"Oh, I'm sorry, Megan. I didn't mean to worry anyone. I'm not really much of a football fan."

"Me, neither, but Chad was thrilled about the tickets. Come on, let's go buy some popcorn and hot chocolate before we go back and sit down."

It was halftime before they got back to their seats.

THE GAME WAS EXCITING ENOUGH that even Sarah got swept up into the action. So much so that she almost forgot her crazy plan. Then Brandy turned up at the end of the aisle as the game clock ran out and waved to them.

Chad and Megan looked at each other and then at Nick and Sarah.

Sarah waved back.

"Why are you waving at Brandy?" Nick asked, frowning.

"Uh, because I invited her to come back to Rawhide with us. I'm going to be lonely without Jennifer."

Megan's eyes widened. "And you just randomly chose *her* to come with you?"

"No. Brandy is a friend of Nick's. I said she could stay with me since I have an empty bedroom."

Nick stared at her, horror dawning in his eyes. "I don't believe this."

Sarah stiffened her back. "It's not like she'll be any trouble. I've got plenty of room."

"And how long is she going to stay?"

"I don't know."

"I'm going to have a word with Brandy," Nick said firmly, pushing past Sarah and the Randalls. When he reached the aisle, he pulled Brandy to the top of the stairs and into the passageway.

Megan looked at Sarah. "This is crazy, Sarah. What are you trying to do?"

"Avoid being alone with Nick. She said she was a friend of Nick's."

Chad said, "Yeah, I know what kind of friend she is. I hope you won't be sorry."

They folded up the blanket and Chad led the way up the stairs. They reached level ground just in time to see Brandy throw herself against Nick and kiss him.

Sarah turned away and prayed her hot chocolate would stay down.

"Thank you, lover," Brandy purred as she snuggled into Nick's body. She turned and saw them. "Nick said I could come. Isn't that nice? What's your name again?"

"Sarah."

"Right. You won't mind if I ride in the front seat, do you? I get carsick in the back."

"No. That will be fine."

Nick glared at her, but Sarah turned away. It was too late now to regret what she had done.

They all trudged quietly to their vehicles. Nick opened the trunk of his car and put Brandy's things in with theirs.

Chad stepped up beside Sarah. "Are you sure you want to do this?"

"It's too late, Chad. I already did it. I must have lost my mind."

"Well, it's certainly going to shake things up in Rawhide."

Sarah shrugged her shoulders. "I'm sure Brandy will reach her goal of getting Nick before too long. She's very pretty."

"Honey, I'd pick you over her any day of the week," Chad said. "Women like you and Megan are rare. That kind is a dime a dozen."

Sarah looked at Chad in surprise. "Thank you for the compliment, but she's very pretty and—and she's the kind of woman Nick needs."

"Poor Nick," Chad said with a grin. "See you in Rawhide."

Sarah told him goodbye and hugged Megan. Then she opened the back door and slid into the car.

Brandy, chatting eagerly with Nick, got in the front seat. Nick glared at Sarah, letting her know her actions hadn't pleased him at all.

By the end of the drive, Sarah thought she'd go nuts if she heard Brandy's giggle one more time. Nick may be upset with her, but she was going to suffer, too.

JENNIFER DIDN'T SPEAK TO GABE at all when he came in to dinner, though she kept up a pretty good conversation with Letty and Blackie. She even talked to Hazel, Blackie's fiancée, who'd joined them this evening.

"Gabe, you've hardly eaten anything," Letty said, looking at his plate. "Are you coming down with something?"

"No, Letty. I'm fine." He looked at Jen, but then away when he didn't see any sympathy in her gaze.

"If you say so," Letty replied. Then she turned to Jennifer. "Did you finish knitting that sleeve I taught you how to do today?"

"I did, Letty. It was so easy once you showed me. Thanks so much."

Hazel leaned forward. "I want to make something for the babies. Have you thought of names yet? I'd like to embroider their names on blankets."

"Oh, Hazel, that would be wonderful! I'm thinking about Robert and Ronald. What do you think?" she asked.

The ladies began giving their opinions and Gabe couldn't stand it. "Don't you think I should be consulted before anyone else?" he demanded in a roar that drowned out the ladies' soft voices.

Jennifer stared at him. Then she picked up her fork to continue eating. "Not particularly," she said calmly.

Everyone at the table suddenly looked at their plates, pretending everything was normal.

"These are my sons. They're going to be Randalls, aren't they?"

"Yes, I believe that's correct," Jennifer said.

"Then I should get a vote on what their names are."

"So, Gabe, what do you think about Robert and Ronald? We can call them Robbie and Ronnie while they're little and Rob and Ron when they're grown up."

He suddenly realized he hadn't given any thought to names for the babies. But then, even when he felt them kicking Jen, they didn't seem real to him. "That sounds fine," he said gruffly.

"Ah. Then Robert and Ronald will be their names, Hazel. Or you can just put Rob and Ron if it's too much to embroider."

Gabe felt like an idiot for having made a scene. But he'd wanted to have a say. "What about their middle names?"

"I haven't thought about that," Jen confessed.

"You could always use the traditional names for twins," Blackie suggested.

"What's that, Blackie?" Jennifer asked eagerly.

"Pete and Repeat," he said, grinning.

Everyone laughed, and then Jennifer said, "If we give them names with the same initial, their mail might be misdelivered the rest of their lives, so I don't think we should do that."

"True," Gabe agreed. "It's bad enough being a Randall in this town."

"We could name Robert, Robert Lee, for the southern general," Jen suggested.

"And name the other one Ronald Grant?" Gabe teased. "That way they'd always be fighting."

"Hmm, maybe not."

"What about movie stars?" Letty suggested. "Name them after your favorite ones."

"Oh, like Robert Brad and Ronald Tom?"

"My father's name was Robert. Did you know that?" Gabe asked Jen.

"You mentioned it once," she replied.

He stared at her. It touched him that she'd name one of the boys after his father. "His middle name was George."

"We could give that middle name to Ronnie so he'd have a name from his grandfather, too."

"Yeah, I like that."

Letty said, "What was your father's name, Jen?"

"James Lucas Waggoner."

"So, do you like Robert James or Robert Lucas?" Gabe asked.

"I think Robert James sounds very distinguished." Jennifer smiled, looking pleased.

"Okay, we've decided," Gabe said. "Robert James and Ronald George. R.J. and R.G."

"Maybe I'd better write them down so I'll get it right when they ask me at the hospital. I might be too drugged-out otherwise."

Gabe frowned. "They'll give you drugs?"

"You think I want to go through natural childbirth? You'd hear me screaming all the way from town," Jennifer told him. "I'm not that brave."

"Lordy, no," Hazel suddenly said. "No point in suffering unless it's necessary."

"Is it very painful?" Gabe asked, concern coloring his words.

The three ladies looked at one another and burst into laughter.

"Now," Letty said, "we know why God chose women to have the babies."

CHAPTER TWENTY-SIX

SARAH GOT UP AT HER USUAL time the next morning. Partly because she was uncomfortable. She'd forgotten there was no bed in Jennifer's room. So she'd given Brandy her room for the night and slept on the sofa.

She gave herself a lecture over a bowl of oatmeal. Then she mixed up some muffins for Brandy's breakfast and put on a pot of coffee. Come to think of it, she could use some caffeine, too. Between gulps of coffee, she set the table for Brandy, put the muffins on the cabinet in a plastic container and left a note on top. It was almost like taking care of Jennifer before she changed.

If things went all right, she intended to visit Jennifer at lunch. She called Letty to ask if that was possible.

"Of course, child. Jen will be glad to see you. In fact, you can ride with Bill Wilson. He's coming for lunch today, too."

"He is? Uh, Letty, I might have to bring a friend who's visiting me. I'm sorry."

"No problem. We'll have plenty. See you at lunch."

Then she called Bill Wilson to ask for a ride.

Still no sign of Brandy.

She went downstairs to find Jeff. She wanted to know how the weekend had gone. If he was upset about being left alone, she might have to cancel her lunch plans. She smiled. For most of her life she'd been tied to the store. Now it seemed hard to work it in to her schedule.

Jeff was enthusiastic. He'd had a good Saturday, and

Sarah was pleased with the amount of sales. He also had several ideas that would improve the store's efficiency. Plus, he had a report on the two teenagers.

"Impressive, Jeff. Will you mind if I go see Jennifer for lunch? We're not leaving until noon, so I can make you a sandwich before I go."

"I'll be fine, but I'd appreciate the sandwich. Uh, Sarah, you said 'we.' Why?"

"Oh. I—I have a guest. Brandy is staying with me."

"Brandy?"

"Yes. She's a friend of Nick's."

"Oh. I guess that's why he's here so early," Jeff said, looking at the front door.

Sarah sighed. Nick didn't look any happier this morning than he had last night. But then, he hadn't had to spend the night on the sofa.

She chided herself. After all, that was her fault, not his.

"I'll let him in. In fact, it's a quarter to nine. We might as well open up."

"Sure. Fine with me."

She let Nick in and he immediately dipped his head and brushed her lips with his.

"Nick! What will Jeff think?"

"You're worried about him? That reminds me. I need to talk to him about his girlfriend."

"Nick, I didn't say she was his girlfriend!"

He smiled in return. "I know. By the way, where's Brandy this morning? I was hoping you'd invite me up for breakfast."

Sarah turned away so he couldn't read her expression. He couldn't wait to see Brandy. That's why he was here so early.

"You can have breakfast with her. I left muffins and coffee ready upstairs."

"So she's not up yet?"

She shook her head. With her back to him, she didn't

see him move. Suddenly he was in front of her, catching
her chin in his fingers. Then his lips covered hers, his arms
encircled her, and she was lost in the emotions that filled
her.

Jeff cleared his throat.

Sarah jerked her lips from his and tried to push Nick's
arms away. He wouldn't let her go. "Good morning, Jeff.
I need to talk to you."

"Nick, turn me loose," Sarah pleaded.

"This lady you know in Buffalo, the legal secretary.
Would she be interested in a job here in Rawhide?"

Jeff's eyes lit up. "I would be, but I'm not sure about
her. She works for a couple of lawyers and really likes the
firm."

"Same job, only it would be one lawyer right now. Me."

"I didn't know you're a lawyer. Are you going to open
an office in town?"

"Yeah, right across the street."

"Hey, super."

"Ask your friend to come down next weekend. I'm sure
Sarah could put her up for the weekend and we could work
things out." He smiled at Jeff, then brought his gaze back
to Sarah, whom he was still holding close. "Okay with you,
sweetheart?"

"*Now* will you turn me loose?" she asked, pretending
irritation, telling herself she must. "And I don't have room
for—"

He stopped her words with a kiss, this time a teasing,
brisk kiss. "Sure I'll let go, if you really want me to. And
we'll work something out for Susan."

Before she could answer, a sleepy voice called from
above. "Sarah?"

Over Nick's shoulder, she saw Brandy staring at them.
This time she didn't hesitate to wrench herself from
Nick's grasp. "Morning, Brandy. Did you see my note

about breakfast? Nick came over to join you.'' And she
shoved Nick toward the stairs.

He amiably strolled in Brandy's direction, but he gave
Sarah a wicked look over his shoulder. "See you later,
honey."

She glared at him.

Brandy pouted at the top of the stairs. As soon as Nick
got within reach of her, she pulled him to her and planted
her lips on him for a death-defying kiss.

Behind her, Jeff murmured, ''That lady knows how to
do mouth-to-mouth like a pro.''

His words broke Sarah from the grip of jealousy. She
turned around and began straightening already-straight
items on the shelf.

"I gather lots happened this weekend," Jeff said.

Sarah ignored him. Fortunately, the doorbell jingled as
two ladies arrived to do their shopping.

All morning, Sarah was distracted, waiting for Nick to
come down. All she could think about was Nick and
Brandy, in *her* apartment. It was driving her crazy. She
finally said something to Jeff about Nick staying so long.

"Oh, he left just a few minutes after he went up, while
you were waiting on that lady in the blue dress who wanted
something from the back. He waved. I guess I should've
mentioned it."

Sarah wanted to scream at him, but instead, she said,
"No, it's all right. I just wondered."

Jeff grinned at her. "Yeah, I bet you did."

"I'd better go up and tell Brandy about our lunch date."

"Will there be any cowboys there?" Brandy asked when
Sarah explained about going to Gabe's ranch.

"I—I suppose so. I don't know if they'll be joining us
for lunch."

"How much time do I have?"

"About an hour."

"Then I've got to get moving." Brandy turned into a whirlwind of activity.

Sarah left her bedroom, reminding herself that she needed to make other arrangements other than sleeping on the couch. Or maybe Brandy's surliness meant she'd be going home right away.

When Bill Wilson came to the store, Sarah was more than ready to leave. She liked Bill. He was a sweet man, kind and patient. He'd moved to Rawhide after his son had come here as a temporary doctor. But Jon found Victoria and married her, and Bill had joined him soon after. Now they were part of the fabric of everyday life in Rawhide. Jon was now the town's doctor and Bill worked for Tori, his daughter-in-law, as an accountant.

"Ready to go?" Bill asked.

"Yes, but I have to see if Brandy is. I won't take a minute."

"No problem. I'm not working today, so we can take our time."

Sarah smiled, but she hurried up the stairs. She hated keeping people waiting. She found Brandy in her bedroom, sitting in front of the dresser mirror. "Where do you put on your makeup, Sarah? I need more space."

She had covered the top of the dresser with jars and bottles. And in Sarah's mind, she had most of the contents on her face. Sarah thought she was pretty without all of it. When Brandy turned around to look at Sarah, she thought she'd ruined the natural beauty.

"Brandy, we have to go right now. Bill is downstairs waiting on us."

"Well, I need a little more time. I need to curl my hair and style it."

"I'm sorry, but we don't have that much time. You can pull it back in a ponytail or I can braid it for you."

Brandy looked at her as if she didn't comprehend what Sarah had said. "I'll be finished in fifteen minutes."

"I'm not going to ask Bill to stand around that long. Nor am I going to delay our arrival when Letty is expecting us." For her friends, Sarah could be firm.

"Well, fine, you can braid my hair. But I want it French-braided, not plain like yours."

Sarah said nothing. But she could French-braid almost as fast because she'd done Jen's hair that way. In two minutes, she was fastening the end of the braid. "Okay, let's go."

"But I think you need to start over. It doesn't feel tight enough," Brandy complained.

Sarah said nothing and kept on going. When she heard footsteps behind her, she grinned. She'd learned a lot during Jen's teenage years.

"Bill, this is Brandy Williams. Brandy, Bill works with my friend Tori Wilson and her cousin Russ. He's also the doctor's father."

Bill nodded in his friendly fashion. Brandy stared at him. "Is your son married?"

Bill seemed surprised by her question. "Yes, he is. He's married to Tori."

Brandy sighed. "Oh." She followed Bill and Sarah out to his sedan. Then she took the front seat, as she had with Nick. Bill opened the back door for Sarah. "I guess you two can trade places when we come back."

Brandy sniffed her disdain and Sarah shrugged her shoulders, grinning. It didn't matter to her.

When they got to the ranch, Sarah jumped out of the car before Bill and Brandy had moved, running toward the ranch house. Jen flung open the door and embraced her sister.

"Oh, Sarah, I've missed you so much. How did things go in Denver?" Jen asked.

Sarah had a lot to tell her sister, but not in public. "Fine. We separated all the furniture. Oh, you know Bill, and here's Brandy Williams. She's an old friend of Nick's. I asked her to come visit.''

Jennifer looked at Brandy and then looked again at her sister.

Sarah tried to look pleased that she had Brandy as a visitor. As she'd reminded herself already today a dozen times, it was her own fault.

"How nice to meet you," Jen said.

Brandy nodded, looking around. "Where are the cowboys?''

"They're out working," Jen assured her. "Gabe doesn't come in for lunch.''

"He did today," Letty said as she arrived to be introduced.

"He did?'' Jen said, surprise on her face.

"He must've heard I was coming," Brandy said, patting her braid to be sure every hair was in place.

"You know Gabe?'' Jennifer asked, her eyes widening in surprise.

"Oh, yes, I kissed him because I thought he was Nick. He's a great kisser.'' Brandy seemed a lot happier with a man around. Not that Bill wasn't a man, but Sarah knew he didn't appeal to Brandy.

In fact, he seemed to appeal a lot to Letty. They were holding hands. Jennifer, however, didn't appear too happy.

"Gabe is my husband," Jen said icily.

Sarah hoped she didn't have to referee a fight between Jen and Brandy.

The sound of a car approaching caught everyone's attention.

"Oh, there's Nick. He wanted to join us. And there's Gabe coming from the barn. Looks like we're ready to eat. Come on in, everyone.'' Letty had the table set and she directed each of them to a specific place.

Sarah was grateful that Gabe was beside Jennifer and on

the opposite side of the table from Brandy. But she didn't like her seat beside Nick.

"Do you mind if I sit by Jen, Letty? We have a lot to talk about. You don't mind switching, do you, Bill?"

Bill shook his head, and Sarah hurried around the table to take the seat on Letty's left.

Since that left Bill still beside Letty, Sarah decided the seating arrangement was now perfect. Nick glared at her from across the table.

Much to Sarah's surprise, Brandy made a play for Gabe. Sarah had felt sure she'd be cozying up to Nick. Instead, she ignored him. It was obvious things weren't going well between Jen and Gabe, but it still seemed to bother Jen that another woman was flirting with her husband.

"Don't worry, Jen," Sarah whispered. "She'll be gone in a few days."

"Not if Gabe has anything to say about it. Look at him. He can't look away from her."

"It would be rude to ignore a guest," Sarah returned. It was the best she could come up with as an excuse for Gabe's behavior. He was staring at Brandy.

"Oh, Gabe, while I'm here, could you teach me to ride a horse?" Brandy asked, batting her lashes at him.

"Sorry, Brandy, but it's a real busy time of the year. We have to check the herd, make sure all the cows are ready for the winter. Sick or weak cows don't make it through one of our winters."

"You'd rather play with cows than with me?" she asked, batting her lashes so fast it was a wonder she didn't stir up a strong wind.

Nick jumped into the conversation. Sarah hoped it was his good nature and not the desperate look on her face. "Gabe doesn't have any horses gentle enough for a beginner, Brandy. I'll take you out to the Randalls' spread. They have an indoor arena we can use."

"Could you come with us, Gabe?" Brandy asked.

"'Fraid not. I have a lot to do here."

Sarah was grateful that Gabe turned her down. She could feel the tension rolling off her sister. "How are the babies, Jen? Oh, Brandy, I don't think I told you my sister's having twins."

Brandy shuddered. "I don't intend to get pregnant. It ruins your figure." She stretched a little to emphasize her slenderness and looked at Jen in a falsely sympathetic manner.

Letty protested. "But surely you and your husband would want children."

"Who cares what he wants. He doesn't have to get fat!"

All the men at the table were staring at Brandy. She responded with, "What? What's the matter?"

"I'm just glad my wife didn't feel that way," Gabe said quietly, smiling at Jen.

Jennifer relaxed slightly and returned Gabe's smile.

Sarah relaxed a little, too, taking a bite of her lunch, when Nick asked, "You don't feel like Brandy, do you, Sarah?"

"No, not at all," Sarah said, deliberately misunderstanding Nick. "I'm delighted that I'm going to have nephews." She smiled brightly at Gabe and Jennifer and ignored everyone else at the table.

"By the way, has Blackie and Hazel's new home arrived yet?" Sarah asked, deliberately changing the subject.

Gabe said it was coming tomorrow. Sarah asked Blackie if he was excited.

"Mercy, yes. Hazel won't marry me until I have a place for her. She said if she moved in here, there'd be too many women in the kitchen."

"I've often wondered," Letty said, "how they manage over at the Randalls'."

"I think it's because Red is in charge. Everyone else just helps out," Sarah said. "Are you two managing all right?"

"Oh, yes," Jennifer answered, a big smile on her face.

"Letty's in charge. But she's teaching me so much. I didn't cook today's lunch, but I helped. Sometime I'll have you to lunch, Sarah, and cook it all myself. You'll be surprised."

"I bet I will," Sarah agreed. "You really learn quickly, though, Jen. Which reminds me, how's the knitting going?"

Letty raved about how well Jennifer was doing and Jen brought Sarah up-to-date on the baby name situation.

Brandy seemed bored with all the homey con· ·rsation. She tried to talk to Nick, but Sarah noticed he ignored her. So she turned to Gabe.

"What do you do for entertainment around here?"

"We watch a lot of movies, television, things like that."

"Want to come to Sarah's apartment and watch a sexy movie with me?" she asked, leaning toward him in her scoop-necked blouse.

Jennifer stiffened and dropped out of the conversation with Letty and Sarah, watching Gabe for his reaction.

"Thanks, but I usually watch those movies with Jennifer."

His easy manner saved any embarrassment.

"Then what else is there to do? I want to meet some *real* cowboys," she said, implying, of course, that there weren't any here.

"Brandy," Sarah warned in a low voice.

Nick, however, had the answer. "I understand they go to the steak house down the street from the store that has a bar and a jukebox. On weekends, they bring in a live band."

"Well, that sounds promising! Do you dance, Gabe?"

"Not without *me!*" Jennifer exploded. "That's what these mean," she said angrily as she showed Brandy her wedding rings. "Go find some unmarried man to play with!"

CHAPTER TWENTY-SEVEN

NICK BREATHED A SIGH of relief when Jennifer put Brandy in her place. He'd been afraid he'd have to intervene for Gabe's sake.

Yesterday, he'd agreed that Brandy could come. She was determined, and he couldn't help hoping that she might make Sarah a little jealous. However, he'd already given up that idea when he got out of bed this morning. He'd had a frank talk with Brandy while he helped himself to coffee and muffins, letting her know that he was absolutely not interested in her.

When he got back to his place, he'd called Letty to be sure everything was all right on the ranch since he'd been gone. He knew that was Gabe's business, but he felt responsible, too. That was how he learned that Sarah and Brandy were going out to the ranch for lunch.

Letty told him she'd called Gabe and he was coming in to join them. Nick decided he couldn't leave the poor man to the woman's clutches. Good thing, too.

When they got ready to leave, he tried to get Sarah to ride with him. Brandy volunteered and Sarah went with Bill. Nick sent Brandy with them, too, because he decided to visit with Gabe a few minutes.

He caught up with Gabe on the way to the barn.

"Everything okay?"

"I guess so, since Jen derailed Miss Brandy," Gabe said with a grin.

"Jen was a little blunt, wasn't she?" Nick said, but he was grinning, too. "Must tell you something."

"Yeah. She doesn't share well. She's always been that way."

"Oh, come on, Gabe. The lady loves you."

Gabe shrugged his shoulders, but said nothing.

"You two aren't getting along any better?"

Gabe suddenly said, "She's naming the boys after our dad."

"She is?"

"Since Dad's name was Robert George, we're naming the twins Robert James and Ronald George."

"Nice."

"Yeah," Gabe said, satisfaction in his voice. "James is for Jennifer's dad."

"Did you go to the doctor with Jen this morning?"

"Yeah, the babies are fine. Getting bigger every day. Jen complains about getting fat, but I think she looks cute like that," he added with a grin.

"Did you tell her that?"

"No. I have to be careful."

"What do you mean?"

"The minute I compliment her, or get too friendly, she thinks it means I love her. Then I get into trouble."

"What kind of trouble?" Nick asked, expecting Gabe to tell him they would argue.

"We—we made love. But afterward I told her it didn't mean that I loved her, because I still couldn't trust her."

"I bet she didn't take that well." Nick knew he was understating the case.

"No. That's what I mean. I get into trouble."

"Yeah. But you do love her, Gabe."

"I know. But I can't tell her 'cause she'd take advantage of me."

"How? Ask you to buy her diamonds? Fur coats? Like my mom?"

"I don't know! I guess I don't understand women."

Nick grinned.

"Don't give me such a superior look. You don't seem to be making any progress, either," Gabe said.

"I made some progress. But Sarah backtracked."

"What does that mean?"

"I made love to her. It was perfect. Then, the next day, she invited Brandy to come home with her."

"How did she meet Brandy?"

"At the football game. Brandy followed her into the bathroom and talked to her there, telling her some sob story, I guess. The next thing I knew, Brandy showed up at the end of the game with her bags packed, saying Sarah invited her to come to Rawhide."

"So we're both in trouble. I guess we are kin."

"Yeah. Know of anyone who can help us?"

Gabe grinned. "The Randalls are famous for their matchmaking. We could give them a visit."

Nick rubbed his eyebrow. "They'd be out working. We'd have to wait until tonight."

Gabe whipped his cell phone out of his pocket and dialed a number by memory. "Red? Are the guys out working? Yeah. Okay, thanks, Red."

"Well?" Nick asked.

Gabe held up his forefinger to ask him to wait a minute and dialed another number. "Jake? Nick and I need to talk to you. Red said you were close to my property. Can we come over? Great! We'll see you in half an hour."

Nick turned around. "Come on. I'll drive."

"No, Nick. We have to go by horseback."

"Whoa! I can't ride. I told you that."

"You also said you were my brother. If that's true, then you can ride. Come on."

With a groan, Nick followed.

SARAH EXPECTED TO HEAR from Nick after lunch. Brandy sulked upstairs until she started getting ready to go to the steak house that evening. Sarah thought Nick would accompany them. She wanted him to in case there was trouble. She couldn't imagine mixing Brandy with anyone from around here and there not being trouble.

Finally, near five o'clock, she called him on his cell phone. When he answered, he sounded strange. "Nick, are you okay?"

"Yeah, fine. What do you need?"

His gruff tone surprised her. "Sorry if I bothered you," she said. "I'll let you go."

"No, Sarah. I didn't mean to sound so abrupt. I'm on a horse and not too comfortable."

"You're horseback riding?" she asked.

"I'm not sure Gabe would call it that, but I'm definitely on the back of a very wide horse."

She chuckled. "A little sore?"

"A lot sore, and Gabe assures me it will get worse before it gets better."

"He's right."

"So what did you need?"

"Thanks to you, Brandy is insisting on going to the steak house tonight. I thought you might want to join us."

"I don't think I'll be able to walk, much less dance."

"You're right. I'll get Jeff to go with us."

Nick groaned. "Let me talk to him."

"Why?"

"I need to warn him about some things."

"But I haven't asked him yet."

"Good. I'll ask him as a favor. That will be better."

Sarah wasn't sure why that would be true. After a moment, she called over to Jeff. "Can you come talk to Nick? He wants to ask a favor."

Jeff looked surprised, but he came over and took the phone. A last-minute shopper came into the store and Sarah went over to help her, trying to keep her eye on Jeff at the same time.

After Sarah made the sale, she followed the customer to the door and locked up, changing the Open sign to Closed. Then she came back to Jeff's side.

"No problem, Nick. Right, I understand."

Then he handed the phone to Sarah.

"We've reached the barn, Sarah. I'm going to get off this moving torture chamber. I'll talk to you tomorrow."

"Nick, ask for Gabe's bottle of liniment. Pour it into the bathtub with hot water and soak for an hour or so. It will make a difference."

"Thanks, honey. Want to come soak with me?"

The offer was so tempting, it took a moment to remember she couldn't. "Uh, no, thanks."

She hung up the phone and turned to Jeff. "Are you coming out with us tonight?"

"Sure. Nick explained."

"*What* did Nick explain?"

"That I was to entertain Brandy and keep her out of trouble. And he said not to worry about dancing with you. You'd understand as long as Brandy didn't cause a problem."

Sarah sighed in relief. "That's the truth. You should have seen her at lunch. She tried to get Gabe out for the evening right in front of Jen's nose."

"What happened?"

"My little sister gave as good as she got. Better, actually. Brandy sulked until it was time to go."

"Good for Jennifer."

"Yes," Sarah said with satisfaction. "I thought I would have to rescue Jen, but she took care of herself."

"Nick also warned me not to fall for Brandy. He didn't have to worry. I know gold diggers when I see them. Not that I have anything she wants, but I recognize the signs."

"But she told me…" Sarah stopped to think. "I thought she was in love with Nick. She said she'd been after him a long time. It didn't occur to me— Oh, dear. I made a big mistake asking her to come."

"*You* asked her? I thought maybe Nick did."

"No. I insisted."

Jeff shook his head in amazement. "Yeah, that was a mistake."

Sarah couldn't agree more. Not that she'd changed her mind about her and Nick. He wouldn't be happy with her. But he'd need to find someone like Brandy, only with a heart. She wanted Nick to be happy. He'd move away, of course, because Rawhide wasn't the right place for him, and Gabe and Jennifer would see him occasionally, but she wouldn't. She'd be busy whenever he came to town. She just had to be strong a little longer.

GABE PUT AWAY THE HORSES he and Nick had ridden over to the Randalls. Molly, Nick's mount, was slow and plodding, but safe. It had certainly given them time to talk. Nick had thought he was an expert on women. Maybe women like Brandy. But he didn't know anything about Sarah. Even Gabe knew more than Nick about Sarah.

He just didn't understand Jen.

When they'd finally gotten to the pasture the Randalls were in, they'd all compared notes. Finally, the Randall men confessed that it was the women who were good about this matchmaking thing, not them.

Gabe couldn't hold back a grin about that. He'd never seen the four older men so embarrassed. But they promised to have a meeting with their wives and see what they could come up with.

Gabe hoped they helped Nick. He wanted his brother to settle down in Rawhide with a good woman, be happy. And Sarah certainly fit the bill. He'd thought Jennifer didn't. But she was knitting and cooking. He'd even caught her sweeping the kitchen floor and doing the dishes.

She and Letty got on like a house on fire. He was beginning to wonder if he really knew her. But it had felt like he knew her when he'd made love to her. It had felt so right, the two of them together.

But he didn't know how to move ahead with their relationship. He'd proposed a marriage of convenience, how was he supposed to change the rules?

So he'd tried to stress Nick's romance to the Randalls. Not his. He just wasn't sure what to do about Jen.

"Is that you, Gabe?" Letty called as he came into the mudroom.

"Yeah, Letty. Is supper about ready?"

He'd hung around the barn until almost six, timing his entrance with suppertime.

"Sure is. Jennifer made us spaghetti."

Gabe came to a halt. Maybe he should go into town. He wouldn't be satisfied with a little bit of spaghetti. Jen didn't know how to cook for a hardworking man. It wasn't her fault. There had only been her and Sarah. But he was tired. Maybe he'd just come out and raid the fridge after she went to bed so he wouldn't hurt her feelings.

"That's nice," he said, coming into the kitchen. Since Jen was putting something on the table, he was glad he'd used tact.

"Gabe, would you please put the spaghetti on the table? I'm afraid it will be too heavy for me." Jen stood there, all innocent-like, waiting for his answer.

"Sure," he agreed, though he thought she was being a little too cautious. A little pan of spaghetti—

He turned toward the stove to discover a deep roasting pan sitting there, a lid on it. "This one?" he asked in surprise. "Do you want to keep the lid on it?"

Blackie came in just then, so Letty told him to leave the lid on the stove. He lifted it off and realized the entire pan was filled with golden spaghetti topped with a thick, fragrant sauce and a lot of meatballs.

He realized Jen had made enough for twice as many people. "Is someone else coming to dinner?"

"No, it's just us," Jen said. "If there are leftovers, we can heat them up for lunch one day...if you like it."

When he set the pan on the table, he noticed a big bowl of green beans and a tossed salad. He was getting hungrier by the minute.

"Jen fixed dinner so I could spend more time with Bill. It was so sweet and thoughtful of her," Letty informed him. "We went for a walk."

"That was nice of you, Jen. Did you take your nap?"

Her cheeks flushed. "No. But I promised Letty I'd go to bed early tonight."

Gabe took a closer look at his bride. He saw dark circles under her eyes and he thought she looked pale. Beautiful but pale. "That would probably be a good idea. I'll help Letty clean up tonight."

Letty praised him for his offer, but Jen looked unsure. "I won't break anything, Jen, I promise."

She nodded and quickly turned away. Why? Was she crying?

Apparently not. She returned to the table and they all joined hands for the prayer.

Since Jen was opposite him this evening, he didn't get to hold her small hand in his. But he wished he could. "Well, shall I serve the spaghetti instead of passing it around? It's heavy." Everyone agreed. Jen told him no more than two meatballs for her. When he got to his own plate, he piled on the spaghetti and got four meatballs. He'd barely left room for the salad and beans.

"Oh, my goodness, I almost forgot the bread," Letty exclaimed. She opened the oven door and brought out two long loaves of garlic bread. "We got these in town the other day. Jen said they go well with the spaghetti."

Half an hour later, Gabe had eaten so much he almost needed to unbutton his jeans. He hadn't made such a pig of himself in a long time. "Jen, that was a wonderful meal."

Blackie agreed. "I guess we'll work a lot tomorrow, since we carbed tonight," he added with a grin. "That's what the athletes call it, isn't it?"

"Something like that," Gabe agreed. "Maybe we should be sure and have this meal the night before we move the herds up to high country. We wouldn't have to eat until we got back home."

"Speak for yourself, boy," Blackie said. "I like to hit the table a little more often than that." He chuckled and added, "Besides, I saved room for dessert."

Gabe looked up in consternation. "Dessert? I can't eat any dessert."

"You don't have to, Gabe," Jen said as she went to the counter and slid a cake pan with a metal lid decorated with flowers toward her. She took the lid off and set a beautiful chocolate cake in the center of the table.

He groaned. "How about I save my dessert until bedtime?" he asked.

"Of course. Whenever you want it. Letty can cut you a piece."

"*I* can cut me a piece."

He'd growled a little too much, he realized. "I didn't mean—"

Letty, however, said, "You sure can, as long as you don't leave a mess in my kitchen to greet me the next morning."

He promised her he wouldn't. Then he thanked Jen again for the delicious meal.

She smiled, but she still looked tired.

"How about if I walk you to bed now, so you can get your sleep."

"Not necessary," she said. "Like you, I can do it myself."

He knew she could, but he wanted to help her. It would be even sweeter than the cake. But tonight, he guessed he'd have to settle for cake.

CHAPTER TWENTY-EIGHT

SARAH PEEKED AT HER WATCH. It was only seven-thirty. They'd come to the steak house at six. There'd been a few people eating, but they'd cleared out by now.

There were a couple of guys in a back booth who didn't look like they wanted to be bothered. Brandy had complained all evening.

"This is the hot place in town? What a joke. In Denver, there are always some guys waiting to pick up a girl." She frowned at Jeff. "All right, let's dance. You're my only choice, right?"

Sarah protested Brandy's rudeness, but Jeff got up and held out his hand.

They went to the jukebox to choose their music.

As soon as they'd moved away from Sarah, she relaxed. She was glad to get some time without Brandy. Then some more men came in. They looked like cowboys to Sarah, so she hoped Brandy would be pleased.

But one of them immediately came over to Sarah.

"Sarah? Is that you? What are you doing here on a week-night?" the man asked.

Sarah recognized him as someone she'd gone to school with. "Hank, how are you?"

"I'm fine, but not as fine as you."

"Oh, Hank! You always were a flirt," she said with a smile.

"Yeah, but you never gave me a chance. Have you married some lucky guy?"

"No, I haven't. But—" She stopped suddenly, shocked by what she'd intended to say. That she was off the market because she'd fallen for someone. That was ridiculous. She'd get over Nick. Of course she would.

"Come dance with me."

"All right." Why not? Hank was handsome, a good guy. He'd gone to college and had a good job in Casper.

He wrapped his strong arms around her, and she had to fight to keep from pulling away. They weren't Nick's arms.

She danced several times with Hank, talking occasionally, while Brandy went through all the men in the place. Jeff seemed happy to sit and watch.

Finally, Hank said, "It's no good, is it? Who's the lucky guy?"

"What are you talking about?" she asked, staring at him.

"Honey, I may not be the world's smartest man, but I know when a woman has no interest in me."

She blushed but shook her head. "Really, Hank, it's not that."

"Don't throw my ego for a loop by telling me I've gotten ugly since I last looked in a mirror."

No, she couldn't do that. "I did meet—that is, I feel—it won't work out. It will just take me a while to get over him, that's all."

"Any way I can help?"

"No, thank you. Maybe you should try your charms with Brandy."

He snorted. "Maybe I should go eat my steak. I don't waste time on ladies like her."

Sarah thanked him for the dances and walked to her table. Why did every man recognize what kind of woman Brandy was, but she hadn't been able to see it?

"Through dancing?" Jeff asked.

"Yes. I'm a little tired."

"Good. I was wondering if I should've interrupted your evening. Nick asked me to keep an eye on you."

Sarah stiffened. "I'm sure he didn't mean for you to do any such thing."

"And I'm sure he did. But no harm done, right?" He watched her closely.

With a sigh, she said, "No harm done."

And she thought that was true until two men started yelling from the middle of the dance floor. Brandy stood between them, a pleased smile on her lips.

JENNIFER STILL FELT TIRED the next morning. But she got up from the breakfast table to put on the athletic shoes she wore for her walks. "Can you go with me, Letty?"

"Oh, child, I know I should, but I need to bake another cake. The Browns were in a car accident. I need to run to the hospital and see them. Then I'll take the cake by their house. Her sister is looking after the kids. Will you be all right on your own?"

"Of course I'll be all right. The cake will cheer everyone up."

"That's true. Now, you be careful out there. Don't hurry."

"No, I won't."

Jen started out a few minutes later. She slowly walked toward the lake. It was her favorite place to walk. Gabe had even built a bench under the tree so she and Letty could rest when they reached the lake. Today, she'd sit for a while, daydreaming about when the babies were born.

She hadn't worked up her nerve to ask Gabe to come into the delivery room with her. She needed his strength, his courage, to help her through the birth. Would he believe her? After all, he'd said he didn't trust her.

How did one prove herself to a man who was determined not to believe her? She didn't know how she could change his mind.

She reached the bench and sank onto the smooth wood. Gabe frequently did little things like building the bench for her. She wanted to believe it was because he loved her. She loved him so much. But if she showed even a little appreciation, he ran away.

She heard some movement and looked around the tree. There was Gabe, in the next pasture, working on the fence. He was so big and strong, a picture of the perfect man. Any woman would want him. Brandy certainly had.

She grew incensed even thinking about that woman's behavior. She'd figured Gabe would be mad about her own behavior, but he didn't seem to mind. She smiled as she recalled his rebuff of all Brandy's suggestions. He'd kept to his agreement to act as if their marriage was real in front of other people.

She looked back at him, working away without knowing she was watching him. Out of the corner of her eye, she caught more movement. She stared as the object grew larger.

It was a bull.

Black Thunder! She'd hear Blackie and Gabe calling him that. He was running toward Gabe, who was wearing a red shirt with his red scarf. The bull was charging him. He was going to kill him.

Jennifer screamed as she leaped to her feet, but Gabe didn't hear her. With a deep breath, she began running toward her husband, determined to save him from the raging bull.

GABE WAS DEEP IN THOUGHT. He'd felt bad all last night about Jen doing so much work for him. And he'd said as much to Letty.

"It's your fault, Gabe," she'd replied.

"What do you mean?"

"She's so anxious to please you, she'd do most anything if she thought you'd like it." Letty had shaken her head. "She loves you so much it's sad."

"She doesn't! She just wants her way!" Gabe had protested.

"And what way is that?"

"She wants me to admit that I'm in love with her."

"Well, aren't you? It's the truth, isn't it? You two might as well be in the fun house, staring into mirrors. It's not doing anyone any good. You could be happy if you'd just admit the truth!" Then she'd gone to bed, leaving him sitting at the kitchen table. But he'd lost interest in the cake.

Now he was wondering if Letty was right. Was he being stubborn for no reason? Jen was his wife, and she'd be his wife for the rest of his life if he had a choice. But how did she feel?

He heard something—it sounded like a scream. He looked up and saw Jen flying at him across the uneven ground, waving her arms as if to warn him about something happening behind him. He turned to see Black Thunder running toward him. Why would Jen be worried about that docile old bull? Damn, he was wearing red. Jen thought that stupid bull would hurt him.

"No! No, Jen, it's all right," he yelled as he jumped the fence, running toward her. Then, before he could cover the ground between them, something tripped her and she hit the ground hard and didn't move.

"Jen! Jen!" he said, gasping, his breathing rapid as he gathered her into his arms. She didn't open her eyes, but she moaned slightly, letting him know she was still alive.

He stood, lifting her into his arms. Then he struggled up the hill as fast as he could. He remembered that Letty had mentioned going to town this morning, so she wouldn't be home.

He had to get Jen to Jon as soon as possible. When he reached the top of the hill, he changed direction and headed for his truck parked by the barn. As soon as he lay Jen on the seat, he crawled behind the wheel, praying as hard as he could that Jen and the babies would be all right.

As soon as he got the truck pointed down the long driveway, he pulled out his cell phone and dialed the clinic's number. He'd memorized it after Jen had come to live with him.

"Doctor's office," a bright, chirpy voice said.

Gabe's voice was hard. "It's Gabe Randall. Tell Jon I'm bringing my wife, Jen, in. She fell and is unconscious." He dropped the phone and didn't bother looking for it. He reached out to put an arm around Jen.

When he arrived at the clinic, fortunately without hitting anything, he was greatly relieved when Jon and several nurses came out with a rolling bed.

"Gabe, what happened?" Jon asked, wasting no time.

"She thought I was in trouble and she was running to warn me! She tripped and went down hard. She hasn't come to yet."

He thought he was under control, but as they put Jennifer on the bed, his vision blurred. He almost panicked again until he realized tears he didn't know he was shedding had impaired his vision. He wiped his face and ran alongside the bed, holding Jen's hand.

"Why doesn't she wake up?" he cried, stepping away so they could get her through the door.

"I don't know, Gabe." Jon followed the bed, and Gabe followed him, anxious to at least touch Jen again. The funeral he'd attended of Abby, Russ's wife, suddenly passed through his mind. "God, no, don't let her die!" he whispered.

"Gabe, we're going to do all we can for her. You stay out here and get hold of her sister. Can you do that?"

"Yes, I can do that," Gabe said, glad to have something to do. Then he remembered he'd dropped his cell phone in the truck.

Before he could go out there, the receptionist pointed to another phone on a table beside one of the sofas. "You can use that phone."

Gabe made a dive for the phone. He dialed the number for the store, a number he'd dialed so many times when he'd been dating Jen. He'd always taken it for granted that he'd hear her sweet voice.

Someone other than Sarah answered and Gabe immediately asked for her.

"She's not working right now. May I help you?"

"It's an emergency. Where is she? Get her! It's Jennifer!"

Gabe waited anxiously, hearing the man call to someone about it being an emergency. Suddenly Sarah's voice came on. "Gabe? Is it you? What's wrong with Jen?"

"She fell!" Gabe said. "She fell, Sarah. I got to her as soon as I could, but she—she won't wake up."

"Where are you?" she demanded.

"At the clinic. Jon's trying—Sarah, I—"

"I'm on my way, Gabe."

He sat there, a dead phone in his hand, crying like a baby as he prayed for his wife and children.

SARAH HAD MADE UP HER MIND to ask Brandy to leave as soon as she got up. Not only wasn't Brandy a nice person, she enjoyed creating problems. She'd been pleased that two men were willing to fight over her. They were so dumb they didn't realize they didn't matter to her at all.

When Brandy got up this morning, Sarah was going to drive her to Casper and pay for her plane ticket back to Denver. It would be worth the drive to have her home to herself again.

She'd already explained her schedule to Jeff. She'd just decided to go awaken Brandy when Gabe's call came in.

Immediately, everything went out of her mind. With a tearful word to Jeff, she ran the two blocks to the clinic. In minutes, she entered the reception area to find Gabe leaning against the wall, tears pouring down his face.

"Gabe! What has Jon said?"

"Sarah. I'm so sorry. I tried to get to her. I didn't know—" He reached out a hand to her as he tried to explain.

"I know it was an accident, Gabe. I know you wouldn't hurt Jen or your babies." She had no doubt of that. Taking his hand in hers, she tried to hold on to her composure.

Jon came out as she got seated beside Gabe. Then they both jumped to their feet. Gabe stared at Jon, but he couldn't ask anything.

Sarah could. "How is she, Jon?"

"She has a concussion. I think she must've hit a rock when she fell. As best as I can tell right now, the babies are fine. They've moved some. We'll be taking a sonogram in a few moments. Jennifer is comfortable now, but still not conscious."

"But she's going to be all right, isn't she?" Gabe asked, his voice choked.

"I hope so, Gabe, but I can't make any promises with head injuries. We just have to wait them out. After we finish, you can sit with her, talk to her. Maybe she'll hear you."

"Now? I can come now?"

"Not yet. Sarah, you'll stay with Gabe? I'll let you know when you can both come in."

"Of course, Jon. Thank you."

She sat down on the sofa, grateful for it since her knees were shaking. Then she pulled Gabe down beside her. There was a box of tissues there and she grabbed a handful. "Here, Gabe, wipe your face. You mustn't sound upset when you talk to Jennifer. You have to sound strong."

Sarah watched Gabe clean himself up, even though tears kept coming. It occurred to her that Gabe would like to have Nick with him. He might be able to do more for Gabe than her. It also wouldn't hurt for her to have Nick there, too.

"Gabe, do you know Nick's cell phone number?"

Gabe told her the number. She let it ring for a long time, but there was no answer. "Was Nick going out of town?" she asked. Maybe Brandy had gone across the street to complain about being thrown out. Or maybe Nick had left with her.

"He's not there?" Gabe asked.

"No, he's not. And there's no answering machine."

"Damn! Where is he when I need him?"

CHAPTER TWNETY-NINE

NICK STEPPED OUT OF the shower. Whatever else he needed to fix in his new home, it wasn't the hot-water heater. He'd stayed in the shower for a long time, easing his sore muscles. But he was a lot better this morning. Probably because he'd taken Sarah's advice.

After dressing, he decided to start his day by seeing Sarah. She'd have hot coffee ready and maybe there'd be a muffin or two left over from the batches she'd made for the Randall women.

He wanted to get a report from Jeff, too, about last night. He figured Sarah was miserable having Brandy in the house. He grinned. He figured even as softhearted as Sarah was, she'd figure out what kind of a person Brandy was soon.

Arriving at the store, Nick found Jeff was waiting on a lady, so Nick headed for the stairs. If Sarah wasn't working, she'd be upstairs with Brandy. He rapped on the door, but there was no answer. However, he found it unlocked and called out a hello.

"Just a minute," he barely heard, the voice sounding muffled. Knowing Sarah wouldn't begrudge him a cup of coffee, he filled a mug and leaned against the counter, sipping it gratefully.

Then Brandy came into the room.

"Where's Sarah?" he asked.

"I don't know. Is there any more coffee?"

He handed her a mug. "I'm going downstairs. She must be down there. Or I'll ask Jeff where she is."

Brandy ignored him.

When he got downstairs, still holding his coffee, Jeff was stacking some new orders on the shelves. "'Morning, Jeff."

"'Morning. I wondered if I was supposed to call you to give you a report of last night."

"You can tell me now."

"Well, everything went okay, except for Sarah, until Brandy started a fight."

"What do you mean 'except for Sarah'?"

"She was fine, but a handsome cowboy came in who knew her. He danced with her two or three times. You could tell he was interested."

"Was she interested?" Nick asked, his heart beating a little faster.

"I'm not sure. Before we could talk, we had to break up the fight and get Brandy out of there. By the time we got back here, we were all too tired."

"Where is she right now?"

"Oh, I thought you knew. I was about to ask you."

"You don't know where she is?"

"No, I meant about Jennifer and the babies. We got an emergency call. I think it was your brother on the phone. Sarah talked to him. Then she ran out of here, crying, saying she was going to the clinic."

Nick ran across the street to his car, which was parked behind his building. In two minutes, he'd covered the distance to the clinic. Then he burst into the reception area, finding Gabe and Sarah huddled in a corner, supporting each other.

"What happened? What's wrong? Why didn't you call me?" he asked, his words getting jumbled.

"We tried," Sarah said. "But there was no answer."

"Jen fell down and knocked herself out on a rock. Jon doesn't know if she'll wake up," Gabe told him.

"The babies?"

"He thinks they're all right. That's what he's doing now, checking them with the sonogram."

Nick put an arm around both of them and held on tight. "I'm so sorry, Gabe. Everything will be all right."

"What if it's not?" Gabe said, unable to stop himself.

"Don't think that!" Sarah protested. "Think good thoughts. We're not going to let anything happen."

The door opened again and Tori greeted them, touching Gabe's arm and then hugging Sarah. "Jon called me. I hope you don't mind, but he thought you should have someone with you."

"Oh, I'm so glad, Tori. It's so terrible," Sarah said, her tears spilling over finally. Tori urged Sarah to sit down, and Gabe and Nick sat down on the sofa next to them.

After fifteen minutes of torturous silence, Jon came back out. "Jennifer's still unconscious, but I did a sonogram on the twins and they're doing fine. You can go in two at a time and see Jennifer. If Gabe or Sarah want to sit with her, they can, but I don't want a lot of commotion."

Gabe leaped to his feet, Sarah with him. They went to the connecting door. Jon leaned over and kissed Tori briefly. "Thanks for coming, honey. You, too, Nick. They were here by themselves for a while."

"I was in the shower when she tried to call," Nick said, feeling terribly guilty. "I got here as soon as I knew."

Jon patted him on the shoulder. "I'm sure you did. Tori, do you think you should call the ranch?"

"Yes, I guess so. How long—I'm sorry, I know you said that you don't know but—"

"I wish I could tell you, honey, but—I think she'll wake up within twenty-four hours, but I can't say for sure. If she doesn't, then we'll need to call in some specialists."

Nick grabbed his arm. "Don't even think about the cost if you need to do so right now. I'll take care of everything."

"Good for you, Nick, but I wouldn't let that stop me. It's too early to bring in someone else now. But I'll keep a close watch on her."

He touched Tori's arm since she was on the phone, and left the room. Nick stood there, not knowing what to do. The door opened and Sarah came out, wiping her cheeks. "Gabe is going to stay in there. Why don't you go in with him, Nick? I think he could use some support."

Nick put his arms around her first and held her tight. Then he kissed her cheek. "I'll be back soon," he promised. Then he went inside to be with Gabe.

Tori hung up the phone. "How is she?"

"She looks like she's sleeping. She kind of blinks her eyes every once in a while, but she never opens them. Oh, Tori! What if—"

"Jon thinks things are looking good, Sarah. Be patient."

"He said—"

"No, no, he'd kill me if he knew I'd said anything. Since he's the doctor, he can't tell you what he thinks. He only tells you what he knows. He thinks she'll wake up within twenty-four hours. If she doesn't, he'll call in specialists."

Tori's words helped Sarah a lot. If the twenty-four hours came and went without improvement, she'd be devastated, but for now she could hope. "Thank you, Tori."

"Mom's on her way in. She said she'd nurse Jennifer."

"Bless Anna. Not that these nurses aren't fine, but Anna, Anna's like family."

"I guess she is family, now that Jen's married Gabe."

"That's true."

"B.J.'s out on a call. They've left word for her. Elizabeth is going to stay there with the kids, of course. Janie and Megan are going over to wait for Letty to come home. They'll pack up a change of clothes for Gabe and Letty will pack a bag for Jennifer. I suspect we'll have to pry

Gabe out of the room, but maybe he'll go shower at Nick's tonight.''

"Maybe," Sarah said, not sure about that. He wasn't budging right now. "Damn, I started to say he could sleep at my place, but I've still got Brandy there. I was going to take her to Casper today as soon as she got up and put her on a plane to Denver. But I can't leave Jennifer."

"We'll find—" Tori began as Nick came back to the reception room.

"She hasn't—" Sarah asked.

"No," Nick assured her softly. "She's still unconscious." Again he put his arms around her, giving her as much of his strength as he could.

"What do you need to find, Tori?" Nick asked over Sarah's shoulder.

"Sarah was wishing Brandy wasn't still around. I'm sure we can find someone to drive her to Casper and get her on a plane."

Nick nodded.

"It can't be anyone with money," Sarah insisted. "None of the Randalls. She's the kind who would claim rape and sue."

"You finally figured her out?" Nick said.

She nodded.

"But how can we—" Sarah began.

"Me. And I'll get Jeff to go with me. She knows I won't put up with that kind of stuff." He took Sarah's shoulders. "I'll have my cell phone with me. Will you call at once if there's any change?"

"Of course. Are you sure you want to do this?"

"Yeah. I know what she's like and I allowed her to come. I could've prevented it. But she needs to be out of our hair. Is it okay if Jeff closes the store?"

"Of course. Thank you, Nick," she said.

He kissed her trembling lips. "I'll be back, sweetheart. Be brave."

"I will," she said shakily. Then he was gone.

Sarah crossed her arms over her chest, as if she were holding him close, staring at the closed door.

Tori said, "Go back inside if you feel like it. I'll wait here for the deluge of Randalls. You'll know when they arrive because Anna will come right in."

"Do you mind?" Sarah asked, knowing it would be wrong to leave Tori all alone after she came to help them.

"I don't mind at all." She hugged Sarah, too. But her hug wasn't as strength-renewing as Nick's had been.

NICK DIDN'T TALK MUCH to Jeff as he drove back from Casper. Brandy hadn't been a pleasant companion on the way in, but they'd got her on a plane and stood there watching it take off, to be sure she didn't get off at the last minute.

"I hope I never see her again," Nick said with a sigh.

"You and me both. Of course, I was fortunate. Without any money, I wasn't of any interest to her. I don't know how you got her to let you go."

"I didn't give her any option."

He'd made one call to the clinic once they were on their way back. One of the nurses told him Jennifer's status hadn't changed. He'd asked if Sarah was there, but she'd been in the room with Gabe and Jennifer, so he'd told them not to bother her.

"How bad off is Jennifer?" Jeff asked.

"The doctor won't say. If she wakes up within twenty-four hours, probably not too bad. But we've got to wait and see. The waiting is tough."

"Yeah, I know. I talked to my girlfriend about the job. She wasn't sure, but now I'm going to insist. Life is too short to spend it apart."

"You're serious about her?"

"As serious as you are about Sarah."

"Yeah. Too bad she doesn't see that."

"I imagine she thinks she's not good enough for you 'cause of all your money."

"You're the second one who's said that. I'll make sure she knows better soon."

Then they fell into silence as Nick drove carefully but fast.

When they got to Rawhide, he dropped Jeff off at the store. "Put out a sign that you'll be closed tomorrow. Probably half the town knows about Jennifer already, so they'll understand."

"Sure. Tell Sarah I'm hoping for the best."

"Thanks, I will."

Nick drove straight to the clinic but didn't find anyone he knew when he entered the reception room. "Where—" he began, but the receptionist interrupted him.

"They're in another room. The first one on the right, across from Mrs. Randall's room."

Nick followed directions and opened a door to find several people inside, including Sarah. "Nick!" she exclaimed. He held out his arms and they met in the middle of the room.

"Any change?" he whispered. She shook her head no.

He stood there, rocking her back and forth in his arms.

"Come sit down, Nick," Jake suggested. "I know Sarah needs to sit down. She won't eat anything."

"Maybe I can talk her into eating with me. All I've had was a cup of coffee this morning."

"O-of course," Sarah said, her voice shaky. "There's lots of food."

Nick led her to a chair, his arm still around her. He pulled another chair to her side. Then he filled a plate from the nearby table. "Have you gotten Gabe to eat anything?"

"No," Chad replied. "That's your next job, as soon as you get Sarah to eat."

"Is Anna in with Jen?" Nick asked.

"Of course," said Anna's husband, Brett.

"Letty was here most of the time while you were gone. She's gone home to cook dinner for everyone. B.J. and Janie went with her." Megan nodded her head in Sarah's direction to remind him she needed to eat.

Nick sat in the chair next to Sarah. "Maybe I should tell you about our lovely ride with Brandy." He gave Sarah a biscuit with butter on it. She reluctantly took it, and he whispered something in her ear. She took a small bite.

"Well, first of all, I hope I never see her again," Nick said.

There were grunts of agreement from those who had met Brandy. "You okay with that, sweetheart?" he asked Sarah.

She managed a small smile. He put a piece of ham inside the biscuit and gave it back to her. "Eat up. Jen's going to need you when she wakes up."

She nodded and took another bite. He fixed himself a biscuit with cheese and beef. Then, after taking a bite, he asked her to taste it. She did as he asked.

Sarah finished a sandwich but refused to eat any more. Nick kissed her and said he'd go in and see Gabe.

There were two people in Jen's room. Anna Randall, wearing a nurse's uniform, was taking Jennifer's blood pressure. Gabe sat on the other side of the bed, holding Jennifer's hand, talking in a low voice.

"Gabe?" Nick said softly. "I'm back. How are you doing?"

"Never mind about me. Jen still hasn't woken up."

"Brother, you need to rest so you'll be strong for Jen."

"I'm not leaving her side."

Nick knew he couldn't change his brother's mind. Hell, he'd be the same way if it had been Sarah lying in that bed.

He sat beside his brother for a long while, his hand on Gabe's shoulder, trying to give him all the support he could. Finally, Nick stood and said, "I'm going back to stay with Sarah. Let us know if there's any change.'' Nick couldn't help thinking about when his parents had died. He'd stood alone at the hospital. How much easier the waiting would have been if he'd had this family surrounding him.

He opened the door to leave, but stopped suddenly when he heard Gabe hoarsely whispered, ''Wait!''

CHAPTER THIRTY

"WHAT IS IT?" Nick asked, his gaze on Jennifer.

"I thought—it looked like—" Gabe stuttered.

"Talk to her, Gabe," Anna ordered, her gaze on the machines that were monitoring Jen.

"Jen, can you hear me? Are you awake?"

Jennifer opened her eyes and, in a weak, wobbly voice, said, "Of course I'm awake, Gabe. Why are you yelling?"

Gabe fell to his knees, burying his face in her pillow. "Thank you, God. Thank you, thank you, thank you!"

Anna immediately pressed a red button on the wall.

Though he noted the running footsteps he heard in the hallway, Nick's first thought was Sarah. He had to tell Sarah the good news. He slipped from the room and crossed the hall. There, he nodded to the others, giving them a thumbs-up sign, but he said nothing, pulling Sarah up into his arms and urging her across the hall.

"Nick—what...?"

By that time, he had Jennifer's door open and Sarah could hear her sister's voice.

"Jennifer! Jen, you're awake!" Sarah left Nick's arms to fly around the bed to see her sister's face.

"Yes, I'm awake. Why does everyone keep asking me that?" She sounded tired and fussy, but Gabe and Sarah were celebrating her awakening, though it was hard to tell by their tears.

"Honey, you fell and hit your head. We were afraid you

wouldn't wake up.'' Gabe was caressing her face, and he dropped several kisses on her forehead.

''I fell? The babies?''

''They're fine. Jon did a sonogram.''

Jennifer felt her stomach. She received a reassuring kick. Satisfied, she turned her mind to what Gabe had told her. ''I fell? What was I— Oh! I remember. Black Thunder was racing toward you. He was going to attack you. I tried to warn you but— You didn't get hurt?''

''No, honey. Black Thunder was racing toward me to get his treat. He's like a puppy. He has a sweet tooth and that's all he thinks about when he sees me.''

''And he's named Black Thunder?'' she demanded, her voice rising in outrage.

He leaned over and kissed her lips softly. ''We'll rename him, I promise.''

Anna had sent the nurse who arrived earlier to get Jon. He came into the room then. ''There's a crowd in here,'' he noted. ''What's happening?''

In her professional voice, Anna said, ''The patient awoke about four minutes ago. She's coherent, shows no speech difficulty and her blood pressure is normal.''

''Is there a chance I can get close enough to examine her?'' Jon asked, grinning at Gabe and Sarah as they beamed at him. Sarah came around the bed, automatically returning to Nick's arms, which pleased him. Gabe backed up a little, but he didn't leave Jen's side. Nor did he turn her hand loose.

Jon listened to her heartbeat. Then he asked her a few questions. ''Very good, Jennifer. I think you're fine, but we'll keep you overnight just to be sure. Are you hungry?''

Jennifer looked surprised at the question. Then she said, ''Yes, I am.''

''Good.''

''Jon, you're sure the babies are all right?''

''Yes. We took their picture and they waved to us.'' His

joke eased the tension in the room. "Now, I know you're all excited that she's recovered, but let's keep the number in this room down to two. Gabe, you can spend the night here, since I don't think Jennifer's arm will reach out to the ranch."

Gabe nodded, as if he'd already planned on being there.

Sarah said, "Gabe, they brought you a change of clothes if you want to shower and change before bedtime."

"Who did?"

"Letty sent them. And Letty packed you a bag, Jennifer."

"Oh, can I change into a nightgown? And wash my face?"

Jon nodded. "Yes, but take it easy. It won't take much activity to exhaust you."

"I'll help her. Gabe can go thank all his family for coming and helping us out," Sarah deliberately suggested. She gave her brother-in-law a firm look.

"But—" he protested.

"She's not going anywhere, Gabe. Go do as I said," Sarah insisted. Jennifer nodded when Gabe looked down at her.

"I won't go anywhere without you, Gabe, I promise."

Gabe gave her a deep kiss and stood. Nick reached out to steady him, sure Nick's legs would be shaky after staying in the same position for so long. "Come on. I'll help you make your appearance."

"Thanks, bro." They went out of the room, arms linked.

Jon looked at Sarah. "Do you need any help?"

Sarah shook her head no, but Anna simply said, "I'll be here."

"Good. I'll check on you later, Jennifer."

As soon as everyone but Anna had left, Sarah hugged her sister, and they hurriedly clarified anything Jennifer wanted to know. Anna gave her a warm washcloth so she could clean up, and Sarah got the nightgown-and-robe set out of the suitcase.

There was even a comb to tidy her hair. "Sarah, could you French braid it the way you used to? It would look better then."

"I'll be glad to. I've even had recent practice." She told her about Brandy and her night on the town. "But she's gone now. Nick took her to Casper and put her on a plane."

"Good," Jen said with a sigh as Sarah finished the braiding.

Anna took her pulse again. "Are you feeling tired?" she asked softly. Jen nodded and Sarah gave her a kiss. "I'll tell Gabe he can come in again."

She opened the door to discover Nick and Gabe leaning against the wall.

"I thanked everyone, Sarah. Can I come back in?" Gabe asked eagerly.

"Of course, Gabe. Your family was really very helpful."

"I know. Nick told me."

"All right. I'll check in later to see how she's doing, but she's pretty tired right now. She may need to sleep." She worried that Gabe would panic if Jen went to sleep.

"I know. Jon told me. And come back when you want. You know Jen will be glad to see you. Me, too."

She reached up and kissed Gabe's cheek.

"Hey, save those for me," Nick said with a smile.

Sarah looked at him, shocked by his words. "What do you mean? We're not—there's no reason for me to kiss you."

Nick stared at her. "Not even to say thank-you?"

"I—of course, I need to thank you. For being here. For taking Brandy away, especially. Yes, of course, a kiss to say thank-you." She leaned forward to kiss his cheek, feeling awkward. He turned his face and their lips connected, his arms went around her and she found herself letting him pierce her armor all over again. When he pulled back, they were alone, Gabe having already gone into Jen's room.

"We called Letty and told her to bring dinner to my place. Everyone's gone on over to help unpack a few things. Come on. You can show them where to put things."

"Me? Shouldn't that be you?"

"I don't know how a kitchen should be set up. You know more than I do."

"I—I should go home. Check on the store."

"Everything's fine at the store. Jeff closed it today and he put up a sign that it will be closed tomorrow. At least I told him to. So there's nothing for you to do but come thank everyone, as you told Gabe to do, for being there for you and your sister."

SARAH HAD NEVER BEEN in the building Nick had recently bought. It had been empty for a long time. Nick drove her there, since she'd run to the clinic. Getting out of the car, she stopped and looked across the street at her storefront.

Her life had been spent in that store. But recently, she seemed to spend more time away from it. She couldn't sell it, like Nick had suggested, but she was going to take a little more time for herself. She'd make Jeff the manager, and she could hire another permanent worker. A woman. Some shoppers were embarrassed to ask for certain products if there wasn't someone of the same sex available.

She'd talk to Jeff about her plans tomorrow. She thought he'd like them. He was a good merchandiser, and she thought he'd be marrying soon.

Nick opened the front door. "You seemed to be lost in thought," he said.

She looked away. "Yes, I was. But it had nothing to do with coming here tonight." It did, of course, have something to do with coming here ever again, but she didn't have to tell him that.

He opened the door wide. "Welcome to my home."

She entered the big living room and stopped in shock. The room was beautifully furnished with rich, dark wood. The floor was covered with several Oriental rugs. She could easily picture it filled with women in furs and jewels.

"I thought we dealt with all this furniture in Denver," she said, still staring around her.

"This is my furniture from my apartment. I've been getting Paul to help me put it in place, instead of painting. But I need you in the kitchen. The Randall women are in there unpacking my dishes and wanting to know where to put them." He had her by the arm, leading her in that direction before she knew what was happening.

"But I can't—"

"But I need help, sweetheart. Won't you help me?"

He knew what he was doing, Sarah realized. Her weak spot had always been someone in need. She arrived in the kitchen, a nice big room, not a small kitchen like hers across the street. The women all suddenly began asking her a dozen questions. While she attempted to sort things out, she wondered what Nick had told them.

She suggested they put the everyday dishes near the sink and dishwasher and the gleaming stemware and china in the cabinets closest to the dining room.

With that direction, they began to fill the cabinets. Sarah couldn't help but admire the beautiful dishes. The daily china was bright and colorful, with an Italian design. Just eating from it would cheer a person up. The elegance of the fine china sent shivers through her. She'd dreamed of one day sitting at the head of a table, her guests chatting to one another, raising their glasses in a toast.

She shook her head, almost overcome with everything that was going on. Nick came into the kitchen. "Good job, ladies. I was dreading having to sort things out. Letty and Janie just got here with the food. Okay if we bring it in here?"

They immediately cleared off one side of the cabinets,

making room for a long buffet. "You have so much room here, Nick. How will you manage?" Megan asked.

"We'll manage just fine. I need a lot of room downstairs for my law library."

Sarah avoided his gaze and asked nothing. When they were ready to serve, she set out the everyday dishes and the silverplate, rather than the sterling silver that had amazed her. She would've felt better if they'd used paper plates.

It was a lively evening. Letty's boyfriend, Bill Wilson, came over. He lived in the apartment next to Russ, over the accounting office across the street. Russ had refused to come.

Sarah sighed. Thoughts of his tragedy had frightened them while they waited to hear about Jennifer. She supposed Russ knew that and thought it would be awkward for everyone. Sarah felt for Janie. He was one of her twins, and she wanted the best for him.

"Don't think about Russ's life," Janie said, squeezing her arm. "Jen is going to be all right."

"I know. I wish Russ had had a miracle happen, too."

"We do, too, Sarah. But we can't plan life. We have to deal with what we're given. And if you're lucky to find love, you hold on to it and give thanks every night. That's what I do."

Sarah smiled. "I think that's what Jen can now do. I think Gabe has finally come to his senses."

"Me, too. Wonderful, isn't it?"

"Yes."

"Now you're next."

Sarah was jolted from her happy thoughts. "What? What do you mean?"

"Don't you want to be happy?"

"I'm very happy, Janie."

"Good. That's all I meant," she said, blinking innocent eyes at Sarah.

Sarah went back into the kitchen to help with the clean-up. She'd thought she would escape Nick that way. But the Randall men were no strangers to clean-up. They'd been raised in an all-male household. Dishes didn't get done unless they did them. They all came into the new kitchen and got to work. In half an hour, it was spotless. And there was nowhere else to hide.

Sarah felt she had to tell everyone goodbye and thank them for their help. Suddenly she found herself alone with Nick. She hastily grabbed her bag and hurried to the door.

Nick stepped in front of her. "Where are you going?"

"I want to see Jen again before I go to bed."

"I called a few minutes ago with the same idea. Jen's asleep and Gabe sounds like he needs to be. You'll only disturb them."

Sarah resented his efficiency, but she didn't doubt his word. Jen had looked exhausted when Sarah had left the hospital earlier. "Then I'll go home and get some rest so I'll be able to help them tomorrow."

"Good idea," he said with a pleasant smile.

Sarah was relieved. Somehow she was afraid he'd stop her. So she smiled back and started to move out the door.

He shut the door in front of her and locked it.

"What are you doing?"

"I'm locking up for the night."

"But I have to go home," she pointed out.

"You are home, sweetheart," he said softly, and put his arms around her. "I know it, and so do you if you'll just stop resisting."

"Nick, this is crazy. We only met a month ago when I slapped your face for Gabe's sins."

He chuckled. "That you did. By the way, have you ever noticed that you don't have trouble telling us apart? Except for that first time when you didn't know I existed. That's strange, isn't it?"

Sarah was getting more nervous. If she could keep her

distance, she could keep her secret. But when he was near her, pressing her, she was in trouble. Like now. "Uh, I know both of you. Jen has no problem, either."

"Right. Because she loves Gabe, not me."

"Yes," she agreed, but hesitantly. She saw a trap.

"And who do you love, Sarah?"

"Nick, this isn't fair."

"Was it fair to let me make love to you—hell, you invited me to make love to you—without telling me you were a virgin?"

"Why? Did you get substandard service? Sorry about that. But I figured I should learn from the best." She was angry now. He was going to be difficult.

"And was I the best?" he asked, a smile on his face.

"How should I know? I don't have any comparisons!"

He took her hand and began tugging it toward the bedroom.

"Nick, what are you doing?"

"I have some more to teach you."

"No! I don't want to learn!"

"Why not? You were willing last time."

"I know, but I made a mistake," she finally said, tears in her eyes. "How can I settle for anyone else?"

He wiped away a tear, his hands curling around her face. "You don't have to settle for anyone else," he said as he kissed her soft skin. "In fact, I forbid you to settle for anyone but me."

"Nick, I'm the wrong person for you."

"No, you're exactly the right person for me."

"But I don't have furs and jewels. I'm not a socialite."

"You did okay tonight."

"But that was just—I wasn't the hostess."

"Yes, you were. And that's exactly the kind of evening I love."

He nibbled at her lips, teasing. Then he dropped his

kisses to her neck. "You are exactly who and what I want for my wife, for the mother of my children."

"Nick, I'm not going to sell the store." She tried to sound firm, but her voice wobbled.

"I'm not asking you to. It was wrong of me to have suggested it before. It's your business. Handle it how you want. If nothing else, Jennifer's accident taught me not to get hung up on silly things. I love you. I want you to be my wife and share my life. And I'll share yours. I may not be a Randall by name—yet, but I'm a Randall in my heart. Marry me, Sarah. Let's raise our children in Rawhide, with their cousins, and be happy."

"Oh, Nick, I love you, too. But are you sure?"

He kissed her and then scooped her up in his arms. "More sure than I've ever been in my life."

There was no more discussion when they reached the bedroom. He placed her gently on the bed and made exquisite love to her.

And he was right. He did have more to teach her.

EPILOGUE

NICK HUNG UP THE PHONE and caught his wife by the waist, kissing her neck.

"Who was that?"

"Gabe. He wants us to come for a visit. He said Jen had made a cake and he couldn't eat it all." He chuckled as Sarah made a rude remark about Gabe's appetite.

"Now, now, he's your brother-in-law."

Sarah laughed. "Twice over, but he can still eat like a horse!"

"I know, but I told him we'd come. I think he just wants to show off the babies again, but I promised him we'd stop by."

Sarah agreed, of course. She loved seeing the babies as much as Nick did. Yet she'd planned on making tonight special, for just the two of them. But she decided she couldn't wait until they got home to tell Nick her news. Putting her arms around his neck, she said, "But you don't have to be envious of your brother, you know."

"Of course not. Because I have you."

She kissed him. "That...and because you're going to have your own baby in seven months."

"Oh, yeah," he agreed calmly, "that, too." Sarah stood there, saying nothing, waiting for her teasing words to hit home. Suddenly, he clutched her tightly. "What? What did you say?"

He picked her up in his arms and swung her around, kissing her as she slid down his body until her feet were on the floor again. "You're sure? That's wonderful! It's not too soon for you?"

They'd had a beautiful wedding in September and gone on a brief honeymoon. Brief because Jen had gone to the hospital to have the babies and they hadn't wanted to miss the event. The babies were born safely and now, with Thanksgiving approaching, they had finally reached an acceptable weight.

"Well, we certainly have something to be grateful for at Thanksgiving. Should we wait until then to tell them?" Their first Thanksgiving was going to be at their new home, and Sarah was going to use the china and stemware she'd so much admired the night they unpacked it.

"We can wait if you want."

He read her mind perfectly, as he often did. "But you'd rather tell them tonight?"

"Yes," she agreed with a grin.

"Okay. We tell them tonight. Ready to go?"

She nodded.

LIFE WAS GOOD.

Gabe sat at the kitchen table. Jen had gone to check on the boys. They'd given them their baths, an Olympic event each evening. Then they'd put them in their bed to play a little.

Yeah, life was good. The boys were wonderful. But best of all was the love he and Jen shared. It colored his life with goodness. And Nick and Sarah were a big part of his happiness, too. Family. He had more than he'd ever dreamed of.

Jen came back into the kitchen. She set out saucers for the cake, with forks. "Are you nervous about this?"

"Yeah. But nothing can take away our happiness, our family. It will probably be sad, but we'll put it behind us." She came over and put her arms around his neck, making

sure he knew she loved him. She took every opportunity
to tell him.

"Has Letty left?"

"Yes. It's bingo night."

"I think I hear a car." He got up and looked out the
window. Then he went to the back door and opened it. Nick
and Sarah ran through the cold wind into the warmth.

"We're here to play with the babies," Nick said at once.
"Sarah is dying to hold them again."

Gabe looked at Jen. "But you said she was just here
today."

Nick chuckled. "You don't realize the drawing power of
those two boys."

"I guess not."

Sarah got to play with the boys and then give Ronnie
his bottle, while Nick and Gabe watched their wives and
the babies. Then Jennifer served the cake, a new recipe.

"This is wonderful, Jen," Sarah said at once. She remembered the time when Jen couldn't bake anything but
cookies. Her sister, and all of them, for that matter, had
come a long way.

"We have news," Nick said casually.

"You do?" Gabe said in surprise. "I—what's your
news?"

"Your kids are going to have a cousin to play with in
about seven months."

There was joyous celebration for several minutes.

Then Gabe cleared his throat. "I hate to bring this up,
but I want to get it behind us."

Nick frowned. "What?"

"A neighbor of Mom's sent me a package this week. It
was the family Bible. I didn't take it with me when I ran
away and I guess it stayed with my stepfather until he died
recently."

Nick waited for his brother to go on. Jennifer reached
out to take her husband's hand.

"Did you think I'd fight you for it, Gabe? It's yours. I understand," Nick said.

"It's not that. There was a letter in it. A letter from Mom."

"Are you going to tell me we're not twins? I won't buy that. Besides, I like being your brother too much."

"No. The letter's to both of us."

Nick fell silent. Then he said, "Me, too?"

"Yeah."

"What does it say?" Nick demanded, his voice rough.

"I don't know. I didn't think I should open it until you were here."

"Damn! You've got the patience of Job. Why didn't I get any of that!" Nick exclaimed.

That made Gabe grin, but he sobered as he took out the white envelope. He carefully opened it and unfolded the paper with spidery writing on it. "She must've written this just before she died," he said, blinking rapidly.

"Do you want me to read it, Gabe?" Jennifer asked softly.

"Yeah. I'd like that."

Jennifer took the paper and began reading.

"My dearest sons,
If this letter ever finds you, I hope you are together. I hope you are well. And may you have it in your hearts to forgive your mother her greatest sin—loving you too much to keep you both.
Please know the choice I made was not easy. It has haunted me since the day I kissed you goodbye, dear Nicholas. My arms still ache to hold you one more time. I pray that your new parents were good and kind and that they loved you enough for me, as well. And Gabe, I'm sorry, too. I realize you had to know some part of me was missing after your brother went away. I'm sorry if I wasn't there for you like a mother should

be. I'm sorry if you ever felt you weren't loved enough.

I pray that time and fate has brought you both together once again. But perhaps time and distance between you will be greater than even a mother's love can bridge. Find it in your hearts to embrace each other as brothers. Forge a family. Forge on. And forgive me. Forgive me.

Love always,
Mom

Jennifer lowered the letter to the table and took a deep breath. Sarah was sniffing. Gabe and Nick stared at each other, tears in their eyes.

"I think we've done exactly what Mom would've wanted," Nick said.

"You're right, we have. I bet she's happy now," Gabe said, his voice wavering. Then the two men hugged each other and then their wives, their hearts at peace at last.

IN THE SPRING, everyone in Rawhide attended the dedication of the new Rawhide library, formally known as the Ellen Randall Library. The plaque read "In honor of a mother who sacrificed her own happiness for the love of her sons, Gabe and Nick Randall. No greater love has man than the love of his mother."

*　*　*　*　*

Don't miss Russ's story,

RANDALL WEDDING,

available December 2002 from
Harlequin American Romance.

DISCOVER
WHAT LIES BENEATH

by
USA Today Bestselling Author
ANNE STUART
JOANNA WAYNE
CAROLINE BURNES

Three favorite suspense authors will keep you on the edge
of your seat with three thrilling stories of love and deception.

Available in September 2002.